"Craig revisits endearing and familiar characters and offers readers an evocative portrait of life in a small Southern town."   —*Richmond-Times Dispatch*

"Everything wraps up in an unexpected and satisfying way in this enjoyable Southern cozy."

—Smitten by Books

Quilt Trip

"Craig's third entry . . . stitches together an updated and creative take on an old favorite and fills the story with a cast of fully rounded characters and a creepy setting."   —*Richmond Times-Dispatch*

"[A] very Christie-esque mystery where all the suspects are trapped together and someone (Beatrice) figures out the who, why, and how."

—Escape with Dollycas into a Good Book

"A great read with a plot that is full of twists and turns that kept it fresh."   —Fresh Fiction

"Has the feel of an old-fashioned whodunit, complete with a group of unsuspecting quilters gathered in a mansion, terrible weather, and a killer in their midst. Craig's use of humor and adventure add to the mix, making this a very enjoyable cozy."   —Debbie's Book Bag

continued . . .

"The mystery has a touch of a Gothic feel, with the killing happening on a dark and stormy night at a Victorian mansion tucked away in the mountains. The loyalty of the quilting friends makes me want to sit in with the Village Quilters Guild even if I don't know how to quilt. . . . And Craig's clever character development and sharp mystery kept me riveted to the story."

—MyShelf.com

Knot What It Seams

"Craig laces this puzzler with a plausible plot, a wealth of quirky characters, and rich local color as Beatrice and her friends try to restore peace for the piecers."

—*Richmond Times-Dispatch*

"There are plenty of descriptions of quilts, fabrics, and patterns, along with a solid mystery, to entice any quilt lover to put down their needle and sit a spell and read."

—The Mystery Reader

"Fans of cozy mysteries, quilting, and well-written fiction will enjoy this book and this series. I highly recommend it." —Sharon's Garden of Book Reviews

Also by Elizabeth Craig

The Southern Quilting Mysteries
Quilt or Innocence
Knot What It Seams
Quilt Trip
Shear Trouble

TYING THE KNOT

A SOUTHERN QUILTING MYSTERY

Elizabeth Craig

AN OBSIDIAN MYSTERY

OBSIDIAN
Published by the Penguin Group
Penguin Group (USA) LLC, 375 Hudson Street,
New York, New York 10014

USA | Canada | UK | Ireland | Australia | New Zealand | India | South Africa | China
penguin.com
A Penguin Random House Company

First published by Obsidian, an imprint of New American Library,
a division of Penguin Group (USA) LLC

First Printing, June 2015

ISBN 978-0-451-46951-9

Printed in the United States of America
10 9 8 7 6 5 4 3 2 1

In memory of Mamma

ACKNOWLEDGMENTS

Thanks first to my family and friends for their encouragement, support, and interest in my writing.

Thanks to my editor, Sandra Harding, for her skillful guidance and direction.

Thanks to my agent, Ellen Pepus, for her responsiveness and business savvy.

Finally and most importantly, thanks to my readers. I appreciate your e-mails more than you know.

Chapter One

"Isn't it wonderful to have a wedding to plan? I don't know when I've been so thrilled." Meadow Downey gave a most un-Meadow-like squeal to emphasize the point. She waved a hand to express her excitement and knocked her red-framed glasses askew in the process. Her long gray braid swished from side to side, punctuating her enthusiasm.

Her friend Beatrice Coleman repressed a wide smile as she pushed back a strand of platinum hair from her face. But she couldn't hold back a grin. "Especially when it's not one's own."

"Well, but for you it's practically a family wedding," continued Meadow. "Wyatt's sister is finally tying the knot after fifty years. It's all very exciting."

Meadow and Beatrice were following up on Meadow's resolution to work in more exercise by walking their dogs through their neighborhood in the tiny mountain town of Dappled Hills, North Carolina. Now that it was April, the air had warmed enough that a morning walk required only a light sweater. The dogwoods were blooming, daffodils were waving in the breeze, and the women could feast on the view of the rolling Blue Ridge Mountains returning to vibrant life after the starkness of winter.

Meadow was wrestling with her gigantic beast, Boris, while Beatrice was taking an easy stroll with her corgi, Noo-noo. Boris was part Great Dane and part Newfoundland, which were clearly visible. It was Meadow's claim that Boris was also part corgi that Beatrice found doubtful. With Meadow always a couple of yards ahead of Beatrice because Boris was pulling her along at great speed, Beatrice wasn't sure if the walk could be considered a success. Or if it really could be termed a *walk* at all.

"It really is," said Beatrice. "Although I would hardly call it a family wedding, Meadow. I haven't even properly met Harper. And Wyatt and I have only just started to date. It's not as if we're married."

Meadow completely ignored this detail, continuing on with her line of thought and yanking back on Boris's halter as he tried to race off after a terrified squirrel. "Can you imagine marrying at fifty? She must be very set in her ways, don't you think? It sure would be tough trying to train a man at that point in your life. Actually," she said in a ruminating voice, "I can't imagine trying to train a man at *any* point in life. You can see what a disaster my training of Ramsay was."

Ramsay was Meadow's long-suffering husband and the police chief of Dappled Hills. He seemed very housebroken to Beatrice. Yes, he had a fondness for losing his reading glasses, writing poetry, and quoting *Walden* a bit much. But he was kind and hardworking. And even seemed to pick up after himself.

"Harper was just waiting for the perfect match—that's all. Wyatt is so happy for her. He felt terrible that she and I haven't met each other, so he invited Harper and her fiancé to have supper with us tonight at his house," said Beatrice.

"What are you bringing to the dinner party?" asked Meadow, a little breathlessly. Beatrice wasn't sure if the breathlessness was because she was always trying to persuade Beatrice to win Wyatt's heart through food, or the fact that Boris was pulling her along as if she were water-skiing.

Beatrice's already brisk walk turned into more of a jog. Noo-noo gave her a despairing look, as if her short corgi legs couldn't possibly keep pace. "I'm not cooking anything," said Beatrice slowly. "I'm just bringing a bottle of wine."

"But it's the perfect opportunity for you to impress Wyatt with your culinary skills," said Meadow, disappointed. "A bottle of wine just shows you know how to shop." She neatly sidestepped a puddle left by a brief spring shower earlier that morning. Meadow finally reined in Boris as he skidded to a stop to inspect a mailbox that apparently smelled fascinating. Beatrice gave a grateful sigh as she slowed to a walk and completely caught up with Meadow again. Noo-noo, tongue hanging out and panting, seemed relieved, as well.

"I think we're keeping it really low-key, actually." Beatrice shrugged. "And my culinary skills are nothing to brag about, as you know."

"A low-key dinner party?" asked Meadow. She sounded a bit scandalized.

"It's not even a *dinner party*. It's really just supper. That way I can meet Harper and her fiancé and we can have a nice evening together."

"I think it's a little odd that you haven't been introduced to Harper before now. After all, she does go to church quite a bit," said Meadow.

"I'm still pretty new to town, you know. Besides, I don't know everyone who goes to church, and there was no real reason for Wyatt to have introduced me to his sister before we started dating. Harper doesn't live in town, anyway."

"She doesn't, but she doesn't live far from Dappled Hills, either. Just let me know how it goes," said Meadow. "I'm curious about Harper's fiancé, Daniel. I know he grew up here, but he was gone for so long. It's been ages since I've last seen him. I remember him as a serious kid. He's younger than I am, and the same age as my youngest sister. He was very smart and kind of quiet. The kind of kid who always had good manners when speaking with adults. He's a lawyer, isn't he? Not that we don't have enough of those around town." Meadow rolled her eyes.

"He is, but I think he works pro bono half the time. Daniel sounds like a good guy."

"Well, be sure to give me the scoop. I'm interested in his best man, too—I've been hearing some gossip lately about Trevor Garber." Meadow waggled her eyebrows in what was supposed to be a telling manner.

"Considering this is Dappled Hills, I can't say I'm

surprised. Everyone seems to know everything around here. What are you hearing about Daniel's best man?"

"I hear he's behaving sort of out of character. And there are rumors"—here Meadow dropped her voice into her usual loud whisper, as if someone could hear them out on the quiet road—"that he might be having an affair." Then she jerked forward abruptly as Boris took off at a full gallop again.

"I doubt I'll hear much about that at supper tonight," said Beatrice, jogging ahead again. But you never knew. Not in Dappled Hills.

Meadow gave a gasping laugh as Boris dragged her forward. "Do you think I'm really getting exercise doing this? It feels like I'm just being pulled along. If I put roller skates on, I bet I'd end up across town in minutes."

"Whatever you're doing, it's exertion, all right." Beatrice smiled ruefully as Meadow went flying forward again. Beatrice decided she and Noo-noo were done with running to catch up and instead ambled toward their friends.

Eventually Meadow was able to tighten her grip on the leash and slow Boris down to a more leisurely pace. When Beatrice caught up with them, she gave Beatrice a curious look. "Have you been able to see much of Wyatt these past few weeks? It seems like he's been in charge of tons of activities at the church lately."

Beatrice cleared her throat. "We've seen each other, yes. Maybe not as much as I'd like to, but I understand about how busy he's been. And when you're a minister, you're never really off. There are always people to visit—folks in hospitals, things like that. It's sort of the point of the job."

"I'm guessing," said Meadow archly, giving Beatrice a sideways glance, "that the best way for you to spend more time with him is probably by spending more time at the church. Right? Volunteering there, helping set up events, attending events. That sort of thing. After all, you're the one who's retired. So, technically, you have more free time."

Beatrice admired a row of azalea bushes as they walked past. She'd have to take a more scenic walk with Noo-noo tomorrow. This one was flying by. "Technically I *do* have more free time," said Beatrice. She was amazed lately how the days seemed to just disappear in a puff. Retirement was growing on her. But Meadow had a point, and it was one that Beatrice had been considering, too. The only thing that was really holding her back was the thought that a lot of extra socializing was going to be in order if she really started spending time at the church. Beatrice didn't mind a little socializing, but always quickly felt as though she wanted to retreat. She thought longingly of her hammock and her book.

"It's something to think about, anyway," said Meadow. She was fond of planting ideas in people's heads. "Although I'll miss seeing you if you spend more time with Wyatt. The sacrifices I make! Well, I'm sure tonight there'll be lots of talk of wedding planning. I hope it will be a beautiful wedding. Although the other night on TV, I saw this really horrifying show. It was sort of like watching a train wreck—I couldn't seem to pull myself away from it. It was called *Worst Wedding Day Disasters Ever!* and there was everything from a typhoon to the groom not showing up and a deer running into the ceremony and charging around the sanctuary. Scary stuff!"

"Well, none of that is going to happen during Harper and Daniel's wedding next month. When was the last time you saw a typhoon here in North Carolina? Daniel sounds too responsible to skip out on his own wedding. And I'll personally ensure that the door to the sanctuary remains closed throughout the ceremony. I defy any deer to run through. It's going to be a lovely service."

Why did Beatrice feel as though she should be knocking on wood?

Wyatt's house was a stone cottage very similar to Beatrice's. It sat on the property of Dappled Hills Presbyterian Church and had been the manse for years.

Shortly after Beatrice rang the doorbell, Wyatt's sister, Harper, greeted her with a warm smile and a hug in Wyatt's small entryway. "I feel as if I know you already—Wyatt has spoken so much and so highly of you, Beatrice. I'm sorry we haven't met before now. I have a bad habit of sneaking into church right before the service starts and then hurrying back out afterward."

Harper was tall and thin like her brother, but didn't yet share his silver-streaked hair. She appeared to be in her early fifties and had an understated elegance about her, reflected in her crisp chinos and cotton button-down blouse with a leaf-and-dot print. She had high cheekbones and a wide, generous mouth. Beatrice followed her into a sparsely but comfortably decorated living room with thick throw rugs on the wooden floors, colorful paintings with scenes from nature, and ultrasoft sofas and armchairs.

Her fiancé, Daniel Kemp, rose to shake Beatrice's hand. He looked as if he had a tendency to be on the serious side, but his eyes were kind and his smile was genuine.

Beatrice took a seat next to Wyatt on a cushy, warm brown sofa. She asked Harper, "So, how did you and Daniel meet? Did you know each other when you were children? Daniel, you are originally from Dappled Hills, aren't you?"

Daniel nodded, carefully adjusting his black-framed eyeglasses. "I knew Harper growing up, but we weren't friends then."

Harper laughed. "That sounds awful. It's just that Daniel seemed much, much older when we were kids. You know how it is when you're in school. He was two grades ahead of me, and that felt like decades. We were in the same youth group at Dappled Hills Presbyterian and saw each other there a little. Wyatt's and my father was the minister then, so we were at about every youth event there was. And Daniel was also there often, although he hung out with the older kids, of course. When he moved back to Dappled Hills from Charlotte, he rented a house right down the street from me, and that's when we finally found out how much we have in common."

Beatrice asked Daniel, "What made you decide to move back home from Charlotte? It must be a huge change for you after so many years."

Daniel smiled at her but seemed to choose his words carefully. "My mother lives in assisted living here and

I wanted to move closer to her. And I always planned on coming back home to Dappled Hills . . . because that's how Dappled Hills feels to me. Like home."

Harper quickly changed the subject, perhaps sensing that Daniel wasn't comfortable as the center of attention. "Beatrice, I understand that you were an art-museum curator in Atlanta, and that you know a lot about setting up exhibits and making displays appealing. I wanted to get your thoughts on some flower arrangements I'm making for the wedding." Harper's intelligent brown eyes gazed earnestly at her.

Daniel gave a good-natured groan. "Wyatt, I guess this is where we bow out of the conversation. We'll have to talk about fly-fishing or football or some other manly activity to counteract the wedding planning."

"I want your opinions, too! You just aren't as experienced in this area as Beatrice is. And, honestly, the biggest parts are already taken care of. We've got the catering set up and the reception location reserved. Now I need to catch up with the decorating, and I'm in a bit of a time crunch, since the wedding is in a month. My thought is that although I want to keep the wedding simple and traditional and low-key, I really want to incorporate quilts and quilting into the ceremony and reception—as a tribute. You've probably heard that Wyatt's and my mother was a member of the Village Quilters," added Harper.

Wyatt looked abashed and Harper said, "You didn't tell her?"

Beatrice blinked. "I'm surprised that *Meadow* didn't tell me. After all, she lives and breathes the Village Quilters guild."

"Not only Mother, but *Granny* was also in the guild. And I have a feeling that Granny's mom was in it, too, but I never asked Mother. You always think you have so much time with your family, and then one day they're gone and you never had the chance to ask questions." Harper swallowed hard and then continued in a firm voice, "So, that's why I want to bring quilting in. Besides, quilting has been a big part of my life, too. One of my earliest memories was of Miss Sissy guiding my hands as she showed me how to quilt my first pattern."

Beatrice gaped at her. "Miss Sissy?"

"Yes. She's Wyatt's and my godmother." A pause. "Don't tell me—Wyatt didn't mention that to you, either?"

Beatrice reflected on Wyatt's patience with the old woman, his continuing visits, and courteous kindness toward her. She should have guessed, she supposed, but he was like that with his entire church congregation.

Wyatt said, "You know, I think I heard a timer go off in the kitchen." He winked at Beatrice and moved quickly toward the door. "Why don't y'all move into the dining room?"

Beatrice decided to help him out by changing the subject. "How do you want to incorporate quilting into your big day?" she asked, as they obediently filed into the dining room and sat around a weathered pine table on farmhouse-style benches. The room was small but warm, with a rug in bright reds and blues under the table, bright lighting, and cheerful yellow paint on the walls.

Harper said, "Oh, I was thinking about several different things. And, Beatrice, you don't know how excited I was to learn that you've become a quilter yourself. I'm so hoping that we'll be able to spend time together, working on projects or showing our quilts at a few local shows. As far as the wedding goes, I'd love our guests to sign quilt blocks that I can sew into a wedding quilt. And Miss Sissy said she was working on a double wedding-ring quilt for us as a gift. I'll be sure to display that somewhere prominently at the reception. And I've got a great idea for putting quilt blocks on the sides of the food and beverage tables. I meant to tell you that Posy said the Village Quilters and I could take over the Patchwork Cottage back room tomorrow to discuss the plans for integrating quilting into the wedding. Will that work for you?"

"Sounds like the perfect plan."

Wyatt walked into the tiny dining room that adjoined the living room and carefully laid down a dish of baked salmon. "All right, I think we're ready," he said, hurrying back into the kitchen for the rest of the supper, which consisted of roasted vegetables, wild rice, and fruit.

Harper blinked at her plate in wonder. "Wyatt, this is a feast! I'm positively amazed. I'd no idea you could cook this well, or I'd have been over for supper way before now. Marian's fabulous cooking must have rubbed off on you." She flushed and put a hand up to her mouth. "Sorry," she muttered, looking irritated with herself.

Beatrice remembered that Marian was Wyatt's late wife. She gave Harper a bright and reassuring smile, but inside her heart sank. She didn't exactly excel in the culinary arts.

"You're right," Wyatt said mildly. "Marian was a great cook. She'd have been proud of me tonight. And surprised. I never displayed any culinary talent during our marriage." He smoothly moved on to another topic. "How are things going for the ceremony itself? In my experience, getting the wedding party organized can be one of the toughest things."

Harper and Daniel exchanged glances. Daniel said, "We've put it together fairly quickly, although it's been a bit harder than we thought. We wanted to keep it small and intimate—and that meant an intimate wedding party, too." Daniel added quickly, "Wyatt, if you weren't officiating, I hope you know you'd be best man. As Harper's brother . . ."

Wyatt's eyes twinkled. "I've no doubt that's the case, Daniel. And I'd be honored to step in. But you're right: it would be tricky to take both parts."

Harper hesitated. Then she said, "There is one thing that's been on my mind that I wanted to bring up. Wyatt, I know you see and counsel many people in your line of work, and I hoped you might be able to offer your opinion on something. I'm afraid that Trevor has been acting out of character." She gave Daniel something of an apologetic look.

Wyatt frowned. "Trevor. He's your best man, isn't he?"

Daniel said, "That's right. Trevor Garber is an old friend. We grew up together here before I left Dappled Hills. We kept up pretty well through the years, and then picked up where we left off when I returned to town. He's always been a fairly upright guy—an anesthesiologist, a good husband to Eleanor, a friend who was always ready to listen. But lately?" He glanced over at Harper to help him fill in.

Harper cleared her throat and said diplomatically, "He's been unpredictable."

"That's right. Unpredictable." Daniel nodded. "He's been acting really erratically—seems to be drinking a lot; speaks without thinking. It's almost as if he's a different person."

Wyatt said slowly, "I haven't seen a problem to that extent, but I've seen dramatic personality changes before. They were almost always caused by drug use of some kind."

Daniel considered this for a moment and then shook his head. "I can't see it. I think he's definitely drinking too much, but I just can't see drug use. After all, he's a doctor."

"Did anything happen in his life to trigger this?" asked Wyatt. "Some sort of personal tragedy that perhaps he needs to seek counseling for?"

Daniel said, "Nothing that I know about. He hasn't lost a close friend or family member. He still has a job . . . Although if he keeps going at the rate he is, I have to wonder if that's going to continue."

"But there's something," said Harper, looking at Daniel. "Remember? You said there was something that Trevor said."

"He has a secret. Something he's not telling me. I don't know what it is that he's trying to keep under wraps, because he shuts me down whenever I try asking about it. I have to wonder if it's his secret that's causing him to act this way." Daniel looked down at his plate.

Beatrice said, "So, you're wondering, obviously, if you can trust him to be part of your ceremony."

Harper sighed. "That's right. What if he shows up intoxicated to the church? What if he makes a big scene at the reception?"

"But, at the same time, he's our best man. I asked him months ago . . . before he started acting so oddly. Remember how proud and excited Trevor was to be part of our wedding?" Daniel asked sadly. "I'm not sure I can take that away from him . . . Not without just cause."

Wyatt said, "Maybe it would be a good idea to talk with Trevor about it. Tell him you're concerned about him. Ask him again what's happened to make him start showing this behavior."

"And think of a good replacement for best man," added Beatrice grimly, "just in case."

Chapter Two

The Patchwork Cottage back room is like a war room, mused Beatrice. Except the generals were the Village Quilters. In attendance were Miss Sissy, Meadow, Posy, June Bug, and sisters Savannah and Georgia. Posy's and Harper's friend Lyla, who was also in the wedding, was the only non–Village Quilter there besides Harper. "Does everyone know Lyla Wales?" asked Posy. "She's not only a dear friend of mine, but she's helping me introduce quilting to a younger generation. Lyla is giving the quilting workshop that will be held soon after the wedding." Posy looked as if she were about to bubble over with excitement. "And maybe we'll even have a quilting booth at the spring festival!"

Lyla was an attractive middle-aged woman with a sleek bob of brown hair and an athletic build. She gave a jaunty wave. "Hi, everyone!"

Miss Sissy gave Lyla a rather rheumy glare. "Foolishness!"

Clearly, Miss Sissy was having one of her bad days. Her wiry gray hair was falling out of her bun, and her checkered dress was nearly as wrinkled as she was.

Everyone decided to ignore Miss Sissy's little outburst. They were used to her temper, and it was definitely worth putting up with her hostility to get her input. After all, she'd been quilting for seventy years; she knew more about the craft than anyone else at the table.

Harper beamed at everyone. "Thanks so much for coming today and for being part of Daniel's and my special day. It means a lot to us—especially having the Village Quilters help out, since Mother was a member of the guild long ago. I wanted to talk about how I wanted to incorporate quilting into the wedding. And if y'all have any ideas, I'd love to hear them."

"Boutonnieres!" barked Miss Sissy.

"Yes, and we're really looking forward to those," said Harper to her godmother. Seeing that everyone looked confused, Harper explained, "Miss Sissy is going to make wool boutonnieres for the groomsmen."

Beatrice couldn't quite picture it, but she knew that everything Miss Sissy created was amazing.

"And June Bug is in charge of our marvelous cake," said Harper with a grin at the little woman who was regarding them all very seriously with her large, buglike eyes. June Bug bobbed her head in shy agreement.

Meadow's stomach announced that she hadn't had breakfast that morning. "How are you incorporating quilting into the cake, June Bug?"

June Bug smiled at her. "It's going to be squares of sheet cake that look like quilt squares."

"It's going to be so pretty that we'll all hate to eat it," said Harper with a laugh.

Meadow shook her head. "I doubt it. It sounds exactly like the kind of cake that I would eat with gusto."

Miss Sissy suddenly lurched to her feet. "Intruder!" she hissed, waving an arthritic fist at the door leading into the shop.

They swung around to see a man with a flushed face and a slight receding hairline peering in through the wooden door of the storeroom. "Can I help you?" asked Posy uncertainly.

Lyla's cheeks were darkly flushed. "Excuse me one minute, please. I'll be right back."

The quilters could hear Lyla's voice whispering angrily to the man in the store. He didn't seem inclined to whisper back. They heard him clearly say, "But I want to see you! When can we talk?"

Lyla furiously whispered back, "Not now. Not ever! Why are you pestering me like this? Leave me alone!"

The quilters looked at each other, startled. Harper leaned over and murmured to Beatrice, "That's Trevor with Lyla . . . the best man that I've been worrying about." Her eyes were clouded with concern, and her voice was tight.

The other quilters were clearly uncomfortable by the whisper. Harper said, "Savannah, tell me about that cute kitty of yours."

Savannah, holding herself stiffly in her starched, high-collared floral dress, relaxed a little. "Smoke? He's wonderful. Let me tell you what he did yesterday— you won't believe it! He's smart enough to know when it's suppertime, but I was busy working on this very tricky section of my 'Tumbling Blocks' quilt, so I was holding off. So he jumped on the coffee table and started pushing off papers and magazines one by one to get my attention. Isn't that amazing?" Savannah positively glowed.

Beatrice said in an undertone to Savannah's sister, Georgia, "It sounds like Savannah is still just as much in love with little Smoke as the day she got him. And hopefully that means she's still giving you more space?" The two sisters were roommates.

Georgia nodded. "It's wonderful. Savannah is happy and distracted and learning about being a pet owner. And I don't feel as if she's is right on top of me—trying to organize my cluttered room, or making plans for the two of us to do things without checking with me first. I'm so glad you introduced Smoke to Savannah. It was love at first sight for both of them, I think."

Meadow homed in on their conversation while the others shared their own pet stories. "What do y'all think *that* was all about?" she asked, nodding her head toward the door until her gray braid swung out over her shoulder. "Do you know who Lyla was talking to?"

Beatrice said in a quiet voice, "Harper said it was Trevor Garber."

"Did I miss something about Lyla and Trevor? I thought they were both happily married. To other people," said Meadow.

Georgia said sadly, "I did hear Trevor and his wife, Eleanor, squabbling one day recently when I was in the grocery store. I never know what to do when I come across a scene like that. I just fled. And I really needed that box of cereal, too, but they kept standing in that aisle, until I started worrying that my ice cream was going to melt all over the store."

Meadow said, "Did you hear what they were arguing about?"

Beatrice frowned at Meadow. "Gossiping?"

"Well, I'm one of the people helping to make this wedding a successful event," said Meadow, drawing herself up proudly. "I need to know if there are factors at play that might create a big problem during the wedding."

Georgia looked thoughtful. "I didn't really hear what they were arguing about, no. I did hear Lyla's name mentioned, though."

Meadow and Beatrice looked at each other. But they didn't comment further because Lyla quickly came back into the room. "Sorry about that," she said. Her face was flushed and her voice sounded gruff, as if she were trying to hold back some sort of strong emotion.

Harper quickly resumed the information session with more details about the types of quilting elements she wanted to include at the wedding reception. She needed quilt squares tilted like triangles to hang from the food tables at the reception. Harper also needed a special quilt, stationed near the guest book, for all of her wedding guests to sign. And she was hoping for quilts to be used for decoration at the reception. The quilters offered up their own ideas, too.

When they were done with planning, they all stayed to chat for a few minutes. Savannah and Georgia joined Posy and Beatrice to talk about the wedding. Beatrice peered surreptitiously over at Lyla, who appeared to be back to normal and was visiting with some of the other ladies.

Savannah said, "I haven't seen a wedding for so long. I'm looking forward to this one."

Georgia smiled. "I know. There's just something about weddings. They're full of hope, aren't they?"

Posy said, "They surely are, Georgia. And this one is going to be lovely. I'm so thrilled that the quilts are going to be part of the ceremony and reception. Harper's mother would be so pleased if she knew. The guild meant so much to her."

Beatrice thought that Georgia looked wistful, as happy as she was for Harper and Daniel. Her own marriage hadn't been a very happy one and had ended in divorce. Although she'd enjoyed living with her sister—at least to a point—it wasn't quite the same.

The women gradually moved to the front door of the Patchwork Cottage, with Posy staying behind to lock up for the evening. As they left, Tony Brock, who worked at the hardware store next door, greeted them. Beatrice thought again how much she liked this nice young man, with his gentle smile and always-neat jeans and T-shirt. She especially liked that he gave a special greeting to Miss Sissy, who preened under his attention. Tony helped Miss Sissy around her house, ran errands for her, and even drove her around town—the few times he could persuade her not to terrorize the town in her ancient Lincoln.

After greeting all the ladies, Tony flushed and said, "Georgia, could I speak with you a minute?"

Georgia blinked with surprise and unconsciously put a hand to her hair, which was loose and flowing today, to smooth it.

The quilters continued walking toward the parking

lot. "What does he want with Georgia?" asked Savannah crossly. "I'm ready to head home."

Beatrice thought the young man's flush and Georgia's response might mean that there was a hint of romance on the horizon. But knowing how protective Savannah could be of her sister, Beatrice asked mildly, "Did y'all drive here? Or bike?" Savannah and Georgia biked nearly everywhere in Dappled Hills. Beatrice was never quite sure how Savannah managed it in her long skirts.

"We biked," said Savannah, gesturing across the parking lot to the bike rack, where two bikes with white baskets were parked.

"You could head on home if you wanted. I can wait for Georgia and let her know that you left ahead of her."

They heard the sound of footsteps behind them and turned to see a rosy-cheeked but smiling Georgia swiftly catching up with them. "Sorry, Savannah . . . I know you were ready to leave. But Tony just . . . well, he asked me out on a date!"

Beatrice said, "Georgia, that's wonderful! I was thinking what a nice young man he is. I hope you have a good time on your date." She glanced over apprehensively to see what Savannah's reaction might be.

But Savannah was much more relaxed about Georgia's news than she could have imagined. She did look confused for a moment at the announcement, but then quickly asked, "You're going to supper?"

Georgia nodded, also looking worried about Savannah feeling left out.

Savannah said briskly, "Okay. Be sure to let me

know what night that will be so I won't cook for both of us. Can we head home now? I'm sure Smoke is wondering where his lunch is."

Beatrice winked at Georgia, and she winked back. The little cat was working out even better as a distraction for Savannah than they'd hoped.

It was about a week later when Wyatt called Beatrice to invite her out to dinner. "I thought we could meet up with Harper and Daniel, too, if you don't mind. They've been so busy with wedding plans that I haven't seen them at all since we had supper at my house."

Beatrice was proud that she managed not to remind Wyatt that she hadn't seen much of him since that night, either. There had been a busy week of events at Dappled Hills Presbyterian—from a consignment sale to benefit the church preschool program to a book-donation drive for a local elementary school and a middle-school car wash that the youth put on to fund a beach retreat. These were all good activities—important activities. But it meant that she hadn't seen Wyatt apart from her volunteering at the consignment sale. And although she was pleased with herself for not harping on his busy schedule, and she certainly didn't feel as if she needed constant companionship, there was a part of her that deeply missed spending time with Wyatt.

Beatrice said lightly, "That sounds like a great idea. And then maybe you and I can spend some time alone together, too. Maybe a walk on Thursday at lunch? The weather is supposed to be beautiful then."

Wyatt sounded abashed. "You're right: we haven't really been able to see each other, either. I'm so sorry.

I'm hoping that things will ease up right after the wedding."

"I miss seeing you—that's all. I understand your huge commitment to the church and your congregation. It's not a regular job. When I was curator at the art museum, I left work and I went home, and that was it. I worked some odd hours because of the museum hours, but basically when I was at home, I wasn't working. But you never know when you might need to be called away." If Beatrice was being completely honest, this was the part that rankled the most. It was somehow tougher to have planned something fun and then abruptly have it canceled than not seeing Wyatt at all.

"I think the fact that it's such a small town and a small church and that I'm the only pastor makes a difference," said Wyatt. "In a larger church, there might be several ministers to divide duties among. Here I'm the only one."

"And you're doing a wonderful job handling all those responsibilities," said Beatrice. "I'm just wanting to keep you all to myself. Or maybe *more* to myself."

"Not at all," said Wyatt staunchly. "And I'll try to work out some ways for me to delegate more to elders and deacons or church volunteers, and make some more time for us. For picnics. I do enjoy going on picnics," he said wistfully.

Although Beatrice would have preferred a quiet dinner with Wyatt, she had to admit that she did enjoy Harper's and Daniel's company that night. She gave an appreciative sniff of the air as they walked into the Italian restaurant. There were red tablecloths with bright white napkins on every table, and each table had a wrought-iron lantern with a lit candle inside. Daniel regaled them in his dry voice with tales from years practicing law, and had them all in stitches. Then Beatrice curiously asked Wyatt and Harper what it was like having Miss Sissy as a godmother.

Wyatt smiled at her, eyes twinkling. "Well, you know, she wasn't always like she is now."

Harper said with a laugh, "She was great, actually. Spry. Childlike. We made her play hide-and-seek with us when we'd play over at her house."

"Miss Sissy was tough to find, too," said Wyatt in a reminiscent voice. "Remember that one time, Harper?"

Harper's eyes opened wide, remembering. "You mean the time we lost Miss Sissy? We gave up and kept calling for her to come out. But she wouldn't! She was determined to keep playing the game until we found her. We were starting to wonder if we should call the police and file a missing-person report."

"That's what we *thought*," said Wyatt. "But remember? She'd fallen asleep in her hiding place. She was curled up in a ball, snoring away, when we finally found her on the floor of her linen closet, under a comforter."

Beatrice laughed and was about to comment on Miss Sissy's hide-and-seek expertise when she noticed that Daniel had grown tense and was staring at something across the restaurant.

"What's wrong, Dan?" asked Harper, noticing. Then she stiffened, too. "Oh no," she muttered.

At the far end of the room, a man was stumbling

toward a table partially hidden by a column. He seemed as if he had once been a good-looking man, but his looks were starting to go to waste. His face was bloated and ruddy, and he looked a bit soft around the middle. Beatrice frowned. Although she could swear she didn't know the man, there was something familiar about him.

The biggest problem was that he was talking very loudly to his dinner companion, a shaggy-haired, middle-aged man with deep-set, concerned eyes. In fact, he appeared to be threatening him.

Chapter Three

Beatrice gazed thoughtfully at the man, who was clearly intoxicated. In an instant, she realized he was the same man who'd argued with Lyla at the quilt shop: Daniel's best man, Trevor.

Trevor's belligerent voice now attracted the attention of the restaurant's manager, who hovered nervously nearby. "I know all about it!" said Trevor, staggering a bit as he clutched the back of his chair in an attempt to stand still.

His chair crashed to the floor, and Harper gave an embarrassed groan. Daniel's face turned nearly as ruddy as Trevor's.

"I know all about it, Patrick. And I'm going to tell everybody. You always thought you were so much smarter than me—made all the great grades in med school. I think everybody needs to know more about their favorite doctor." Trevor's voice was slurred and angry.

The manager, gaze darting anxiously around at the other diners, moved quickly next to Trevor and murmured to him in a low voice the others couldn't hear. Trevor said, "What if I don't want to leave? What if I'm not done talking?"

Wyatt moved his chair back and said swiftly, "Daniel, let's talk with Trevor before this situation gets worse."

Daniel, who'd been frozen in his chair, snapped to. "Of course," he muttered, also pushing his chair back. The two men hurried across the restaurant. Wyatt spoke with the manager, while Daniel appeared to be quietly trying to persuade Trevor to let him drive him home.

Trevor's dinner companion decided to make his escape. He threw down some money, told the manager to keep the remainder, and rushed out, shooting worried glances at the other diners as he left.

Unfortunately, Daniel didn't appear to be making much headway with his approach. Trevor became even more combative. He shoved Daniel, but the shove turned into a bit of a stumble, with Trevor already so off-balance. Daniel quickly caught himself, but Trevor fell over the chair that he'd knocked to the floor.

The entire restaurant appeared captivated by the scene in front of them. Trevor lay on the floor, looking as if he might stay down there for a while to fully recuperate.

Wyatt squatted down next to Trevor and spoke gently to him. Although Beatrice couldn't hear what he said, the words seemed to be effective, and Trevor accepted the hand that Wyatt held out to him.

Since Trevor didn't seem inclined or able to pay his dinner bill, Daniel quickly paid it with his debit card, as Harper collected Trevor's reading glasses and windbreaker from the table and Beatrice helped Wyatt take Trevor outside.

Daniel caught up with them once they were out the door, which wasn't difficult, since they were moving slowly with Trevor weaving from side to side and occasionally stumbling. Daniel remotely unlocked his car. "I'll drive him home," he said grimly. "Trevor and I have something to discuss." He looked at Wyatt. "Do you mind giving Harper a lift home?"

"Of course not," he said.

After Daniel and Trevor left, Beatrice, Harper, and Wyatt got into Wyatt's car. "Well, *that* was interesting," said Harper. "I knew Trevor's behavior was getting worse, but I had no idea things had gotten quite this bad."

"Who was that man he was with?" asked Beatrice.

"The guy he was threatening, you mean?" asked Harper dryly. "I've no idea. But he sure wasn't happy with him. It sounded, from their conversation, like maybe it was somebody he works with at the hospital."

Wyatt said, "I'm sorry Trevor's behavior is getting to be such a worry for you. If there's anything I can do, I'd be happy to try to speak to him, if you think it would help."

Harper gave a dark laugh. "I'm sure it would help, but I'm not sure he's in the right frame of mind to be looking for help. I'm hoping . . ." She bit her lip. "Well, I'm hoping that Daniel is telling Trevor that he's going to be using a different best man. I know that sounds really selfish of me. It's that it's a special day for us and

I'd hate for any . . . incidents—to happen. And it seems like Trevor's behavior is spiraling out of control."

Beatrice asked, "Do you have any idea what might have happened to trigger this? It sounds like it's a pretty dramatic change from the way he used to act."

Harper sighed. "I sure don't. I know he's been drinking heavily lately, and he's clearly someone who doesn't handle alcohol well. He's had other personal issues, too, I think."

Beatrice hesitated. "And do you know what his relationship with Lyla Wales is?"

Harper said slowly, "No, that's a mystery to me. Lyla's mother and ours were great friends, and Lyla has always been a friend to me. But there are definitely parts of her life that she keeps private. I did wonder, though, when Trevor interrupted us at the Patchwork Cottage, if there was something going on between the two of them."

From what Beatrice had heard, maybe whatever relationship there had been had ended. Lyla certainly didn't seem interested in talking with Trevor Garber.

The following weeks passed quickly, and the May morning of Harper and Daniel's wedding was bright and sunny. Beatrice was up early and was just feeding Noonoo when there was a knock at her door. She peered out the side window and saw Meadow there, waving at her. Meadow had Boris with her, which meant that Beatrice needed to quickly put her kitchen on lockdown. Boris was big enough and hungry enough to take food right off Beatrice's counters.

She perked a large pot of coffee and got both Boris

and Noo-Noo some treats, in the hopes that Boris would settle down and not go on a kitchen expedition. Meadow poured them both coffee, and they sat in Beatrice's tiny living room on her overstuffed sofa. It had taken Beatrice a while to adjust to the cottage after her home in Atlanta, but this one room had helped her do it. She'd hung folk art on the walls, scattered colorful throw rugs over the hardwood, and proudly displayed the quilts in warm reds and bright yellows. Quilts she still couldn't believe she'd made with her own hands.

Meadow, sadly, had a talent for zooming in on the one thing that didn't feel completely perfect about the room. She squinted at the back wall. "You have a real houseplant cemetery going there, Beatrice. I mean, I know you usually do, but isn't there a new resident?"

Beatrice sighed. "The peace lily? It's not dead yet, although it seems to be giving up hope. I don't know what it is about houseplants. I never have this problem with any of the plants out in the yard. But as soon as something comes inside, it immediately gives up the ghost."

"I'm going to have to invest in some mother-in-law's tongue for you. Or ivy. You wouldn't be able to kill that stuff with a stick," muttered Meadow, still staring in wonder at the houseplant graveyard.

Beatrice laid down her coffee and walked over to the plants. She pointed to one of the pots that held a plant with tall and spiky upright green leaves. "This one *is* mother-in-law's tongue. I thought those plants were supposed to be indestructible." She gave Meadow a reproachful look.

"Ah. That's right—we did have a very similar con-versation to this one about six months ago," mused Meadow. "Sorry it didn't work out." She squinted across to the plant. "Although I'll admit I've never seen a dead one. You must have really worked hard to kill it." She paused. "Perhaps some kudzu, then. I doubt you'd be able to kill that."

Beatrice plopped back down on the sofa, picked up her coffee again, and took a long drink. She was ninety-eight percent sure that Meadow hadn't come here at the crack of dawn to discuss her gardening deficien-cies. But it took her forever to get to the point, and she absolutely couldn't be rushed. Beatrice drew in a deep breath. This was going to be a great day—Harper's wedding day—and she wasn't going to start out with being irritated. She simply drank her coffee and waited, willing herself to be patient.

Meadow absently spewed some ideas for potential hardy, long-living, stubborn houseplants for Beatrice to try out, and Beatrice nodded along at her. Then Meadow abruptly broke off, took a deep breath as if suddenly remembering the point of why she'd dropped by, and said, "The wedding."

Beatrice said encouragingly, "Yes. The wedding. To-day."

Meadow knit her brows. "You didn't tell me about the best man."

"What about the best man?"

Meadow said indignantly, "That he's been replaced!"

Ah. Beatrice said slowly, "Actually, I didn't *know* he was being replaced. But I'm not very surprised."

"So you *do* know about it." Meadow clucked, giving Beatrice a reproachful look.

"All I really know is there was a scene in a restaurant a couple of weeks ago. Trevor was drinking too much—was incredibly intoxicated—and had some sort of altercation with the man he was eating supper with. The restaurant was on the verge of kicking him out when we managed to get Trevor outside and drive him home. Daniel did say that he wanted to discuss something with Trevor. He must have told him that he couldn't have him as best man any longer," said Beatrice.

"So, Daniel found someone else to step in as best man," said Meadow, "after Trevor got fired. I guess Trevor can't come to the wedding now?"

"Oh, I don't know about that. They're still friends, right? Trevor might be fine as a guest. He just doesn't need to be in the spotlight—that's all. And, besides, I think his wife, Eleanor Garber, is also friends with Daniel and Harper. It would be hard to *un-invite* them. I'm sure his wife will be keeping an eye on him." Beatrice took a sip of her coffee.

"It sounds as if it could be a real mess," said Meadow, unconvinced. "And I'm wondering what the deal between Trevor and Lyla is. Did you see them together at the Patchwork Cottage?"

"Whatever the deal is, it looked like Lyla didn't want anything to do with it," said Beatrice. Changing course a little, she asked, "What time are you going to the church? Are you on the church setup team or the reception team?"

"Definitely the reception. I think the church is going

to be decked out as usual, with maybe a nice arrangement and some white bows on the ends of the aisles. But the reception . . . that's something else," said Meadow.

They reflected on this a minute. Then Meadow stood up and walked to the kitchen to rinse out her coffee cup. "Better get to it," she said briskly.

The Forces that Be did not appear to be working in Beatrice's favor that afternoon. After Meadow left, she did have a relaxing morning, which included taking Noonoo on a walk. She'd had a healthy lunch with fresh tomatoes, black beans, and feta cheese on spinach leaves. And Beatrice gave herself plenty of time to get ready. This was a good thing, because she ripped the sleeve of the dress she was planning on wearing to the wedding. She quickly found a replacement in the closet, but realized it had some sort of mysterious stain on the hem. Finally, she found a midnight blue, lacy sheath dress with short sleeves and a scalloped hem. Beatrice carefully slipped it on, feeling as if whatever curse she was under might fell yet another garment. The third time was the charm, though.

The phone rang, and Beatrice—one heel on and one heel off—stumbled to answer it. Wyatt was on the phone. "Would you like me to pick you up? I know I'm going early, but . . ."

Wyatt sounded as if he might want the company. It *was* his little sister getting married, after all. Beatrice gave herself a look in the mirror next to the back door and grimaced. "Sure, Wyatt. Thanks. What time do you think you'll be coming by?"

"Actually . . . I'm in your driveway. I'm sorry. It didn't occur to me to offer you a ride until I came upon your house."

"Be right there," said Beatrice. She hurried to the bathroom, where she put half of her makeup on. At least she'd done her eyes. She crammed a powder and a couple of lipsticks in her dressy purse (which was a little too small for all the things she was stuffing into it), and quickly left.

Despite Beatrice's mad scramble before getting to Dappled Hills Presbyterian, everything for both the ceremony and the reception was lovely. The sun shone through the stained-glass windows, illuminating the sanctuary with light. "Double Wedding Ring"–pattern quilts made by Harper and Wyatt's mother hung on the double doors leading into the church. Miss Sissy was courteously escorted into the sanctuary by an usher with as much ceremony as if she were the mother of the bride. She had a fierce pride in her eyes, and Beatrice was relieved to see that she had dressed up for the occasion and had even managed to tame her wiry gray hair into a semblance of obedience. Wyatt choked up a bit during the vows, but cleared his throat and quickly recovered. His choking up made everyone else misty-eyed, too. Beatrice loved seeing these two people, who obviously cared about each other so much, joined together.

The reception, under large tents on the church grounds, was a treat both visually and gastronomically. Colorful quilt squares in bright colors hung like pennants around the white-tablecloth-covered tables full of hors d'oeuvres. Lyla Wales oversaw the guest-book table, where guests signed a wedding quilt with their warm wishes inscribed in each square. Tables were stacked with jars of Posy's blackberry preserves, covered with quilt squares, as favors for the guests.

There was a variety of different foods served, all finger foods and heavy hors d'oeuvres with a Southern flavor. There were two delicious spreads—one a cucumber spread that was a light, refreshing topping served chilled on toast points; and the other a warm mushroom spread that melted in Beatrice's mouth. There was also an amazing asparagus casserole with hard-boiled eggs and a sharp cheddar cheese that kept being replenished by the catering staff.

But the best part, decided Beatrice, was June Bug's cake. The little woman, always so bashful, had carefully dressed up in what were clearly new clothes. Her creation resulted in an amazing display: fondant-covered square cakes that resembled quilt blocks with piped icing for stitches. It really was a work of art, and Beatrice felt an unusual reluctance to eat it. Miss Sissy, however, apparently felt no such compunction. Beatrice walked up to the old woman, hair now not nearly as tamed as it had been in the church, as she was greedily chowing down on a square of wedding cake. June Bug shyly walked over to join them.

Beatrice said, "June Bug, you've really outdone yourself with this wedding cake. I've never seen anything like it. Miss Sissy, don't you think that June Bug's cake is really too pretty to eat?"

The old woman gave her a scornful look. "Foolishness," she muttered, finishing off her piece and eyeing the others with a canny expression. "Foolishness!" she repeated again with feeling.

"Thank you, Beatrice," said June Bug with a smile. "It was fun to make. I love baking."

"And we love to gobble up the things you bake!" said Meadow, sweeping in behind them. She'd eschewed her usual flowing garments for a more tailored silk suit jacket in lime green over a long black skirt. Her long gray braid was much tidier than usual, and she was even sporting makeup. Meadow pointed to a nearby photographer. "June Bug, the photographer was saying that he wanted to have a picture of the cake baker with the cake."

June Bug's round eyes grew rounder with dismay.

Meadow said stoutly, "Come on, June Bug. It's easy. You stand there and smile. And then Harper and Daniel will have a lovely picture in their wedding book."

June Bug trotted off with an expression that evoked a prisoner heading to the gallows. Miss Sissy had already slunk off to stand innocently near the cake, apparently waiting for an opportunity to swipe another piece.

Meadow leaned over toward Beatrice and said in her stage whisper, "What's the scoop on Trevor? Have you been able to keep tabs on him?"

Beatrice gave her an alarmed look. "Meadow, I didn't think I was supposed to." She frowned, thinking back over the past couple of hours. "I did see him in the church—he was wearing a suit and looked rather solemn, I thought. His wife was next to him, and she didn't look very pleased. But I wasn't sure if she was unpleased with Trevor being sacked as best man or just upset with Trevor in general. Has he been misbehaving at the reception?"

Meadow's husband, Ramsay, walked up next to Beatrice. "*Who's* been misbehaving at the reception?" he asked in a grim voice.

"Maybe Trevor," said Meadow. "At least, we don't know he has, but we're voting him Most Likely to Misbehave if someone does."

Ramsay relaxed a bit. Although the Dappled Hills police chief was clearly off duty, he never knew when he would have to quickly go on duty again in the small mountain town. He was a short, balding man with a quiet air of authority and a stomach that testified to Meadow's good Southern cooking. Although he seemed to be enjoying the reception, and Beatrice had spotted him dancing with Meadow to the music of the local folk band that was playing, she knew if he had his way, he'd be at home in his favorite armchair, drinking a glass of Cabernet Sauvignon and reading *Walden* for the millionth time.

"So no immediate threat," he murmured. "Just Meadow's imagination running rampant again."

"My imagination is doing no such thing!" said Meadow indignantly. "We've got precedent! Trevor Garber is a real mess."

Ramsay squinted as he scoured the tables under the huge tent. "Oh yes, he's a real mess, all right. Sitting quietly over there by himself at the table, watching everyone."

Beatrice glanced over. Trevor was indeed slumped rather sadly in his chair, watching people dance, eat, and drink. He had a Coke in front of him, which Beatrice assumed was rum and Coke, but this time Trevor didn't appear intoxicated. Beatrice frowned as she glimpsed a shadowy figure peering around the side of the tent. The figure seemed to be trying to get Trevor's attention. After a quick glance her way, however, he was gone. Beatrice frowned. Was it her imagination, or was that the man who'd been arguing with Trevor in the restaurant?

Lyla Wales briskly walked away from her guestbook duties to get a plate of food. Beatrice noted that Trevor tried to catch Lyla's eye, but she seemed determined not to look his way.

Meadow sniffed. "He's probably sitting quietly by himself because he's alienated half the people here."

Ramsay said thoughtfully, "That I can believe. I had to pick him up on a drunk-and-disorderly lately, trying to start a fight in a bar."

Meadow gaped at him. "With whom?"

"Half the bar," said Ramsay with a shrug. "He didn't seem to realize he was slightly outnumbered. Perhaps I should have pulled him in for inciting a riot."

Beatrice said, "What's set him off like this? I'm sure Daniel wouldn't originally have chosen Trevor as his best man if he'd always been this way. This is a small town . . . You don't remember having any other problems with him previously, do you, Ramsay?"

Ramsay shook his head. "No. He's been a reputable doctor. He did talk to me in the car when I was driving him back home. I don't think he was really looking forward to going back home. Apparently, his wife had found out about a relationship he was having with someone."

"With whom?" Meadow was starting to sound a bit repetitive.

"He didn't say, and I didn't ask. Wasn't any of my business. But I got the impression that this illicit relationship of his had ended—and that Trevor was pretty upset about it."

They reflected on this a moment, looking at Trevor's back. Then Meadow abruptly changed the subject. "By the way, Beatrice," she said with a delighted grin, "did you see Georgia and Tony Brock dancing with each other? I don't think I've seen any sweeter sight. And Savannah didn't seem to blink an eye. Savannah even said that she'd made that pretty sundress that Georgia is wearing. I can't believe how relaxed Tony looked in a suit, when I've only ever seen him in blue jeans and a T-shirt. He looks as if he's worn a suit every day of his life."

Ramsay rolled his eyes at the romantic gossip. "You'll be glad to know, Beatrice, that your salvation is on its way. Wyatt's heading over. Maybe he wants you to dance."

Meadow said, "Have you caught your breath yet from our last dance together, Ramsay? Because I'm ready for another spin."

Wyatt held out a hand to Beatrice. "Have I told you how lovely you look tonight?" he asked in a low voice. "I'm so proud that you're here with me."

The folk-music trio, on cue, started playing a slow song, and Beatrice relaxed into Wyatt's arms. She glanced back over at Trevor's table but didn't see him there. Probably gone to get another drink. With any luck, one with no alcohol in it.

The rest of the evening was a pleasant blur of toasts and dancing, great food, and time with friends.

Until Beatrice once again caught sight of Trevor Garber.

Chapter Four

The bride and groom had just left the reception, smiles on their faces, well-wishers blowing bubbles as they ran to their car on their way to a short, weekend honeymoon, since Daniel had a trial in Lenoir on Monday. The car had, blissfully, escaped much tampering with, although someone had written *Just Married* in shaving cream on the car's back window.

Wedding guests were gathering their things and leaving. The band had stopped playing and was packing up instruments and gear. The catering crew was busily cleaning up, with June Bug helping them out. Meadow, Posy, Beatrice, and other Village Quilters were gathering the quilting decorations for Harper to keep.

Meadow grimaced at Trevor, napping at the table with his head on his folded arms. "Guess we spoke too soon," she hissed. "Looks like he's tanked, after all."

"Well, we weren't worried about him being tanked. We were worried he'd make a scene. And he didn't," said Beatrice. "I guess there must have been alcohol in that Coke of his."

"Falling asleep at a wedding reception seems to qualify as a scene," said Meadow as she removed pennants from the table of refreshments. "At least, it does to me."

"Where's Eleanor?" asked Beatrice. "Isn't she keeping an eye on her husband?"

"It looked like she was trying to avoid him all evening," said Meadow. "Oh, except for one time. Once I saw her with him at the table, but it looked as if they were arguing."

Beatrice poked her head out of the tent and scanned the church grounds. "I think I see her. She's talking with some friends." She paused and looked at Trevor. The catering company was in the process of packing away the chairs and tables, and kept stealing glances over at Trevor, as if hoping he were about to get out of his chair so they could put it away. One of the staff members rolled her eyes at the sight of the sleeping Trevor and glanced at her watch in frustration. Beatrice said to Meadow, "The caterers look like they're ready to wrap things up. It's time to wake up Trevor."

Beatrice walked over and put a hand on Trevor's shoulder, half expecting him to jolt awake.

But he didn't.

"Trevor?" asked Beatrice sharply.

No response.

Beatrice shook him by the shoulder insistently, with no response. Finally, she put a shaking hand to the side of his neck to feel for a pulse . . . a pulse that wasn't there.

Beatrice looked up to see Meadow gaping at her. "Is he . . . ?" she asked.

"I'm afraid so. Where's Ramsay?" asked Beatrice grimly.

Before Meadow could answer, they saw Lyla walking by, holding the guest quilt and some of the candles used as decorations. She gave only a furtive glance their way at first, as if still trying not to engage on any level with Trevor. But when she noticed their serious faces, she quickly put the quilt and candles down on a table and hurried over.

"What's wrong?" she asked sharply.

"Trevor's dead," said Beatrice.

"He can't be," she snapped, as if impatient with Beatrice. "Trevor?" She shook him by the shoulder, as Beatrice had done.

Lyla took a deep breath as she finally accepted the truth. White-faced, she knelt beside him and touched his arm with a tenderness that Beatrice hadn't seen from her. She whispered, "Why couldn't we have loved each other at the same time?"

A sharp exclamation from across the tent made the women quickly look up to see Eleanor staring angrily at them. "What's this? What's going on?"

Lyla slowly backed away from Trevor. "Nothing is going on, Eleanor," she said gently. "It's going to be okay."

Eleanor's piercing gaze transferred to her husband, still slumped on the table. "What's wrong with Trevor?"

"I'll get Ramsay," muttered Meadow, scampering off.

Beatrice strode over to Eleanor's side. "I'm afraid

that something terrible has happened." She took Eleanor by the arm in a supportive way. "Trevor has . . . passed away."

Eleanor stared at her, slack-jawed. "Trevor? He can't have. He was fine a few minutes ago."

"Was he?" asked Beatrice intently.

"Of course he was. Well, he was a little too relaxed— sleeping. But he gets that way when he drinks." Her voice was sounding faint, and Beatrice helped her to a chair.

Meadow returned a bit breathlessly with a grim Ramsay in tow. Wyatt, seeing Ramsay and the others huddled around the table, walked quickly over to Beatrice. "He's gone?" asked Wyatt quietly, so that Eleanor couldn't hear him.

Beatrice nodded, unable to speak.

Wyatt took her hand, giving it a reassuring squeeze. There was a muffled sob from Eleanor, and Wyatt murmured to Beatrice, "I'll stay with Eleanor. Why don't you go back and speak with Ramsay?"

After a quick examination of Trevor, Ramsay pulled out his phone and called the State Bureau of Investigation to assist him.

Beatrice asked in an undertone, "Does calling the state police mean that you suspect foul play?"

"I don't really know what I'm looking at, so I've got to call in people with the equipment to help. For all I know, he could have had a massive heart attack. I don't see any outward signs of foul play—there aren't any knife wounds evident, for example. But would I see that at a wedding?" He rubbed the side of his face, thinking. "Knowing what I do about Trevor, I was more inclined to consider alcohol poisoning. But I don't smell alcohol on him, and there's no drink at his table."

"Even if he were drinking alcohol, he seemed to be nursing the same drink, from what I could tell," said Beatrice. "He did have a drink earlier, when the band was playing. But it might not even have had alcohol in it. I guess the caterers must have removed his glass already."

"You weren't watching him the whole evening, though. Is that correct? Or were you keeping an eye on him to make sure he wasn't acting up?" asked Ramsay.

"No, I only glanced his way a few times during the reception, so he could have been drinking more. He didn't appear intoxicated, though. Of course, if something had been put in his drink, we wouldn't necessarily know it," said Beatrice.

Ramsay asked the remaining guests and the caterers to vacate the tent and move to the church parking lot. Wyatt supported Eleanor, extending his arm to her for balance. He asked, "How about if I open up the sanctuary—would that work better? The night air is cool and there's a breeze, too."

The remaining guests and caterers moved into the sanctuary. Wyatt brought Eleanor a glass of tea, and she now sat quietly in a pew, her face pinched but looking more composed. Lyla was very pale and seemed agitated, checking her phone one minute and then walking around the sanctuary, looking at the stained-glass windows the next.

Ramsay said to Beatrice, "While I'm waiting for the

SBI, I'm going to start getting some statements. Can you tell me what you observed tonight and what, if anything, led up to your discovering Trevor's death?"

Beatrice related what she knew, and then paused for a moment. "There was something else, but I doubt it was important. It might have been my imagination going into overdrive."

Ramsay raised his eyebrows. "That sounds like exactly the type of thing I'd like to hear. You can discount it, but frequently those impressions or gut instincts are exactly the kinds of clues we need to crack cases."

Beatrice still hesitated. "All right, but like I said . . . I'm not sure how important this is. At one point during the reception, I saw a figure peering in around the tent. He was in the shadows, but I thought he resembled the man that Trevor had had the argument with in the restaurant. He was looking in Trevor's direction and seemed to be trying to get his attention."

Ramsay's eyes narrowed. "Interesting. And could you tell me again about this public argument that Trevor was having with this man? I'll listen more closely this time."

After Ramsay had spoken with Beatrice, he started the process of taking the other guests' statements, or at least getting their contact information. He said to Wyatt, "I know your sister and her husband have left for their honeymoon, but if you have access to their guest list at all, that would be very helpful for the state police and me."

Wyatt nodded. "I actually do have one—Harper wanted me to make sure that she hadn't forgotten to invite any old family friends. I'll e-mail it to you when I get home."

"Do you know when Harper and Daniel will be back in town?" asked Ramsay.

Wyatt looked a bit startled. "They'll be back tomorrow night, actually. They were just going away to a bed-and-breakfast for tonight and tomorrow, since Daniel has a case in Lenoir on Monday. Then they were planning on taking a longer honeymoon later on."

"Thanks," said Ramsay. He turned to speak with another guest who was hovering nearby to ask him a question.

In an aside to Beatrice, Wyatt said, "You don't think Ramsay believes that Harper or Daniel could have something to do with this, do you?"

"Oh, I'm sure Ramsay simply wants statements from them. Maybe they noticed something that could be significant," said Beatrice. Wyatt was still staring absently at Ramsay's back, and Beatrice asked quietly, "You don't think they could be involved?"

Wyatt quickly answered, "No, of course not. Harper really doesn't even know Trevor."

"And Daniel couldn't have, could he?" asked Beatrice. It really hadn't occurred to her to suspect him—bridegrooms are fairly busy at wedding receptions, and it seemed hard to imagine that he'd have had an opportunity.

Wyatt shook his head, but there was a worried expression in his eyes. "I can't imagine that he would. Of course he couldn't. But Ramsay will know that Trevor was supposed to be Daniel's best man and that there was a falling-out."

"A falling-out, sure. And I have a feeling that Ramsay would be the first to understand, since he knows that Trevor has been getting into some trouble lately. Besides, a falling-out is one thing. Murdering your friend at your own wedding is another," said Beatrice, trying to get at least a small smile out of Wyatt.

He gave Beatrice a small smile in return. "I should sit with Eleanor—she looks as if she needs someone to talk this out with." Wyatt walked over to sit and talk quietly with Eleanor, who was looking rather stressed again. Lyla met Beatrice's eyes and walked over to talk with her.

"Was he . . . dead for long before you discovered it?" asked Lyla quietly. She made a face. "It just seems awful that he might have been dead throughout the reception and no one took any notice."

Beatrice asked, "You didn't see Trevor yourself during the reception?"

Lyla quickly answered, "No. That is . . . not really. I may have glanced his way once or twice when I went into the main tent. But since I was in charge of the guest quilt, that's where I was most of the time. When I saw him, he wasn't slumped on the table like that. But I wasn't in there often."

"He wasn't slumped for very long," said Beatrice gently. "I'd seen him not long before that, and he was .silently looking on." She gave Lyla a searching look. "From all accounts, Trevor hasn't been himself lately. Of course, you probably know that he was originally supposed to be Daniel's best man. Harper and Daniel felt that he didn't need to have that type of responsibility."

Lyla flushed. "Well, I wouldn't know very much about it, no. Harper and Daniel didn't say anything to me about it when Harper and I were talking about the guest quilt and some of the other preparations. But she and I were so busy with the wedding plans that maybe it just didn't come up."

"Wouldn't you have known, anyway? It seemed as if you knew Trevor somehow." Beatrice noticed that Lyla was picking at her fingernail polish until it was nearly gone.

"No, I didn't really know him. Not well. But as a casual observer, yes, I'd say that Trevor's behavior had changed a lot lately. I'd heard gossip about him drinking too much and making scenes publicly. I didn't know he was supposed to be the best man, but it makes sense that Harper and Daniel wouldn't want him to be—especially in light of his recent behavior." Lyla shrugged and took a small step backward, as if she were ready to end their conversation. She didn't seem as if she were going to say anything about the fact that Trevor had shown up at the Patchwork Cottage when they'd had the planning session with Harper. Or Lyla's tender words shortly after Trevor was found dead.

"You don't know what might have happened to make this sudden change, do you? It seems so abrupt."

A splotchy flush crept up Lyla's neck. "I remember Eleanor telling me that Trevor had made a few bad investments and had lost a lot on the stock market. She mentioned them having a lot of debt—a large house payment, cars. Maybe Trevor just sort of gave up. Started drinking and making bad decisions. It happens when you have financial problems."

"Eleanor told you this?" Beatrice frowned. She hadn't gotten the impression that Eleanor and Lyla were friends.

The flush crept farther up Lyla's face. "Eleanor and I used to be very close. Before. . . ." Lyla hesitated, darting a look in Eleanor's direction before glancing away and starting over again. "Before she and I had a disagreement. Now we really don't talk anymore." She took a step backward and pulled her phone out of her pocketbook. "If you'll excuse me."

Lyla quickly walked, heels clicking, to a pew that was far away from everyone.

Beatrice spotted a hunched-over, lifeless-looking figure in one of the pews across the sanctuary. Her heart froze for a second as she thought in that moment that she was seeing another victim. But then she relaxed when she realized the figure was only Miss Sissy, sleeping.

Beatrice joined her. She knew the wily old woman frequently spotted odd bits and pieces of information that no one else did—and the bits and pieces often added up to solid clues. It was easy to discount her; her lucidity could be fairly low, depending on whether she was having a bad day. And there were plenty of bad ones. Still, Beatrice had learned to listen to Miss Sissy's observations.

"Miss Sissy?" asked Beatrice gently, sitting down next to the old woman.

Miss Sissy erupted from sleep with a snort, looking around her wildly. Seeing Beatrice, she rolled her eyes and slumped back into the pew. "Thought you were the killer," she muttered.

Beatrice blinked. "Do you *know* who the killer is, Miss Sissy?"

"Course not!" she barked scornfully.

Beatrice framed her next question carefully, considering how agitated the old woman was acting. "You always do an amazing job observing the world around you, Miss Sissy."

Miss Sissy squinted suspiciously at Beatrice.

"You know that Trevor Garber passed away during the reception. We don't know how he died, so Ramsay is also checking into the possibility of foul play. Did you notice anything at the reception? Unusual people? Guests who might have been talking with Trevor? Anything at all about the reception?"

Miss Sissy said, "Food. Good food there. June Bug's cakes were very good."

Beatrice sighed. "Thanks, Miss Sissy. You can go back to sleep now."

It appeared that Miss Sissy had been too enamored with June Bug's baking; she'd had eyes only for the food. Beatrice stood up and walked toward Wyatt and Eleanor, hoping to sit in the pew behind them.

"How long do you think this is going to take?" asked a voice behind her, and Beatrice turned to see Savannah there. Savannah had traded in her long floral dress for a starched high-necked blouse and a long navy skirt for the day. Her thin hair was still captured it its usual severe bun. Her brow was wrinkled with worry. "I do feel bad for Eleanor and Trevor, of course," she said quickly, as if realizing that her question sounded selfish. "But I was hoping to get back to Smoke. Usually I've fed him some canned cat food by now."

Beatrice glanced over at Ramsay, who seemed to be making some slow progress taking statements, or at least everyone's phone number and address. The sound of voices entering the sanctuary behind them made them turn to see the state police coming in. "They must have been close by," said Beatrice absently. Ramsay interrupted his statement taking to go talk with them. "Yes, it might take a while."

Meadow joined them in time to realize what Savannah and Beatrice were talking about. She said, "Ramsay can be fairly deliberate when it comes to taking statements. You could ask him if he'd speak to you next . . . that's one of the nice things about being friends with the local police chief." She fidgeted with her watch, spinning it around on her wrist. "I can't believe this happened. And at a wedding! But thank heavens it didn't happen before Harper and Daniel left, so all they'll remember is the happy day they had." Meadow asked Savannah, "Did you see anything? Is that why you're wanting to talk with Ramsay so urgently?"

Savannah said, "I didn't see a thing. I just want to get home to feed Smoke. I was busy overseeing the food and the helping direct the photographer and explain who he should take pictures of so he wouldn't miss anything important."

Beatrice hid a smile as Meadow gave her a knowing look. Savannah was being bossy, then, as usual. She'd forgotten about the photographer, though. Maybe he'd have some footage on his camera that would be interesting. She glanced around the sanctuary and saw that Ramsay was sitting down to speak with him.

Beatrice said, "Maybe you actually saw something important without realizing how important it was. For instance, did you happen to see a man who didn't seem to be a guest at the reception?"

Savannah tilted her head to one side, thinking. "He was looking around the side of the tent a couple of times."

Beatrice nodded. "Sounds like the one I saw."

Meadow heaved a gusty sigh. "Why don't I ever notice mysterious people lurking around?"

"That's all I saw, though," said Savannah briskly. "The only reason I noticed him at all was because I was suspicious that maybe he was looking for purses to steal. You know? It seems as if it would be really easy for a thief to read the engagement announcement in the paper, figure out the wedding day, and then look for women's purses lying around while people are dancing or up getting food or whatever. I didn't see him go near Trevor. And I guess someone would have had to go near him for him to be the victim of foul play."

Beatrice considered this. "Not necessarily. We don't know what happened, but what if Trevor's glass of Coke was somehow tampered with? Maybe Trevor left his glass unattended for a moment for some reason—to get a plate of food or to visit the church restroom, or even to confer with our mysterious lurker. Someone could have seen that he was away and then casually walked to the table and added something to his glass. I remember one time I looked back at his table and he wasn't there."

Savannah said, "Wouldn't the caterer have taken away Trevor's glass, though? I mean, if he left the table for a few minutes."

Meadow snorted. "Probably not. They were slow on the uptake, I thought. Especially if his glass had been halfway full when he got up . . . these caterers weren't looking for any extra work—that's for sure."

Savannah frowned, her heavy eyebrows pulled together in thought. "Actually," she said, "I did see something, I guess. It irritated me, so that's why I remember it. You know how I was keeping everyone on schedule? There's a timeline of events at a wedding, you know. It's very important. Greeting guests, cutting the cake, dancing, tossing the bouquet . . . there are things that *must* be accomplished in a certain period of time." Savannah made swift cutting motions with her hand to emphasize the necessary uniform production schedule of your average wedding.

Meadow rolled her eyes at Beatrice.

"Well, Daniel had slipped away at one point. We were in the slot on the schedule where the couple was supposed to be visiting with guests, thanking them for coming, hugging people, and whatnot." Savannah's hand now made a whirling motion through the air to signify airy frippery. "I lost track of him, which was annoying, since it was time for the—erm—garter toss."

Savannah blushed, as if any mention of undergarments was in violation of some sort of strict moral code.

"When I finally caught sight of him, he was talking with a couple of guests who seemed to be on the verge of leaving. And then I saw him sit down briefly at an empty table." She pursed her lips. "I do believe it was the same exact table that Trevor was discovered at a short while ago. He appeared as if he were waiting for someone."

Beatrice's heart sank, and Meadow said sharply, "Daniel? For heaven's sake, Trevor was his *friend*. He was going to be his best man."

Savannah gave her a stern look. "I don't know what happened. I only know what I saw. That's what I saw. And then I got myself over to that table and told him it was time to toss the garter and take pictures, and to hurry up. He stood up and followed me off."

Beatrice and Meadow stared at each other. Could Daniel possibly have been involved in Trevor's death? If so, why?

Savannah said briskly, "Here comes Georgia now. You could ask her if she noticed anything." Her tone suggested that she very much doubted that Georgia had anything remotely helpful to add.

Georgia blinked at them. "What?"

Savannah said, "Beatrice is asking questions about the reception." Without giving Beatrice the opportunity to slowly introduce the subject, Savannah said, "Did you see anyone approaching Trevor's table? Did you notice anything unusual?"

Georgia was flustered. "Did I? Hmm." She looked at Meadow and Beatrice for help.

Meadow grinned at her in understanding. "Or did you only have eyes for Tony?"

Beatrice nodded. "Which would be natural for a first date."

Georgia blushed. "I don't think I noticed anything at all except for Tony. I'm not even sure I could tell you what food I ate or what beverages they served or what songs the band played. But we had a lovely time."

Meadow said in a bubbly voice, "You both looked so cute together!"

"Thanks," said Georgia, eyes dancing. She glanced around the sanctuary and saw Tony looking her way.

She flushed and gave him a small wave. "I'll talk to y'all soon . . . I'm going to go stand with Tony." She stopped short suddenly, looking guiltily toward Eleanor. "I feel bad being so happy at such a tragic event."

Meadow made a dismissive sound. "No worries, Georgia. We've all been there. It's a nice reminder that life does go on."

Beatrice looked curiously at Savannah to see if she was troubled at all by her sister's obvious delight in spending time with Tony. But she was checking her watch impatiently, her mind clearly back home with the little gray cat. Seeing her chance with Ramsay, Savannah hurried off.

Meadow yawned. "I think I'm going to sit down in the pew for a while. And, Beatrice . . . maybe you can give me a ride home when Ramsay's released us? Ramsay is my ride, and I'd like to get home before, oh, three in the morning."

Chapter Five

It wasn't that late when Beatrice finally dropped Meadow home, but it was after eleven. Meadow said sleepily, "I'll get the scoop from Ramsay when he gets home, and then I'll come by and see you tomorrow and fill you in."

"Won't Ramsay be too tired to talk it out when he gets home?" asked Beatrice. "It looked like he might pull an all-nighter there."

"Even better. If he pulls an all-nighter, then, when he finally comes in, stumbling from exhaustion, I'll leap out of bed—somewhat rested, hopefully—and start pulling out the frying pan to make a good, old-fashioned country breakfast with his favorite fixings. Because you know he's not eating there. He'll tell me anything I want to know if I whip up a feast for him after a crazy night."

Beatrice smiled. "Okay, sounds like a deal."

She'd slept like a rock that night. Apparently, the long day before, with its surprise ending, had affected her more than she'd thought. Noo-noo must have realized that she needed the company, because she lay at the foot of Beatrice's bed, protectively watching over her as she slept instead of staying on her own bed in the living room, as she usually did.

Beatrice overslept a bit. Usually, the morning sun coming through her window would automatically wake her up; this time, she slept through it and didn't awaken until after nine. Beatrice dressed quickly and made Noo-noo a bowl of dog food and warmed up a couple of blueberry muffins for herself. She also made a large pot of coffee. She was sure it wouldn't be long before Meadow was knocking at her door. Her next thought was that she should probably have some treats ready for Boris, since she'd surely have the big dog in tow.

Beatrice was pouring her first cup of coffee when that knock came. Beatrice heard Boris barking wildly outside, and Meadow gently scolding him. "Silly Boris! You only need to bark when someone knocks on *our* door."

Beatrice was glad she had the big treats ready, and some prepared for Noo-noo, too, so her feelings wouldn't be hurt. She opened the front door.

Meadow leaped in, pulled by Boris, as if she were water-skiing through Beatrice's living room. "Hi, Beatrice!" She gave Beatrice a closer look, taking in her combed silvery hair, eyeliner, and lipstick. "You've even gotten dressed and have makeup on," she said reproachfully. "It doesn't look like spending a day at a wedding and a night at a murder investigation even put a dent in you."

Beatrice said, "I slept really hard, though, which did me a world of good."

Meadow made a face. "I didn't. I kept waking up, thinking I heard Ramsay coming in and that I needed to leap into action with my breakfast-making, information-gathering session. But all I was hearing was Boris making that loud, squeaky yawn of his, or his toenails scraping on the wood floor as he got comfortable. I don't think I slept a wink." She pointed to the circles under her eyes as evidence. "I'm haggard. Absolutely haggard."

"I'm surprised you're here now. You could always have gotten some sleep and visited later."

"What?" Meadow lifted her eyebrows archly. "And miss mulling over our murder suspects? No way. That's my favorite part of being a sidekick." Meadow quickly proceeded to make herself at home by pouring a cup of coffee and dosing it liberally with cream and sugar, while Beatrice kept Boris from roaming into the kitchen by offering him treats and tossing some to Noo-noo.

They settled down into Beatrice's overstuffed chair and sofa with their coffees. "So, it *was* murder? At least, you mentioned murder a minute ago."

Meadow nodded. "Oh, it was murder, all right. Some really powerful prescription sleeping pills were ground up and put into Trevor's Coke. Carbonation and the taste of Coke apparently mask the bitterness of the pills. It was a fatal amount and, because it was ground up, it would have taken effect right away. Somebody wanted Trevor dead—and quickly."

"Sleeping pills. But Ramsay doesn't think Trevor placed them in his own drink? Trevor looked pretty solemn at the reception. Maybe he took his demotion from being best man particularly hard," said Beatrice, absently petting Noo-noo.

"Well, Ramsay wondered that. Although it seems like kind of a weird thing to do at a wedding. But Ramsay talked to Eleanor, and she said there was no way he could have put those sleeping pills in his own drink. He hadn't been prescribed any sleeping pills, apparently." Meadow, who'd also discovered the muffins while she was making coffee, took a bite.

Beatrice said slowly, "But Trevor was a doctor. It seems like he would have access to medication if he really wanted it."

"True. But Eleanor also stated that Trevor had told her he was determined to start turning his life around. He was going to cut out drinking, be a better husband to Eleanor, mend fences with his adult children, and be a better friend. So he wasn't *that* down. She said he was . . . resolute. That being demoted as best man had served as a wake-up call."

Beatrice scratched Noo-noo behind the ear, and the corgi grinned up at her lovingly. "So Trevor made plans to change. Which doesn't exactly go hand in hand with someone who is depressed and wants to end his life."

"Right. Although I have to say that it didn't look as if Trevor had exactly made up with Eleanor at the wedding. She seemed pretty remote whenever I saw her. And I thought she was trying hard to avoid Trevor most of the time," said Meadow flatly. "She sat next to him in the sanctuary, but for all intents and purposes, there might as well have been a wall separating them. As it was, she left about a foot of space on the pew between them."

"He had a lot to make up for, though," said Beatrice. "I'm sure Eleanor thought that it was great for him to *want* to make amends, but she wanted to see Trevor live up to his promise before she was ready to let bygones be bygones. And maybe she wanted to punish him a little bit. It would have been only natural."

Meadow shook her head sadly. "But then he died before he *could* make good on his promise. I wonder if she feels guilty for not spending his last night closer to him. She might even have prevented someone from tampering with his drink if she'd stayed near."

"Unless she was the one responsible for it," said Beatrice. "The spouse is always the first suspect the police consider."

They quietly sipped their coffee as they considered this possibility. Beatrice snapped her fingers as she remembered something she'd wanted to ask Meadow. "Did Ramsay talk to the photographer? Did the photographer take any interesting footage that might be useful for the investigation?"

Meadow gave her a baleful look. "Nothing. Ramsay said it was the most boring footage he'd ever seen. All the photographer took were lots of close-ups of Daniel and Harper. There were no revealing photos of criminals surreptitiously putting sleeping powder in a disgraced former best man's drink."

"Well, it *was* a wedding. He was simply doing his job. Still, it's a shame the pictures didn't give Ramsay any leads to work with," said Beatrice.

When there was a sharp knock on the door, they both jumped. Boris and Noo-noo, startled out of their naps and, embarrassed at being caught sleeping on the job, began barking up a storm.

Beatrice peered out the window next to the door.

"Oh, it's Piper," she said with a smile, opening up the door for her daughter.

Piper was the reason Beatrice had retired from curating at the art museum and left Atlanta for Dappled Hills. She wanted to be close to her schoolteacher daughter. She'd missed seeing Piper's unrepentant grin and twinkling gray eyes that matched Beatrice's. Her dark hair sported a pixie cut, and she wore slim-fitting jeans and a cheery yellow cotton top that emphasized her cute figure. Piper was also becoming increasingly important to Meadow because she was dating Meadow's son, Ash.

Piper gave her mother a hug and a fleeting kiss, "Figured you'd be up." She spotted Meadow in the living room and said, "Oh, hi, Meadow! Didn't see you over there."

Meadow raised her coffee cup in greeting. "Piper! Glad you came by. I've been wanting to catch up with you."

Beatrice gave Piper a rueful look as they walked into the kitchen to get Piper a coffee. Ash had recently moved from the West Coast back to North Carolina to take a position teaching marine science at a local university . . . and to spend more time with Piper. Meadow was tickled pink by their relationship. Sometimes she was *too* excited about it and started wistfully talking about quilting diaper bags.

Meadow called to them from the living room. "Piper, have you had a chance to see Ash's new house? I know it's just a rental while he's getting settled here, but I think it's so cute. Don't you?"

Piper stirred cream and sugar into her coffee, and they joined Meadow. "I do think it's cute, although I don't think that was the word Ash used to describe it. *Cozy* was how he put it."

Meadow laughed. "It sure is. Although—and I wouldn't hurt Ash's feelings in a million years by telling him this—I think it needs a woman's touch. You know? It's sort of plain with all that white paint and cold hardwood floors." She leaned over to pet Boris, who had laid his massive head on her foot.

Beatrice rolled her eyes at Piper.

Piper gave her a reassuring smile. She could handle Meadow well. "Oh, I don't know. There's something masculine in the sheer starkness of it." Meadow's face fell comically, and Piper added quickly, "Although I did go yard-sale shopping with Ash to buy a few finishing touches. We found some throw rugs that looked brand-new. And a great tablecloth for his kitchen table, too. Makes the whole kitchen look so cheerful."

Meadow beamed at her. "I can't wait to see it."

Piper turned to her mother. "So, how's everything going with you, Mama? I meant to check in with you last night, but then I got distracted, and when I looked at the clock again, it was too late to call."

Meadow spluttered into a chuckle. "Oh, I doubt that. That it was too late, I mean."

Piper raised her eyebrows. "Late night? Must have been quite a party."

Beatrice sighed. "I'm afraid not, Piper. Trevor Garber died during the reception last night."

"What?" Piper's eyes opened wide.

"Did you know Trevor, Piper?" asked Beatrice curiously.

"Not directly, no. But one of his children, Anne, was

a friend of mine when I moved to Dappled Hills. I met her father and mother a couple of times when she and I were out getting coffee or lunch. She moved away about a year after I got here, unfortunately. I know she and her brother will be devastated—she seemed to think the world of her father. I'm sorry to hear that he passed away."

"And your poor mother discovered him," said Meadow. "The rest of us thought he was taking a nice little nap at the table."

"What an awful thing to happen on their wedding day," said Piper.

"It is, but at least it happened at the very end of the wedding, and Harper and Daniel had already left. But yes," said Beatrice.

"And what's more, it's murder!" said Meadow, shaking her head.

At that point, Piper demanded to hear the entire story instead of having it come out in dribs and drabs. At the end, she leaned back in the cushy armchair, thinking. She said, "Were you able to sleep at all last night, Mama? What a terrible experience for you to go through!"

"Actually, I slept like a rock," admitted Beatrice. "I think I was just exhausted from the events of the day— both good and bad."

"Tell Piper about your mystery man," said Meadow with an impish grin. "The one that you've got the SBI searching for now."

"I wasn't the only person who saw him," said Beatrice indignantly. "Savannah noticed him, too, remember? You're making it sound as if I were hallucinating."

"What mystery man?" asked Piper. She took a long

sip of her coffee, as if she needed to be more alert to take this all in.

"I saw this man peering into the tent from the shadows," said Beatrice. "He didn't seem to be an invited guest. What's more, I thought I recognized him. He looked like someone that Trevor had been arguing with recently."

Piper said, "Did he have a shaggy haircut that was heavy on the gray? Deep-set eyes? Sort of a bloated look about him?"

Beatrice frowned at her daughter. "That's him. How did you know that?"

"I saw that man arguing with Trevor, too," said Piper simply.

Meadow exclaimed, "Were you at the restaurant with Beatrice and Wyatt, too? Was I the only one in town who wasn't there?"

"No, this was only a few days ago, in downtown Dappled Hills. I was just guessing that it would be the same person, unless Trevor was making a point of having arguments with lots of people. I was in the bank parking lot, and they were arguing outside of Trevor's car. The mystery man's eyes were bulging, he was so agitated. Trevor gave the man a huge shove and hopped into his car, locked the doors, and sped off." Piper made a throwing motion with her hand to indicate how fast Trevor drove off.

Beatrice and Meadow blinked at her.

"So, you never found out what that was all about," said Meadow.

Piper shook her head. "And that's about all the information I have on Trevor Garber." She shrugged.

"Sorry about that." Then she paused. "Wait. That's not quite true."

Meadow grinned. "You're a font of information today, Piper!"

"This is more under the category of gossipy stuff," said Piper slowly. "Except, I guess, in a murder investigation, it's exactly the kind of thing that's relevant."

"This is gossip you heard?" asked Beatrice.

"No, this is something I *saw*. And I didn't tell anyone about it because I didn't want to cause any trouble. But it's . . . sort of like a soap opera, I guess. A love triangle." Piper sighed. "I felt bad for Eleanor."

Beatrice and Meadow exchanged glances.

Beatrice asked, "Did you spot Trevor and Lyla Wales together, perhaps?"

Meadow put her hand to her face. "Oh goodness. I just remembered. Eleanor signed up for that quilting workshop that Lyla's teaching. Oh dear. I wonder if she signed up only to make trouble for Lyla."

Piper said, "Am I the last person in town to know about their relationship? I thought I was the only one who knew. Wow—they must not have been very careful about keeping it under wraps."

"No, you're not the last person to know it. Actually, we hadn't confirmed that they had a relationship until you brought this up. Meadow and I saw Trevor trying to talk to Lyla, and Lyla furiously trying to get rid of him," said Beatrice.

But Beatrice also remembered what she'd heard Lyla say to Trevor after they'd discovered his body: *Why couldn't we have loved each other at the same time?* That had confirmed a relationship right then.

"They were embracing. In a car," said Piper. "I'd gone up the Blue Ridge Parkway for a hike on this gorgeous Sunday. And there they were, at the top of the mountain, at the lookout. As soon as I recognized them, I slipped away before they could see me. I wanted to avoid the embarrassing situation, so I escaped."

"It sounds as if the relationship was over," said Beatrice thoughtfully. "Lyla certainly didn't want anything to do with Trevor when we heard her arguing with him at the Patchwork Cottage."

Piper gaped at her. "At the Patchwork Cottage? So they'd gotten that sloppy about keeping the relationship quiet?"

Meadow said, "No, it was *Trevor* who had gotten sloppy. He was the one who was seeking Lyla out in a public place and in front of everyone."

"Maybe Lyla ended the relationship and Trevor didn't want it to be over," said Beatrice. "Could that have played into his unusual behavior over the past few months?" She remembered that Ramsay had suggested something similar.

"Unrequited love," said Meadow, clasping her hands together. "I guess it ruined him. He started drinking, carousing, getting more and more daring about contacting Lyla."

"Everything must have seemed as if it were in a downward spiral. Lyla probably didn't want her comfortable lifestyle with her husband disrupted," agreed Beatrice. "Especially considering that we know Trevor was also having financial problems."

Piper frowned. "Eleanor and Trevor were having financial problems? Where did you hear this? I would never have dreamed that. They've got a big house and nice cars and always seem so well dressed."

"That's the point," said Meadow, slapping her leg and making Noo-noo wake with a start. "They've got too many nice things. It sounds like they didn't spend their money wisely."

"Or, to be fair, they *had* money to spend on the cars and the house and the clothes, but then Trevor mismanaged their money and it disappeared," said Beatrice. "Lyla told me that Eleanor had informed her that Trevor had lost money on a lot of bad investments."

Piper gave a low whistle. "Y'all are full of news this morning. And here I thought I was coming over for a quiet visit."

Meadow peered hopefully at Piper. "You could perhaps share news of your own today."

"I have news?"

"Well, not news, per se, but maybe information. I don't think Ash wants me visiting his house again in the very near future because he thought . . . ahh . . . that I was trying to be an interior designer there."

Piper smiled at Meadow, eyes dancing. "So, you want me to give you the scoop on the changes we made to it?"

"Please," said Meadow, dragging her chair closer as Piper described the rugs and tablecloths and other things they'd found at the yard sales.

.

Chapter Six

The next day, Beatrice received an early-morning phone call from Wyatt. "Beatrice? I was wondering if you'd like to grab breakfast with me. And, well, I had one other thing to do before breakfast and before going to the office. Harper and Daniel came back into town late last night. The SBI and Ramsay have already talked to them. On the phone, Harper sounded understandably upset."

"I'm sure she must be," said Beatrice, wincing a little.

"Would you mind running by there with me before breakfast? It shouldn't be a long visit," said Wyatt.

"I'll be ready in ten minutes," said Beatrice.

Harper and Daniel's new house they'd bought together had an unfinished feel about it that was exacerbated by the fact that their suitcases were still at the bottom of the stairs from the night before. Both Harper and Daniel had circles under their eyes and tense faces.

"Were you able to get any sleep at all last night?"

asked Beatrice sympathetically. She and Wyatt gave both of them hugs.

Daniel shook his head. "Not a wink. As soon as we got back into town, the police came over. After they left, Harper and I started talking, and I don't think we stopped until two this morning. We tried to sleep then, but I think we were both tossing and turning."

"Who could have done such a thing?" asked Harper tearfully. "Especially during a wedding, of all times. Trevor was dealing with some personal issues, but he certainly didn't deserve to be murdered."

Daniel said in a flat voice, "I blame myself for this. I'm the one who created this situation."

"It wasn't your fault," said Wyatt steadily. "Whatever stress was present between the two of you was a separate issue."

Daniel nodded but glanced away, as if he couldn't look Wyatt in the eyes. Was he hiding something? Or simply feeling guilty that his wedding factored indirectly into Trevor's death? "I still say it might have been an accident," he said gruffly.

"An accident?" asked Beatrice.

"Maybe Trevor didn't realize how much sleeping-pill powder he was putting in his drink. Maybe he thought it would help him relax," said Daniel.

Harper reached over and squeezed his knee. "Daniel, Ramsay and the SBI are pursuing the idea that it wasn't self-inflicted. Remember? He said Eleanor told him that Trevor didn't have a prescription for sleeping pills. Besides, I doubt most people would grind their pills up and add them to a beverage."

"Right, right," Daniel said, rubbing the side of his

head as if it were throbbing. "I forgot. Lack of sleep, I guess." He glanced at his watch and said ruefully, "And now I've got to get to court. My forgetfulness doesn't sound promising for my client, does it?"

Harper stood up, "Let me give you a coffee refill to take with you."

In a few minutes, Daniel had left, still looking deeply absorbed in his thoughts.

Harper said with a short laugh, "I'm not starting out my married life as a very good hostess, am I? Can I get you two something to eat or drink?"

Wyatt said, "No, thanks, Harper. Beatrice and I are actually going to get some breakfast when we leave here. We're trying to work in some time to visit with each other." He turned to Beatrice. "By the way, I'm afraid the funeral for Trevor is probably going to impact our lunch plans for Wednesday. That's when Eleanor is planning for the funeral, and I'm going to be officiating."

"Of course," murmured Beatrice. "I'll see you at the funeral, then. Maybe you can come by my house for a glass of wine afterward." She was definitely planning on being at Trevor's funeral. Who knew? Perhaps she'd see the mysterious man there and get another chance to identify him.

"I'll need to check with Daniel to make sure that he clears his schedule for Wednesday, if he's not in court," said Harper absently. "He and I should both be at the funeral. I feel so terrible about all of this. I called Eleanor as soon as the police left last night. It was very late, but I knew she'd be up. And she was. She sounded absolutely worn-out and sad . . . but rather matter-of-fact."

Harper paused. "Have you heard if Ramsay has any leads? Anyone that he's pursuing as a suspect?"

Beatrice said, "I haven't spoken with Ramsay, but Meadow has, of course. I got a little information from her. But a lot of it seems like hearsay right now."

Harper gave her a sharp look. "Hearsay? About what?"

Beatrice stared at her in surprise. It was almost as if she thought she might know the gossip. "Well, the usual kind, I guess. About Trevor and another woman."

Harper seemed to relax. "I see. I'm sorry to hear that. I didn't know anything about Trevor having an affair. I hope Eleanor didn't know. She's had enough to deal with lately. And now this on top of it." Harper shook her head.

"What has Eleanor had to deal with?" asked Beatrice.

Harper hesitated. "I shouldn't probably say, because it could create a problem for Eleanor. In fact, I was going to call you this morning, Wyatt, and ask your opinion on whether or not I should share this with Ramsay. It's just that Eleanor and Trevor had been having financial problems. Eleanor and I are friends but not *especially* close, but I guess she thought I was someone she could confide in. Which makes my telling others about it feel even worse. I don't think Eleanor has a lot of friends—she's the kind of person who keeps to herself."

Beatrice cleared her throat. "If it helps at all, I've actually already heard from someone else that they were in financial difficulty. Although I didn't really get any details."

"Oh." Harper considered this. "Then I do feel better

about talking about it. She and Trevor had a good deal of debt to contend with, and they weren't really working on it. They had a sizable mortgage and car payments, and a few credit cards that were maxed out. Eleanor had even been looking at returning to work. She'd been talking to the bank about the possibility of her working there, even as a teller. They really needed that extra income."

"Did Eleanor say why they'd gotten into that situation?" asked Beatrice.

"She said that Trevor had made some bad investments in the stock market. That he'd thought he could be a day trader in his spare time. Eleanor was actually pretty caustic when she was talking about Trevor. She felt he'd put them in a terrible position by experimenting with something he didn't know anything about. So, basically, he lost their nest egg, but he also lost the money they used to supplement Trevor's regular income," said Harper.

Wyatt said, "They must have really been worried. That can't be a good feeling to be in a hole like that."

"I think that Eleanor was worried, yes. But she said that Trevor always had other things on his mind. Plus, Eleanor said he never liked owning up to his mistakes," said Harper.

Beatrice asked slowly, "Do you think the financial situation is better now, with Trevor's death?" She said, "Although it's hard to think it would be, considering that they depended on Trevor's income, and now that will be ending."

"As a matter of fact, that was one of the first things

Eleanor said after she'd thanked me for calling her last night, and after I told her how sorry I was that this had happened. She said, 'Well, at least this financial mess is finally over. I can take the money from Trevor's life-insurance policy and pay off the outstanding bills. Then I'll sell Trevor's car.' Eleanor had it all planned out, and it sounded very organized. She'd get rid of the debt, sell off assets like the car and the house, move into a small place, and start working again, living on her own income." Harper looked thoughtfully out the window as she repeated what Eleanor had told her.

Beatrice said, "It does sound very organized and practical. But that's how I see Eleanor in general—that seems like her personality."

Harper nodded. "It is. I know it might sound suspicious to Ramsay or the state police, which is why I hesitated to mention it—they'll think that Trevor's death so nicely solved Eleanor's problems that she was the one who was behind it. But I think she's working through a problem in a meticulous way. I think she's being smart. I just have the feeling the police won't see it the same way—that's all."

Beatrice said, "At the wedding, I'm sure it was all a blur—at least, that's how I remember my own wedding day years ago. A blur of well-wishers and food and cake cutting. But did you happen to see if Eleanor was anywhere near Trevor's drink? Or, I guess, near Trevor much at all?"

Harper said ruefully, "Eleanor was certainly trying to avoid Trevor—that's for sure. That much I picked up on. I did spot Trevor sitting by himself quite a bit at the table." She paused. "At one point I did look over there and think, Oh good. Eleanor and Trevor are talking. And that was it. I didn't notice her putting anything in his drink, but I did see the two of them together at one point during the evening." She made a face. "I guess that won't sound good to the police, either."

"And I guess Eleanor should think about what she says," said Beatrice. "Telling people that Trevor's death is taking care of their financial mess isn't exactly putting her in a good light."

Harper sighed. "No, it's not. Although I don't really feel that I know her well enough to tell her that. Maybe I can hint at it when I go there—I need to return the vases I borrowed from her for the wedding. She did a lovely job with the arrangements."

"A woman of many talents," said Wyatt.

"Eleanor has a great eye for arrangements and has been doing them on the side for a few years now—I think that was a way for them to get some extra income. Maybe she could kick that into high gear now," said Harper.

Beatrice said, "I'll take those vases back for you, if you'd like." She gestured at the suitcase and the boxes still on the floor and the empty walls. "You've got things to do here. Moving is tough enough without having to run so many errands. And let me know if there's anything else I can do. I don't mind unpacking boxes or putting things up on the walls."

Wyatt smiled at her. "I have the feeling that your curating experience puts you in the expert category at decorating."

"Well, walls and display tables, anyway," said Beatrice dryly.

"If you wouldn't mind," said Harper slowly, "I really would appreciate it. They're kind of heavy, though."

Wyatt said, "I'll load them into Beatrice's car when I'm dropping her off home after breakfast. And, Beatrice, call me before you go to Eleanor's, and I'll help you unload them."

"Meadow mentioned that she wanted to pay a visit on Eleanor, so how about if I get her to help me this time?" Beatrice was pretty sure that when she'd glimpsed the church calendar online, this week had been pretty full. Wyatt had thought his schedule would ease up after Harper and Daniel's wedding, but it looked as if the calendar had filled up in the meantime. And that was before a funeral had been added to it.

Harper smiled at her. "Thanks, Beatrice. That's a huge help. Once I get a few things put away here, I'll feel a lot more at home, I think. Plus, I need to make some progress before Lyla has that quilting workshop. I offered to help out with that. And I guess after that is the spring festival. It just doesn't stop. I clearly wasn't thinking about the fact that I was going to be in the process of moving! Are you going to help out with the workshop, too?"

"Posy asked me if I could," said Beatrice. "I like the idea of introducing quilting to a new generation of quilters, so I told her I'd help the new quilters. Although I really still feel like a new quilter myself."

Harper said, "Oh, believe me—that feeling never really goes away. I think I learn something new every time I'm with other quilters. And when I'm around a quilter like Miss Sissy, I immediately feel like a novice."

Beatrice and Wyatt made their good-byes and headed off to the restaurant, vases in the backseat. Beatrice consumed most of the huge pancake, egg, and bacon breakfast she'd ordered, while trying very hard to focus on Wyatt and not think about the murder. When she thought Wyatt seemed to be on the verge of talking about the murder, Beatrice quickly said, "I desperately need you to share your secret with me."

"Secret?" asked Wyatt with a quizzical smile.

"That's right. The secret of how you manage to stay so patient in a job that must demand a lot of it. You might have noticed that patience is a virtue that I'm trying—and failing—to cultivate." Her eyes smiled at him as she took a sip of her coffee.

"It's not so hard. I remind myself that each member of the congregation is special in some way. If I think about their gifts and if I can treat situations with humor, then I can handle just about everything."

Beatrice said, "But you must encounter some situations where you really wonder what you've gotten yourself into, right?"

Wyatt grinned. "You mean like when Miss Sternbough-Collins led a petition that insisted we get new large-print hymnals? And then we discovered they were so thick that they wouldn't fit in the pew racks?"

He was, in his kind way, trying to change the subject by telling gently funny stories of various characters who'd been in his congregation over the years. He was clearly genuinely fond of them despite some of their oddities (several of them made Miss Sissy appear normal in comparison), and Beatrice laughed out loud at one point when he told of a particular disastrous wedding he'd officiated. The groom had had cold feet at the very last minute, delaying the start of the ceremony for a good twenty minutes. A guest had had a choking fit at the reception and had to have the Heimlich maneuver applied by the DJ. To top it all off, the couple's car hadn't started when they were ready to leave for their honeymoon. Wyatt had Beatrice laughing out loud.

But part of her mind kept drifting over to the murder.

The morning of the funeral dawned. It was a somewhat dreary day, with an overcast sky and brisk wind that had enough bite to it to make Beatrice decide to don a light sweater.

Meadow picked her up to drive her there. She was wearing a rather un-funeral-like outfit composed of a white skirt and a festive chartreuse top. Meadow noticed the direction of Beatrice's gaze and made a face. "My funeral dress fell off the hanger in the closet, and Boris has made it into a bed. If I'd tried to resuscitate it, we'd have been desperately late."

They weren't particularly early now. Beatrice asked, "You probably don't have a lot of navies or browns or blacks in your wardrobe, do you?"

Meadow took this as a compliment. "I certainly don't. It's good to be cheerful, right?"

Maybe a funeral wasn't exactly the place or time to be cheerful, but Meadow definitely had the ability to raise everyone's spirits.

"So, we're going to deliver the vases to Eleanor,

right?" asked Meadow with a jerk of her head toward the backseat where the vases were stored in boxes.

"Not today, though. She's probably going to be exhausted after the funeral," said Beatrice. "Let's try to run by tomorrow instead."

"It's a good thing you've got an excuse to stop by her house," said Meadow, taking a curve too wide. "She's not being good about letting people come over and help her. She was discouraging people from bringing her casseroles and isn't having a visitation at her home, only the funeral home. It seems like she wants to be left alone."

Meadow continued speeding along the mountainous curves, and Beatrice gripped her armrest. "The caring of others can be really overwhelming. There would be an army of church ladies bearing casseroles with heating instructions jotted on the top, maybe a well-meaning gentleman or two to cut her grass if she didn't use a yard service, and people coming by to sit and chat and comfort. They're being kind, but it's a lot of activity. Maybe Eleanor simply wants some quiet time to digest what's happened."

"Maybe," said Meadow. "Although it's definitely out of the norm here in Dappled Hills. The key to being able to talk with her are those vases of yours."

They arrived at the cemetery and stood with the others for the simple graveside service. Eleanor had asked for the ceremony to be as basic as possible. Wyatt read a Biblical passage. There was one rather short hymn and a brief prayer, and then the service was over.

"No longer than a skinny minute," Meadow said

huffily to Beatrice in her stage whisper. "For this I put panty hose on?"

"Meadow, I don't think it's really fair to rate funerals, do you? Considering that the person organizing them is the grief-stricken party," said Beatrice mildly.

"This is why you allow the army of church ladies to come in your house!" objected Meadow. "They tell you your obituary is rather pitiful—which it was; did you see it in the paper? They tell you that you need to accept casseroles from people who'd like to feel as if they're helping you, and that you should have some sort of a eulogy at the service. This just doesn't look good," said Meadow, shaking her head. "Especially under the circumstances. And I disagree that Eleanor is grief-stricken. She seems entirely too composed, if you ask me."

Eleanor did look exceedingly calm. She wore a somber dress, and looked tired but not particularly mournful. A young woman about Piper's age whom Beatrice figured must be Eleanor's daughter, Anne, held her mother's hand. A slightly younger man in his early twenties sat on Eleanor's other side. Both of the adult children appeared exhausted and not nearly as calm as Eleanor. On the other hand, Lyla Wales was having a hard time maintaining her composure as she stood behind the tent. She clutched a handful of used tissues.

Beatrice was about to stress that people mourned in different ways when her attention was diverted by a man standing at the back of the group, under a small grove of trees. A shadow fell across his face, but she could see his height and a shaggy shock of gray hair. Before he could disappear again, Beatrice clutched

Meadow's arm, cutting Meadow off from giving more of her general philosophy on appropriate Southern funerals.

Meadow jumped, "What? What is it?" she hissed.

"The man over there . . . No, to the right of the group. See him? Standing at the back. He's tall and you can see his gray hair."

Meadow said, "Yes, I see him. What about him?"

"That's that mystery man that I saw at the wedding!"

Chapter Seven

Meadow squinted. "That man there?" Then she frowned, focusing on the figure with great intent. "I know who he is," she said thoughtfully.

Beatrice stared at her. "Who is he?"

"My doctor," she said simply. "Dr. Patrick Finley. He's a surgeon in Lenoir and he took care of a gallbladder issue I had a couple of years ago. Pretty decent guy," she said with a shrug. Then she drew her brows together. "Wait. So, you're saying Dr. Finley is the man you saw arguing with Trevor that night you and Wyatt and the Kemps went out to supper? The reason that Trevor was dumped as Daniel's best man? And you think he might have slipped a fatal dose of sleeping pills into Trevor's drink at the reception?"

Meadow's wheels were turning, but, unfortunately, her stage whisper was getting even louder than usual as she made her revelations.

"Shh," said Beatrice. "And yes. That's the man. He

wasn't really the *reason* that Trevor was dumped as best man, though. Trevor's poor behavior was the reason. What do you know about him?"

"Well, he lives in Lenoir, but he has an office here with appointment hours. He was friends with Trevor and Eleanor, and he and his wife would have supper and do other things with the Garbers. And Wyatt should know about Dr. Finley, too, because he volunteers at the church quite a bit."

Beatrice said, "He and Trevor must have had a falling-out of some kind. I guess they must have known each other from the hospital. Trevor was an anesthesiologist, and Finley is a surgeon. They might have worked together on various surgeries."

"Why on earth would he have wanted to kill Trevor, though?" Meadow asked. "It doesn't make any sense to me. Especially since they've always been such good friends."

"But everyone has said that Trevor's behavior has changed radically over the past few months. Doesn't it make sense that maybe Trevor's odd behavior created trouble in a lot of different ways?" asked Beatrice.

"I guess. I certainly don't think anyone believes Trevor changed for the better—that's for sure." Meadow said, "People are starting to walk to their cars now. Weren't you hoping to try to talk to someone while you had the opportunity?"

"I'd like to talk to the mystery man—I mean, Dr. Finley. But he's already leaving." Beatrice watched with frustration as the tall man climbed into a large SUV.

"How about Lyla?" asked Meadow, nodding in Lyla's direction. "Hurry! She's going to leave, too. And we know she has no intention of speaking with Eleanor, since they're not getting along."

Beatrice strode quickly to the parking lot and caught up with Lyla, who was fumbling to find the keys to her car. When Beatrice called to her and Lyla turned around, she saw that Lyla's eyes were full of tears, which probably hadn't helped in the search for her keys.

"Are you all right?" asked Beatrice with concern. "Sorry—I didn't realize you were feeling sad when I called out to you. I was . . . going to talk with you about your workshop and let you know that I'll be there."

Lyla's tousled bob was windblown, and some wayward strands were sticking to the tears on her face. She brushed them away in irritation. "No worries . . . It's silly for me to have gotten so emotional. It's just that Trevor and I used to be friends once. Eleanor, too. I guess I'm feeling like there have been too many changes in my life lately—that's all. And thanks for offering to volunteer for the workshop. I really appreciate that."

"I like the idea behind the workshop, and I think you could really help bring younger quilters to the craft. I know that sometimes when I mention quilting to a younger woman, her immediate reaction is that she doesn't have time for all the intricacy of quilting," said Beatrice.

Lyla nodded, momentarily forgetting her sadness in her enthusiasm for the project. "That's right. I'm planning on giving information and demonstrations on machine quilting and basic tools that will help them starting out. And Posy and I are also making plans for a booth at the spring festival that might help encourage younger people to try quilting."

Beatrice hesitated and then said quickly, before anyone else could approach the parking lot and overhear their conversation, "You mentioned just now that you and Trevor and Eleanor used to be friends. What changed that, if you don't mind my asking?"

Lyla gave her a sharp look, as if she were thinking about refusing to answer. But then she slumped back, leaning on her car.

Beatrice said gently, "Were you and Trevor having an affair? Is that why you and Eleanor had a falling-out?"

"Who told you that?"

"Is it true?" asked Beatrice quietly.

Lyla said, almost to herself, "I guess it really doesn't matter if I tell you. My husband already knows, and Julian was the whole reason I was trying to keep it under wraps." Her hazel eyes contemplated Beatrice for a moment before she said, "Yes. Trevor and I did have an affair. But I ended it. I realized it was foolish to jeopardize everything in my life that I cared about. I ended things with Trevor."

Beatrice saw that several people were starting to move to their cars from the cemetery. "Trevor didn't want it to end, though, did he?"

Lyla ran a hand through her windblown hair, which did nothing to help smooth it down. "No, he sure didn't. I'd known he cared about me, of course. It was very flattering, actually," she said, raising her chin. "I've been married for twenty years, so I was very foolishly flattered by his attention. Trevor fell very hard, though, and I didn't realize it was happening. When I tried to break it off, he started making my life miserable."

"In what way?" asked Beatrice.

"By being completely indiscreet. Somehow, he'd become totally obsessed with me," said Lyla, shaking her head in bewilderment as she remembered. "He was ringing my doorbell during the day, when he should have been over at the hospital. He knew Julian would be gone at work then, so Trevor would skip work, show up at my front door, and keep banging on the door until I'd let him in."

"Did you open the door to him?" asked Beatrice. "It almost sounds as if he was a little dangerous in those moods."

Lyla said quickly, "He was. He certainly was. That's because he didn't care at all about anything but what he wanted and himself. He became completely absorbed with me and completely self-centered. He didn't care if I was afraid the neighbors were going to see this man pounding on my door and call the police. I let him in to shut him up and to try to keep our secret—the secret that he didn't care about anymore."

"After you let him in, did he settle down?" asked Beatrice.

"Not a bit. I could always tell he'd been drinking, too, which definitely didn't help things. Alcohol made him aggressive and loud. It was a bad combination. As soon as I'd let Trevor in, he'd start begging me to continue our relationship. He'd promise that he'd leave Eleanor and assure me that I could easily leave my husband. My answer was always the same: that the affair was over. That I needed him to leave, or else I was going to call the police." Lyla pressed her lips together tightly.

"Would he leave?"

"My response to him would sort of take the wind out of his sails . . . for that day. He'd leave with this hangdog expression on his face. But the next day he'd show up at my house or my work and start harassing me again. He'd follow me around. He'd call the house and my cell number until I ended up having to block him. But then he'd call from another phone at a business or at a pay phone. He was driving me crazy," said Lyla.

"And you think Eleanor found out," said Beatrice.

"There was no way she *couldn't* find out," said Lyla, spreading out her palms in front of her. "Trevor was acting so erratically. He was drinking, not going into work, spending all his time following me around Dappled Hills. She went from being my friend to giving me the most frigid looks you've ever seen. And you know what? I can't really blame her. I never meant to hurt Eleanor. I didn't think it through. I wish I had." She gave a bitter laugh.

"You told all this to Ramsay?" asked Beatrice intently.

"I did once he started asking questions about Trevor and me. I don't know how Ramsay knew about it . . . Maybe the neighbors talked to him. Of course, I realized right away that this gives me a huge motive, doesn't it? Every day I was worried that my husband would find out about Trevor's and my . . . indiscretion.

Every day, Trevor's erratic behavior escalated. I had a lot to lose. Why *wouldn't* I have killed Trevor?" Lyla looked as if she were choking up again . . . this time with fear.

"But you didn't do it," said Beatrice. She made sure there was a faint question mark at the end.

"Of course not," she said crisply. "I really cared for Trevor. He was driving me nuts with his behavior, but I'd loved him once. And now Julian *does* know—the police had to ask their questions. Obviously, he'd have been a suspect, too. Luckily, he was out of town at a business conference for the past ten days, so he's out of the picture. And now he and I are having to work through this huge issue of trust."

"Who do you think might be behind his death, then?" asked Beatrice.

Lyla looked at her in surprise. "Isn't it obvious? Eleanor. She's livid, Beatrice. Absolutely livid. She feels betrayed, angry, vengeful. Who can blame her? She clearly murdered Trevor . . . no doubt about it."

After Lyla had finally driven away, Beatrice walked slowly back to the cemetery. Still thinking about what Lyla had said, she gave her condolences to a composed Eleanor. Harper and Daniel spoke quietly to Eleanor before giving her a tight hug. Harper looked as if she still hadn't caught up on her sleep, and Daniel looked a bit strung out himself.

"I still can't wrap my head around it," he said, shaking his head. He continued walking toward the car as Harper walked slower, keeping pace with Beatrice.

"He's been in such a state over Trevor's death," she

said, shaking her head. "I've honestly been glad that we've had all the moving in to do, in addition to that court case—at least he's had some kind of a distraction while he's at home."

Meadow caught up with them breathlessly. "How long has Daniel known Trevor? It was ages, wasn't it?"

Harper nodded. "There was a break in the middle when Daniel moved away and was practicing law in Charlotte. But they'd grown up together and gone through school together. They always got along really well. It's a shame that the only time they've ever had words with each other was right before Trevor's death."

Beatrice said, "But Eleanor thought that Trevor was planning to make some real life changes, though. It sounded as if they were in response to his being removed as best man. So, Daniel removing Trevor as best man could have worked as a good thing, right? At least Eleanor has the comfort of knowing that Trevor was trying to get on the right path again."

Harper gave Beatrice a quick hug. "Thanks for that. And you're absolutely right. I'll remind Daniel of that the next time he brings up feeling guilty."

Meadow fished out her car keys from her cranberry-colored straw purse. "Ready?" she asked Beatrice.

Thankfully, Meadow took the curves more gently than she had on the way to the funeral. "So, did you find out anything? I saw you talking with Lyla."

"She confirmed that she and Trevor were having an affair. Lyla said that she was the one who realized she was making a mistake and broke it off. Trevor didn't accept that their relationship was over and basically started stalking her and generally making her life miserable. She was worried her husband would find out," said Beatrice.

Meadow snorted. "I bet he's found out about it now! Hard not to if the police are questioning you." Beatrice raised her eyebrows questioningly, and Meadow said with a shrug, "Ramsay told me. He figured if there was some sort of love triangle, Julian Wales might be looking for revenge. But Ramsay said he had a rock-solid alibi. Apparently, he was on the other side of the country and speaking to hundreds of people at a conference." She pulled into Beatrice's driveway. "Okay, so we're visiting Eleanor tomorrow, right? And you've spoken to Lyla. Who else is there?"

"I'd really like to speak with your doctor friend," said Beatrice. "Although I'm not really sure how best to manage that."

"Pity you don't have any problems with your gallbladder," said Meadow thoughtfully.

"Ugh. I'll pass, thanks," said Beatrice.

"Dr. Finley does volunteer at Wyatt's church pretty frequently, but I don't know when. We couldn't even really ask Wyatt about the doctor's church volunteering times if it meant we were going to ambush him with questions about a murder. Wyatt probably wouldn't go in for that," Meadow said.

She was now so deeply in thought that she was no longer focusing on the road in front of her. "Meadow!" hissed Beatrice, putting a hand on the wheel to help yank the van back on their side of the road.

Meadow ignored this intrusion by Beatrice. She snapped her fingers. "I know. Dr. Finley was trying to convince me to get more exercise." Meadow looked down in exasperation at her solid shape. "Anyway, he said that if I set an appointment for exercise, I'd have an easier time keeping up with it."

"An appointment? Like, with a personal trainer?"

"Well, yes. That, too. But he was thinking more of a casual setup. He said that if I made a set day and time to meet a friend for a walk or a swim at the indoor pool or an aerobics class, that would help me keep up with the exercising. And he *said*"—Meadow paused for maximum impact—"that he always meets a friend of his for racquetball at the community center every Friday morning."

Beatrice was impressed. "That's some memory you have, Meadow."

"Not really. I remember because I realized that's why I could never get in to see Dr. Finley on a Friday morning. It annoyed me and stuck in my mind. So maybe you should accost him in the community-center parking lot on Friday," suggested Meadow. "I could go with you, to explain that you assist Ramsay with his inquiries."

"Is that what I'm doing?" asked Beatrice dryly. "I thought I was simply being nosy. Will we stake out the place and see if we spot him?"

"We can even stand by his car, if you want. He's got one of those vanity tags, so he's easily recognizable. Doctor Number 1," said Meadow, spelling out the number abbreviation. "It does sort of stand out. And it's a Mercedes, I think."

"Thinks rather highly of himself, doesn't he?" Beatrice shook her head.

"He's a great surgeon, so I guess he can get away with it. But, no, I wouldn't have said that he has an inferiority complex or anything. Okay, so that takes care of Dr. Finley and Eleanor. Were you . . . going to speak to Daniel?" Meadow asked delicately.

"Do you think I should?" asked Beatrice.

"Well, I know it's a touchy area—him being family and all."

Beatrice gritted her teeth. It was most annoying when Meadow's matchmaking extended to the point where she made far-reaching and blanket statements on relationships. She'd gotten better about handling it, though. Beatrice took a deep breath and said, "But what makes you think I should talk with Daniel?"

"Because Ramsay and the SBI are talking to him. Think about it. Daniel pushed Trevor out as best man. There were hard feelings there, big feelings. It's worth the police pursuing and worth your pursuing, too. Besides, I get the feeling that Daniel is hiding something. I'd really like to know what it is. Wouldn't you?" asked Meadow as she pulled the van into Beatrice's driveway.

Beatrice found herself nodding in response. Yes, she thought Daniel was hiding something. He'd known Trevor for a long time—it would have been natural for the two of them to have shared secrets with each other. She remembered how Daniel had seemed to blame himself for Trevor's death and had avoided Wyatt's gaze. "I'll add Daniel to my list, then. But I'll have to make my questioning pretty gentle."

Meadow and Beatrice were thinking that through when Beatrice laughed. Noo-noo, hearing a car in the driveway, had decided to check it out. At first, all you could see were two big, pointy ears. But then she put her legs up on something, probably the little footstool in there, and her eager face was plainly visible as she grinned at Beatrice.

"Looks like you'd better head in," said Meadow with a laugh. "Call me when you want to go see Eleanor. I guess you're driving, since the vases are already in your car, so I won't offer to help lug them around for you."

And because Meadow's enthusiastically speedy driving on the mountain curves probably wasn't the best thing in the world for crystal vases.

Chapter Eight

The next morning was so foggy that Beatrice couldn't even see the road in front of her house. Noo-noo, however, didn't care a whit whether it was foggy or not. She stood by the door, looking expectantly at Beatrice as Beatrice finished eating her breakfast. "Is it that time again?" asked Beatrice, as Noo-noo grinned at her and then looked pointedly with her big brown eyes at the leash and collar hanging on the coatrack near the door.

Beatrice hadn't completely woken up yet and the idea of walking through fog and not even having any scenery on the walk wasn't particularly appealing. But some days, if she didn't fit that walk in first thing, it wouldn't happen at all.

Ten minutes later, she and Noo-noo were walking in the direction of Dappled Hills's little downtown, since they'd walked yesterday toward Meadow's house. The old gas station was hidden by fog until Beatrice and Noo-noo got right up on it. Beatrice squinted to see if the two old fellows were sitting in front of the gas station as they did most mornings—drinking their coffee, cutting up with each other, and waving at cars. Finally, she spotted them and they waved to her and called out a greeting.

She passed Bub's Grocery and the row of shops that the Patchwork Cottage was part of. Then she made a loop around the park located right in the middle of the town, and headed back home, since Noo-noo looked as if her short corgi legs might not make it for a much longer trip. They were about to exit the park when she spotted another dog walker in the fog.

As the figure drew closer, Beatrice saw that it was Daniel with a golden retriever. She greeted him with a bit of surprise. "I didn't realize that y'all even had a dog!" Noo-noo and the golden retriever touched noses, and the golden gave Noo-noo a happy lick on the face.

"This is Sunny," said Daniel with a smile. "Wyatt was good enough to watch her for us while Harper and I went away for that brief honeymoon. He also handled her the first day or so after we got back, since we were trying to get moved in." Daniel reached down and patted Sunny, and the golden immediately flopped over so that he could rub her tummy.

"Sweet dog," said Beatrice. "How's the moving in coming along?"

"You wouldn't even recognize the place, Beatrice. It's so much better than it was when you first saw it. Harper has done an amazing job pulling everything together. She's unpacked boxes like a veritable whirlwind. Pictures are hanging on the walls, the furniture is arranged, and there are even those homey touches like picture frames on tables and quilts on the backs of the sofa. It looks beautifully lived-in. I've helped unpack and organize when I've been home . . . but, then, I guess I've been at the courthouse half the time." Daniel stopped rubbing Sunny's tummy and scratched Noo-noo behind the ears so she wouldn't feel left out.

Daniel studiously avoided looking at his fellow dog walker. "Beatrice, I was wondering if . . . well, you spend a good deal of time with Meadow and probably Ramsay, too. If you're in their house a lot. I was wondering if you've gotten a sense of who the suspects are in this case."

Beatrice hesitated. "I wouldn't say I know very much, Daniel. You probably know more than I do, with your court connections."

"I know Ramsay pretty well, of course. I've known him from growing up in Dappled Hills, but I also know him from work—I've reacquainted myself with him since moving back here from Charlotte. But I wouldn't presume to ask him about a case that I'm so closely associated with. At least, I'd rather not." Daniel's hands played with the leash he was holding.

Beatrice blew out a deep breath. "I have an idea about who might have had problems with Trevor, yes."

Daniel's eyes met hers. "Do you know if I'm considered a suspect?"

Beatrice said, "Daniel, I have no idea. It seems to me that it would be hard to consider you a very serious suspect, considering all your duties as groom and all the people watching you."

"I did sit at Trevor's table with him," said Daniel stiffly. "At one point of the reception there was enough of a lull in people coming up to talk to me that I was able to talk to Trevor. I wanted to tell him that I was sorry with the way things had worked out but glad that he was able to share such an important day with me, and indicate that I hoped we could work things out between us in the future." His voice got a bit choked up on the last words, and he cleared his throat impatiently.

"I'm sure Trevor must have appreciated that," said Beatrice gently. "When you were talking with him, did you notice how Trevor was doing? Did he seem intoxicated at all, or sleepy? I was wondering when his drink might have been tampered with."

Daniel shook his head. "He seemed clearheaded for once. I thought that maybe getting bumped out as best man might have somehow jolted him enough to realize that he needed to make some changes in his life. I was delighted to see that he appeared completely sober."

"It seems like the police would realize it would have been tough for you to slip sleeping pills in Trevor's drink with him sitting right there," said Beatrice, frowning.

Daniel's stiff reserve returned. "I headed to Trevor's table as I saw him returning to his seat with another plate of food. So, technically, I suppose I did have the ability to stoop over his drink and very quickly tamper with it. But I didn't. I was completely dedicated to the prospect of starting over with Trevor. I certainly wasn't trying to enact any type of revenge on him—I wanted to move forward and be friends again."

Beatrice said, "During your reception, I saw a man looking in the tent. He didn't appear to be invited. I wondered at the time if he might be the same man we saw at the restaurant, and now I believe he is. I also saw him at Trevor's funeral, hanging back and watching the proceedings."

Daniel pushed his black-rimmed glasses up his nose and regarded Beatrice seriously. "Who is he? Did you find out a name?"

"Apparently, his name is Patrick Finley, and he's a surgeon who may have worked with Trevor. At least, I know he knew him. I'm just guessing that he worked with him." There was a spark of recognition on Daniel's face, and Beatrice asked, "Do you know who he is, then?"

"I do. I mean, I don't know him personally and had never seen him before. I'd only heard him mentioned by Trevor." Lines of strain pulled from the sides of Daniel's mouth.

"What had Trevor said about him?" asked Beatrice.

Daniel sighed. "This was recently, when Trevor was really spiraling out of control. He wasn't being himself at all. Eleanor had called me, as a matter of fact. It was one morning where I didn't have an appointment at the office until afternoon, so I came over. Eleanor was upset that it was morning and Trevor was already drinking. When I arrived, it was clear that Trevor was in no shape to be able to go to work. The last thing he needed to do was be anesthetizing patients at the hospital—not in his condition."

"Did he explain anything to you? About why he was drinking or what was going on?"

"Not really. As I mentioned before, he seemed to be keeping a secret—something that he didn't want to let me in on. The police asked me if I'd known that Trevor was having an affair with Lyla Wales." Daniel's face was bewildered. "I'd had no idea. I suppose this was the secret that he was keeping from me. He wouldn't have wanted to tell me about it because he'd have known I'd have disapproved. I'd gotten very fond of Eleanor and would hate for her to get hurt."

"What did Trevor tell you?"

"He wasn't making a whole lot of sense. But he did tell me about his financial problems—that he was buried in debt. I reminded him that not going to work wasn't exactly the best approach in the world for getting out of financial trouble." Daniel made a face. "He wasn't listening to me, though. Trevor was coming up with his own plan to get out of the mess, and it had something to do with Patrick Finley. That was the name he kept repeating."

"Why would Patrick Finley help him?" asked Beatrice.

"Apparently, Trevor knew something about Patrick. Something pretty bad. He said that Patrick could lose his medical license or practice or whatever if people knew about it. I didn't really want to hear more than that. I cut Trevor off and asked him if he really thought blackmail was the solution to his problems. Because, to me, that's what it sounded like he was planning."

Beatrice raised her eyebrows. "That's a pretty big leap for Trevor to make, isn't it? First he's an upstanding doctor in the community. Then he becomes someone who gets intoxicated in the mornings and considers blackmail to escape a huge financial problem. Would you have said that Trevor was capable of acting like that?"

Daniel reached down and patted Sunny, who wagged her tail and looked lovingly at Daniel in response. "No, of course not. I'd never have thought he could behave that way."

But when he straightened up, Beatrice saw a haunted look in his eyes.

Back at home, Beatrice reached for her phone, then hesitated as she was about to dial Eleanor's number. It was hard to know why she felt so reticent about phoning her, but she had the feeling that it had something to do with the fact that Eleanor clearly wanted privacy and time to grieve by herself. That was something that Beatrice would ordinarily respect. Eleanor hadn't hosted anyone at her house; hadn't been receiving at home. She hadn't lingered at the cemetery too long, either, after the funeral.

But Beatrice did have a couple of things she needed to accomplish. For one, she'd promised Harper she'd give those crystal vases back to Eleanor. The longer they rattled around in Beatrice's car, the worse off they'd be. For another . . . she really hoped that Eleanor would open up and, in an unguarded moment, provide Beatrice and Meadow with some useful information.

Beatrice released a deep breath and dialed Eleanor's number. "Eleanor? Hi. It's Beatrice Coleman. I know this can hardly be a *good* time, but I offered to bring the vases you loaned Harper back to you. Is it possible for Meadow and me to run by and return them to you?"

There was a pause on the other end, and then Eleanor's voice drawled, "Of course. Thanks, Beatrice. I appreciate it." Another pause. "Do you want to leave them on the front porch for me?"

She was definitely avoiding them, then. Beatrice could hardly blame her, though. "I would . . . except they're so heavy. That's why I'll have Meadow with me—to help me carry them in. I don't think it's a one-person job." Beatrice winced after she said it. She didn't mean to point out that Eleanor was on her own now.

Eleanor hesitated again. "Well, everything is a disaster inside the house. Anne and David decided to get hotel rooms in Lenoir instead of staying here with me at the house. I'd hate for y'all to think it was always that way."

"Of course we won't! I can't imagine what you've been through the past week. Cleaning house would be the last thing on my mind, if it were me," said Beatrice.

"All right." Another pause. "Actually, if the clutter doesn't bother you, I could probably use the company." Eleanor quickly added, "But not if you have somewhere you need to go."

Beatrice had thought it would be like pulling teeth to arrange a visit with Eleanor. She made her voice as level as possible to conceal her surprise and said, "No, we don't have anything going on today, Eleanor. And we'd be happy to visit for a while."

Twenty minutes later, Beatrice had swung by to pick up Meadow, and they were on their way to Eleanor's house.

Meadow said, "I'm shocked that she's letting us come in her house. The women of the church were telling me that Eleanor politely refused both their casseroles and their sympathy. Same with the garden-club ladies. What makes us so special?"

"I think," said Beatrice, carefully navigating the

mountain curves, "that what got us in is my insistence that you and I don't mind a bit if her house is a little messy."

Meadow raised her eyebrows. "Well, I'm glad you gave me a heads-up. My house is cluttered most of the time, but I'd probably have shown some sort of surprise at Eleanor's being that way. She always seems so organized. I mean, *my* house would be a wreck if I'd just lost Ramsay. In fact, I'd probably ask those women from the church to come in with their casseroles *and* do some cleaning on the side."

"I've never seen your house less than lived-in-looking, Meadow," said Beatrice.

"If you say so. Okay, so on to this visit. We're coming in with the vases . . . and I do think they're pretty heavy, right? So we'll be super careful with those. And then we need to sit down with Eleanor and be an ear, probably. Right? Because I'm imagining if we start grilling her with questions about her husband's murder, that's likely not going to go off so well." Meadow pulled down the visor on her side of the car and looked at herself critically in the mirror. She tried to smooth down the errant strands of hair from her long gray braid, and then made a face at herself and pushed the visor back up.

"That's right. We need to try to elicit information in the gentlest, most sympathetic way possible," said Beatrice.

"I certainly don't want to trigger an outpouring of grief," said Meadow in a worried voice. "I didn't even bring any tissues with me."

"I remember how hard it was for me when my husband died," said Beatrice. "It wasn't only the fact that I'd lost my soul mate. It was also that *everything* had changed. We'd been together for twenty years, and suddenly my entire daily routine abruptly shifted. It's a very, very hard transition."

Meadow nodded, considering this for a moment. Then she gave Beatrice a sideways glance. "Thinking of relationships, have you seen much of Wyatt lately?"

Beatrice sighed. Meadow could be very nosy, but she also did have good advice sometimes. Maybe Beatrice could use some advice. "We did have breakfast together the morning we talked with Harper and Daniel after they'd returned to town."

"Have you seen him besides that?" asked Meadow.

"Oh sure. I saw him at Trevor's funeral, of course. And Harper and Daniel's wedding, too." Beatrice's hands tightened on the steering wheel.

Meadow made a scoffing sound. "Seeing someone at a funeral or wedding is hardly a date, Beatrice. Especially when you're there with the minister who's presiding over those events. What about that volunteering you said you were going to do? In order to see more of Wyatt at the church? What's become of that?"

"I'm still planning on doing it. I know I have an ulterior motive, but I really do believe in volunteering and supporting the community I live in. I think, with Trevor's murder, I've been sort of sidetracked," said Beatrice.

Meadow said thoughtfully, "Mmm. There were a couple of things in the church newsletter that maybe you'd be good to help with. I know you enjoy working with the elderly, for instance."

"Aren't I elderly myself?" asked Beatrice with a snort. "It's more like just visiting."

"Early sixties—elderly? Absolutely not! The elderly are our octogenarian and nonagenarian friends," said Meadow, sounding fairly miffed.

"Oh, I see. What type of volunteering is it?" asked Beatrice.

"The type where Wyatt goes," said Meadow simply.

Beatrice said in a warning tone, "Now, Meadow, I mentioned that my volunteering won't simply be a scheme to spend more time with Wyatt. That's just a pleasant by-product of it. So, what type of work is it?"

"A group goes to a local retirement home and visits with the residents," said Meadow. "It's one of those multifunctional retirement homes, so there's also a nursing unit there. Sometimes the group eats with residents. Sometimes they play a game of checkers or help work on a jigsaw puzzle. Most of the time they're simply providing fellowship." Meadow registered Beatrice's look of surprise. "I'm not one of the volunteers, but I know someone who is and loves it. She talks about it all the time."

"Who is that?" asked Beatrice, pulling into Eleanor's shrub-lined driveway.

"Miss Sissy."

Beatrice nearly took out one of the shrubs as she looked at Meadow. She carefully corrected the wheel and slowed down a little. "Miss Sissy! She should be in a retirement home herself!"

"Probably. But she only wants to visit there. Wyatt takes her along with the others in the church van." Meadow mused, "I think one of the big draws for Miss

Sissy is the snacks. The staff always provides snacks there."

"I don't know if spending an afternoon with Miss Sissy is something I'm really up for right now. But I'll keep it in mind."

Beatrice focused on parking close to the house and missed the look on Meadow's face. She'd have recognized it, if she had—it was the look of Meadow on a mission.

Beatrice looked admiringly at Eleanor's yard as she and Meadow approached the front door of the white Colonial Revival–style home. "I can certainly tell she enjoys gardening," said Beatrice. "No wonder she's a florist."

Crepe myrtle shrubs framed the front porch, and tall hollies created a natural hedge between the neighboring houses. Forsythia bushes with branches full of delicate yellow flowers waved gently in the breeze. It was clear that Eleanor took great pride in her yard and had already spruced it up with annuals, despite the chilly May temperature.

Eleanor managed a smile when she opened the door, but her eyes still held an exhausted expression. "Here, let me help you with those boxes," she said quickly.

Beatrice and Meadow demurred. "It's one of those things that if we tried to hand one to you, we'd probably drop the boxes," explained Beatrice. Although that wasn't really the truth. The truth was that Eleanor Garber looked frail beyond her years and didn't seem capable of holding any boxes herself. It was as if she were truly carrying the weight of the world on her shoulders.

"Where should we put them?" asked Meadow in something of a belabored voice as she tried to shift the large box she was carrying to a slightly more comfortable or secure position.

Beatrice blinked as she faced the room in front of her. Where indeed should they put the boxes of vases? She very carefully kept her features neutral as she looked out at the foyer and living room and into the dining room. There didn't seem to be a single spot anywhere that was clear. There was, actually, no way that the house could have gotten in this shape since Trevor's death. This type of clutter was surely years in the making. And it was such a shock after the carefully tended front yard.

Beatrice saw Meadow's eyes widen as she surveyed the rooms before she carefully arranged her expression into one as blank as Beatrice's.

Chapter Nine

There were unopened boxes from mail-order companies stacked floor to ceiling. As well, there were brand-new appliances, stacks upon stacks of folded clothing for men and women and even children, empty containers, books, catalogs, mail, and newspapers.

Eleanor gave them an uneasy look, and Beatrice and Meadow smiled reassuringly back at her. "Let's see," said Eleanor slowly. "What group should I put the vases with?" She frowned as she tried to figure out what stack the vases belonged with.

Meadow said, "Kitchen items? I usually keep my vases in my cabinets with my glassware." She stopped elaborating on that when her eyes fixed on a stack of cans that were there in the living room, right next to tubs of what appeared to be craft items.

Eleanor's grouping system didn't make immediate sense to Beatrice, so she decided to stay quiet and await her instructions.

Eleanor's decision making was painstakingly slow, however, and Beatrice shifted the medium boxes she was carrying to try to hold on to them better. Then Eleanor's face cleared. "I know. The dining-room table. It's this way."

The reason that Eleanor had to lead the way is because there was a specific path one had to take to navigate the piles and stacks of things in her home. Meadow, following behind Beatrice, gave Beatrice an alarmed look. Beatrice nodded back. This was much worse than just a little clutter or falling behind on housekeeping.

When Beatrice finally spotted the dining-room table, she had to bite her tongue to keep from asking Eleanor how they could put the boxes there. The entire table was covered with stacks of newspapers, catalogs, and old paperback books.

By this time, Beatrice's arms were groaning with the strain of carrying the heavy lead-crystal vases. She couldn't see even a conceivable spot to put the boxes down where they might not topple over and break. "Eleanor, do you think this is a good spot?" she asked weakly. "I'm worried they might break here."

"Oh! Oh, not up on top of the table. Underneath it. Can you put them underneath?" asked Eleanor a bit uncertainly.

Beatrice and Meadow stooped to check. Beatrice found that although the stacks under the table were pretty tall, there was still room to put their boxes on top of them. She finally unloaded the boxes with relief and slowly stood back up.

"Thank you so much for bringing those in for me," said Eleanor, real gratitude in her voice. "I can see now that there was no way I'd be able to do it myself." She shyly asked, "Would you like to sit for a few minutes? I could get you some lemonade, and we could visit. It's the least I could do after you had to haul those heavy boxes."

Meadow, standing behind Eleanor, raised her eyebrows. Like Beatrice, she must have been wondering where on earth they would be able to sit.

Eleanor quickly added, "Why don't we go into the kitchen?"

Beatrice wondered if the careful stacks hadn't yet extended into the kitchen. But they had. Most of the stacks there didn't appear to be kitchen related, either. Beatrice and Meadow hung back by the kitchen door as Eleanor swept in and started pulling glasses out of the cabinets and poured them some lemonade from a pitcher in the fridge.

"You know," Eleanor said, "I usually like to perch on those piles right there." She gestured to a newspaper pile and a magazine pile. "They're pretty comfortable. And you can reach the table from there."

Beatrice wondered what had become of the kitchen table that Eleanor was referring to. It must be somewhere, buried under the folded clothing. A sense of sadness rose in Beatrice as she surveyed the cluttered house. No wonder Eleanor hadn't wanted anyone over here. And what kind of stress or unhappiness had she been dealing with for it to manifest in this way?

Eleanor handed Beatrice and Meadow some glasses of lemonade, and then she settled down on a third stack to give them a tired smile. She said, "I wanted to thank you, too, for coming to the funeral yesterday. It meant a lot to me, and I'm not sure I showed that to everyone. I was just trying to make it through the day."

Meadow said staunchly, "Everyone knew you appreciated their being there. And they all *wanted* to come, after all. To show support for you."

Eleanor said with a faint smile, "You think so? To show support for *me*?"

"Absolutely!" said Meadow. "After all, it wouldn't mean anything to poor Trevor whether people were there or not. They were there for you."

This seemed to please Eleanor, and a rosy glow tinged her pale features as she thought about it.

Then Eleanor looked down at the floor. Or, rather, at some brown paper grocery bags that were stacked there. She said, "I had a lot of mixed feelings about being there yesterday. I was trying to be strong and not show them."

Beatrice said, "I'm sure you must have. My emotions would probably swing from one extreme to another on a day like that." She took a cautious sip of her lemonade. But Eleanor's lack of housecleaning or organizing didn't seem to extend to her beverage production. The glass was pristine and the lemonade tasted homemade.

Eleanor gave Beatrice a relieved look, as if glad that someone understood. "That's exactly right," she said. "Extreme emotions. You see, in some ways—this is horrible to say—but it was something of a relief when Trevor died."

Beatrice and Meadow froze. Beatrice hadn't dreamed that Eleanor, as fragile as she seemed right now, would be so up front with them about that.

"Trevor hadn't been acting like himself for months," Eleanor explained. "Our relationship was experiencing a lot of stress." She sighed, and the lines on her face showed in sharp relief as she reflected on the problems she'd had with her husband. "But then I did feel this huge sadness, because Trevor was determined to finally turn things around. When Daniel dropped Trevor as best man, it made Trevor realize that he needed to start behaving better. It made me very sad that he never had the chance to prove that he could make changes."

Eleanor paused again. "I'd also told Trevor that *I* was going to make some changes," she said quietly. She glanced around the room absently. Then she gave a small smile. "I'm sure you've noticed that things are a little cluttered in here."

Beatrice and Meadow didn't say anything, just smiled at her encouragingly. It seemed like the best thing to do.

"I'd told Trevor that I was finally going to be able to clear out my things here." Eleanor grimaced, as if it pained her to say the words. She swallowed and continued. "It's hard for me, you know. To throw things out that I might be able to use in the future. And there's so much information here that I might need to read and learn from." She indicated the stacks that Beatrice and Meadow were sitting on. "But I knew we both wanted to be able to have people over again. To host our grown children at Christmas. To have friends over for supper—that kind of thing. We were both going to work on changing." Eleanor's eyes were full of sadness.

Beatrice said, "That's why this is such a tragedy. I'm actually trying to help figure out who might be behind Trevor's death, Eleanor. I've had some success in the past with helping solve local cases. Did you see any-thing during the wedding or hear anything, or have any idea who might be responsible for this?"

Eleanor's eyes widened in surprise. "Of course. I know exactly who did it. It was Lyla. Lyla Wales."

Beatrice stiffened and said urgently, "Have you told Ramsay this?"

Meadow fussed. "Why wouldn't Ramsay have ar-rested her already, if you saw Lyla tamper with Trev-or's drink? I swear, that man can be so poky sometimes."

"I did tell him. But he wasn't really listening," said Eleanor. Her hands tightened as she clasped them until her knuckles were white.

"Not *listening*?" Meadow gaped at her. "I mean, I know he's not listening sometimes when I tell him gos-sip that I've heard at a guild meeting, but he was inter-viewing you. He *should* have been listening, by golly!"

Eleanor shrugged a thin shoulder. "Ramsay asked if I'd seen Lyla actually putting powder in Trevor's drink. I told him I hadn't, but that I hadn't had to, that I knew she'd done it, sure as anything."

Meadow snapped her mouth shut again and gave Beatrice a wiggle of her eyebrows to signify that Ram-say might need a spot more evidence than Eleanor's say-so.

"Why are you so certain that Lyla is responsible?" asked Beatrice intently.

"She's responsible for a lot," said Eleanor with a bit-ter laugh. "What's one more thing? She was the one who flirted with Trevor and lured him away from me. Then, once they'd had their affair, she was finished with him. Done. She called it quits, but Trevor couldn't seem to accept it was over. He kept embarrassing himself . . . embarrassing me. He'd follow Lyla around and try to convince her that they should be together."

"And you knew about it?" asked Beatrice. She winced as she said it.

"He was so focused, so driven, that at that point he wasn't even thinking about me. The only reason I could handle my own pain is because he was in so much pain himself. Then he started drinking, and everything started into a downward spiral. We were already deeply in debt, already in trouble. Not receiving paychecks certainly wasn't helping. And Trevor had gotten to the point where he really wasn't functioning—all he was doing was chasing Lyla," said Eleanor. She said it in a very matter-of-fact way.

"Why do you think that Lyla would have killed him?" asked Beatrice again.

"Because she needed to get rid of him." Eleanor waved her hands in a *poof* motion, as if making something disappear. "He was obviously driving her nuts. She was clearly trying to avoid him. Lyla was probably worried he was going to make her lose her job, since he was showing up at her office so often. And she wouldn't have wanted her husband to know about their relationship. I can't imagine he *wouldn't* have known, except that he's been traveling for work so much."

Beatrice said, "Why do you think Lyla got involved with Trevor to begin with? I know the two of you were friends."

Eleanor looked directly at Beatrice and said, "Because she *could*. She had the ability to make Trevor fall for her, and she did. It's all a game to her."

Beatrice nodded. She wasn't totally convinced about Lyla, but she could see that Eleanor was certainly convinced. She decided to take their conversation in another direction.

.But she was interrupted by Meadow, who was looking anxious. "But you signed up for the quilting workshop that Lyla is giving at the Patchwork Cottage tomorrow. Why would you have done that if you feel so strongly about her?"

Eleanor raised her chin. "Because I want to show her that I'm not intimidated by her. That I know exactly who—what—she is. And that she shouldn't think that she's won." Eleanor's voice was fierce, and a sort of feverish gleam lit in her eyes. Then she added, a bit more quietly, "Besides, I've always wanted to learn to quilt. That's really the way to connect here in Dappled Hills, isn't it? Now that I'm going to clear the house, I'll need to find some ways to connect here in town. I should invite people over when I'm done tidying. I've got all these craft tubs, too." She gave a vague wave around her to indicate that the craft tubs were somewhere.

"You're not there to start a fight?" Meadow asked in a protective voice. "This workshop is important to Posy—to all the quilters. We're trying to show a younger generation that quilting doesn't have to be hard or time-consuming. It would be terrible if something happened to overshadow what we were trying to do."

Eleanor said, "I'm only going to show her that I'm not a pushover." There was a mulish tone to Eleanor's voice that made Meadow shift uncomfortably.

Before Meadow and the quilting workshop could completely hijack the conversation, Beatrice quickly injected, "Eleanor, I was also wondering if you could shed some light on something for me. Before Trevor died, I saw him in a restaurant, having an argument with a tall man with shaggy gray hair. Then I saw what looked like the same man standing outside the wedding reception. He was also at the funeral."

Eleanor knit her brows. "Sort of deep-set eyes? That's Patrick. Patrick Finley."

Meadow gave Beatrice a confirming nod.

"Were you and Trevor friends with him?" asked Beatrice. "I was just wondering at the connection, since he didn't seem as though he were invited to the wedding, judging from the way he was acting, and then there was that argument they had."

Eleanor squeezed her hands together in her lap. "Patrick was a friend of ours, yes. But then Trevor . . . well, he wasn't acting like himself, as I've already pointed out. It wasn't like the Trevor I married to do *any* of the things he was doing. But he told me, on one of those days where we actually had a conversation, that he had seen Patrick make a huge mistake in the operating room. Trevor, you might know, was an anesthesiologist. Trevor and Patrick were both on call and had been out drinking with each other. Trevor was starting to fall into some bad habits. They both got called in—it was the same surgery. Some sort of an emergency surgery—maybe a car wreck."

Meadow looked horrified. "And they worked on the patient even though they'd been drinking? How much had they drunk?"

Eleanor shook her head. "I'm not sure. At any rate, it was enough for Patrick to really botch the surgery."

Beatrice asked, "The patient died?"

"He did. But Patrick covered it up. He didn't admit to any wrongdoing. Instead he said that the trauma from the car accident had been irreversible. Trevor was the only one who knew the truth—that Patrick had been drinking and was incompetent to perform surgery."

"What did Trevor say?" asked Beatrice. "Did he threaten to do something with the information he had?"

Eleanor sighed. "He did. We've been in terrible financial shape, and Patrick was sitting on a fortune. Trevor basically asked Patrick for a payoff to keep quiet."

"Blackmail," murmured Meadow.

Eleanor flinched at the word. "I guess so. He told Patrick that he would tell the truth about that surgery unless he gave Trevor some hush money." She quickly added in his defense, "Patrick came off a lot cheaper than he would have if he'd lost his medical license or if the patient's relatives had sued for malpractice, believe me."

"So Patrick *did* pay Trevor?" asked Beatrice.

"Some. He paid a bit of money. But then he didn't seem to want to pay any more," said Eleanor.

That might explain why the man was looking for an opportunity to talk with Trevor . . . And why they'd had an argument. It sounded as if Trevor kept asking Patrick for more money instead of allowing the payoff to be final.

Eleanor looked out the window. She said in a quiet voice, "Now I'm okay, though."

Beatrice and Meadow looked questioningly at Eleanor. "In what way?" asked Beatrice.

"The huge financial mess we were in? It's all over

now. Trevor had a life-insurance policy—a pretty big one, since he was really the sole provider. And now all the debts will be taken care of." A complacent look settled on Eleanor's face. "At least I've got that."

Back in Beatrice's car, Meadow whistled. "Well, I can sure see why they had financial problems. Poor Eleanor! I've never seen anything like it. And what a surprise after walking through such a meticulously kept yard!"

"Eleanor obviously has a problem with hoarding," said Beatrice. "It's really very sad."

"I know, but I think of hoarding as being a collection of things with no value. There were a lot of boxes of merchandise in there—some of them opened, some of them not. None of it used. And Eleanor didn't even need that stuff! I saw swimming-pool cleaning equipment, for heaven's sake. The Garbers don't have a pool!" Meadow flapped her hands around in the air.

"I'm sure the reason she was hoarding was a reaction to stress," said Beatrice slowly. "Maybe the onset of the financial problems started it. Or maybe when their children left the nest. Of course, she said she's ready to get rid of it all."

Meadow said, "Eleanor and whose army? It's going to take forever to get that stuff out of there, and she's probably going to have more of a struggle letting it go than she thinks. No wonder her children stayed in a hotel—they'd have had to use bulldozers to get to the guest room at Eleanor's. She needs to stop hanging out in her yard and spend some time working on the inside."

"I wonder if her children have tried to help her unclutter before? Surely they couldn't have simply abandoned her to it."

"Haven't you seen all those shows about hoarding? Family always tries to help, and the help is almost always resisted," said Meadow.

Beatrice accepted this as true. Meadow watched a lot more television than she did.

Meadow said thoughtfully, "On another subject, did you notice that she sure was down on Lyla?"

Beatrice glanced across quickly at Meadow before turning her attention back to the road. "Understandably, though."

"But it was almost as if she blamed Lyla for everything that happened—as if Trevor were somehow the victim," said Meadow.

Beatrice nodded. "She certainly didn't seem very angry with Trevor, even though he clearly was the source of a lot of personal pain for her."

"It might have something to do with the fact that he's dead. No one really likes to speak ill of the dead, after all," said Meadow reasonably. Beatrice frowned and Meadow asked, "Why? Are you thinking that Eleanor is trying to set Lyla up as the murderer?"

Beatrice shrugged. "It's awfully convenient, isn't it? Eleanor's money problems are now all taken care of. Maybe she can persuade the police to really focus in on Lyla, and then she's taken her revenge on her. I don't know. It seems like it would have been pretty easy for Eleanor to have slipped something in Trevor's drink—that's all. And I'm not sure that Eleanor is totally mentally healthy, either. And she did seem fixated on Lyla as a suspect. I thought that was kind of odd, considering that your doctor sure seems to have a pretty strong motive."

"Dr. Finley? Oh, he's a sweetheart," said Meadow with a pooh-poohing motion of her hand. "I'm sure he wouldn't hurt a fly."

"Maybe he wouldn't hurt a fly on *purpose*. But this was obviously accidental, even though it was clearly malpractice. Who knows what Patrick Finley might have done to protect his livelihood and his reputation? Trevor Garber was a disaster—exactly the kind of person you wouldn't want privy to any dark secrets," said Beatrice, pulling into Meadow's driveway.

"True. But, boy, Eleanor didn't seem to think it was such a big deal. She was totally minimizing Trevor's role in that whole mess. She remained convinced that Lyla was the one behind Trevor's death," said Meadow, taking off her seat belt and gathering up her pocketbook from the floor of Beatrice's car.

Beatrice said, "It's going to make the quilting workshop a lot more exciting than Posy had bargained on—that's for sure."

Meadow groaned. "I know. I was hoping to persuade Eleanor not to come. It's obvious that she only wanted to go to it because she's planning on rattling Lyla."

"She did say that she had a lot of supplies, which I took to mean fabric and some notions," said Beatrice mildly.

"If she can find them! I don't think she could," said Meadow, shaking her head. "No, mark my words, Beatrice: this quilting workshop has *disaster* written all over it."

Chapter Ten

Meadow's words rang ominously through Beatrice's head as she opened the door to the Patchwork Cottage. She half expected to see Eleanor already advancing on a hapless Lyla. Instead, she saw Miss Sissy, snoring away as usual in the sitting area in the middle of the store. Savannah was there with Smoke, and was gazing at the cat adoringly as he drowsily curled up in her lap, looking as if he were heading in the same direction as Miss Sissy.

Beatrice walked over to join Savannah. She said eagerly to Beatrice, "Isn't he the cutest? Can you see what he's wearing?"

Beatrice couldn't, not with him curled up, so Savannah held him up for a moment to show she'd put a little polka-dot bow tie on the cat. Beatrice smiled. "He must be a good boy to put up with wearing a tie."

"He's such a good boy. I wanted to thank you again for giving him to me," said Savannah for about the fiftieth time.

Beatrice said, "I'm glad he's worked out so well for you. I certainly couldn't have kept him—Noo-noo kept looking at me with these hurt eyes when he stayed with us. No, Smoke is definitely with the right owner." She sat down across from Savannah and next to the sleeping Miss Sissy on the sofa.

Miss Sissy abruptly woke up with a jerk, glared at Beatrice, and then promptly fell back asleep.

Savannah shook her head and, eyebrows drawn down in concern, said, "Don't you think Miss Sissy might scare away some of the young quilters?"

Beatrice hid a smile. Savannah was usually fairly scary herself, with her bossy attitude, sternness, and perfectionism. She suspected that Smoke was proving a miracle worker by softening Savannah up a bit. "Well, you've got Smoke here to charm them, at least," she answered.

Savannah's gaze fell to the large tote bag that Beatrice had with her. "What are you working on today?"

Beatrice reached into the bag and pulled out her work in progress. "I know we're demonstrating the easier side of quilting for the beginners. My last quilt was such a tough one that I was actually excited about doing something simpler this time."

She opened up the quilt to show off the white background with small blocks of various shades of blue and forest green. Beatrice had machine-quilted a small brown owl perching on a leafy branch about three-quarters of the way down the quilt. The owl stared quizzically out at them.

"I thought it might be a nice gift for Piper, since she's a teacher," said Beatrice.

Savannah was usually a fan of very precise, geometric patterns, so Beatrice was surprised when she beamed her approval. "It's very cute," she said. "That will be a great quilt to demonstrate machine quilting to some of the group."

"Speaking of the group, has anyone come yet?" Beatrice sat up and craned her head to look around. "I probably need to skedaddle to the back room and help Posy set up."

"You're here pretty early," said Savannah with a shrug. Beatrice was amazed at how relaxed the uptight Savannah was these days. "Georgia hasn't even made it over here yet. I haven't seen any of the new quilters."

"How is Georgia doing, by the way?" asked Beatrice.

"Busy!" said Savannah. "She's spending a lot of time with Tony these days." But instead of pursing her lips in disapproval like the old Savannah would have done, she smiled.

"That's good," said Beatrice. "He seems like such a nice guy."

"Hard worker, too," said a voice approaching them. It was Meadow, holding a couple of rolled-up quilts. "Just like Wyatt." Meadow gave Beatrice a meaningful look.

"Yes, he is. And, before you ask, I did go onto the church Web site and volunteer for the outing to the retirement home," said Beatrice. All she needed was for Meadow to go off on another Wyatt-related tangent.

"Did you?" Meadow's face lit up. But then it quickly darkened again. "So, you've decided to actively pursue spending more time with Wyatt. That means *I* won't get to see you as much. And that makes me sad. We already don't spend as much time together as I'd like to, Beatrice. The sacrifice that I've made by suggesting that you volunteer in order to spend more time with Wyatt—it boggles the mind! Now you're condemning me to spend my free time visiting with *Ramsay*. Ramsay, who will nod as I talk but actually be thinking about the last incredibly boring book he read."

"You could always watch *Wheel* with him," said Beatrice, hiding a smile. Ramsay, literary as he was, was a huge *Wheel of Fortune* fan.

Meadow made a face at her and stomped off to the store's back room to help Posy with the setup.

Miss Sissy woke up with another start and glared around her suspiciously. "What's going on?" she croaked.

"Meadow was having a hissy fit," said Savannah absently. She tickled Smoke under his chin.

Miss Sissy turned her attention to the cat. "I want to hold him," she said, with a stubborn set to her chin.

Savannah demurred. "Smoke isn't really used to anyone but me, Miss Sissy. He might not like it."

Miss Sissy growled, "Cat! I want the cat!"

"I'd better get going with the setup," said Beatrice, hastily leaving before Savannah recruited her to protect Smoke from Miss Sissy's clutches.

The back room was already fairly set up. There were extension cords on long tables, and the sewing machines were ready to go. Posy was busily hanging some machine-quilted quilts up for demonstration, and Beatrice helped her hang a few. "How many new quilters are we expecting today?" she asked Posy.

"It looks as if we'll have eight altogether," said Posy

in an excited voice. "I think that's a nice size, don't you? It's a large enough group so that we're not wasting our time, but small enough that we're able to give individual help. Thanks so much for being one of the helpers, Beatrice."

Lyla was helping Meadow lay handouts by each sewing machine. She grinned at Beatrice and pushed a strand of wavy hair out of her pretty, heart-shaped face. "It's exciting, isn't it? If we can hook a younger generation into quilting, it will bring fresh ideas to the craft, too. And it's not as if you have to be retired to have the time to quilt. There are ways to fit it into a busy schedule."

"Oh, you don't have to convince me," said Beatrice with a laugh. That laugh cut off as she noticed that a glowering Eleanor entering the door. She looked a bit more disheveled than usual, and her gray hair in its pixie cut looked as if it had either been windblown on the way over or hadn't been brushed that day.

Beatrice heard Posy take a deep, steadying breath before she said in her sweet voice, "Eleanor! So good to see you here at our class. But you've come a little early—we're still setting up. Would you like to have a seat out in the shop? I put out some refreshments out there, too—you could have a pimento cheese square and some iced tea."

Meadow caught Beatrice's eye and winced. This was exactly what Meadow had been worried about.

Eleanor didn't appear to be listening to Posy at all. She continued staring darkly at Lyla, who was looking increasingly uncomfortable. Lyla said quietly, "It's great to have you here, Eleanor. You could always put down your pocketbook wherever you want to sit and we could keep an eye on it for you while you're waiting in the store."

Again, Eleanor didn't seem to register what Lyla was saying; she just continued staring at her with a cold fury.

Miss Sissy scurried into the room with her oddly galloping gait, followed by an anxious Savannah, who hovered closely, as if Miss Sissy were on the continual verge of dropping Smoke. Miss Sissy was in a much more cheerful mood and held what looked like a very contented Smoke in her arms. "Nice cat," she grunted. She seemed oblivious to the tension in the room, and plopped down in a chair against the back wall to stroke the cat.

Finally, Eleanor started talking. And she spoke as if no one were in the room except for her and Lyla. "You killed Trevor." Her gray eyes were fixed on Lyla.

Lyla, sleekly dressed in a black knit top and jeans, gaped at the disheveled woman in front of her. "Eleanor. Eleanor, you don't know what you're saying."

"I do! Don't act like you don't know what I'm talking about. You wanted Trevor, you got Trevor, and then you wanted rid of Trevor. Then you wanted rid of him for *good*. I know what you did." Eleanor's voice was steady and without inflection.

Lyla's face was white, and the hand holding the handouts trembled. "Eleanor, you've had a huge shock with Trevor's death. I understand that. But you know I wasn't anywhere near Trevor during the reception. I was trying to avoid him, actually, and I was very busy at the sign-in table with the guest quilt."

Eleanor's voice grated. "Maybe you were at the

guest quilt some of the time. In fact, I know that you weren't there *all* the time. All I know is that you're the one responsible. You killed him, just as sure as if you'd held a gun to his head and pulled the trigger."

Miss Sissy, eyebrows pulled together in a ferocious expression as she clutched Smoke protectively, barked at Eleanor. "Enough! Go!"

Eleanor still stayed focused on Lyla. "You didn't even *want* him. Why did you have to mess everything up?"

Lyla glanced around at the other quilters and said in a quiet voice, "Eleanor, there's a time and a place to discuss this. But it's not now. The students are going to be arriving any minute for my workshop, and this is important to Posy and to all of the quilters. I'll speak with you about this later, I promise."

Eleanor still stood still with a bullish expression on her face until finally Miss Sissy again bellowed, "Go!" Eleanor bolted out the door.

Lyla swallowed, and her shoulders seemed to relax as they heard the door to the Patchwork Cottage close behind Eleanor. She'd really left. "May I ... Could everyone excuse me for a couple of minutes?" she asked. Lyla quickly strode out of the room in the direction of the ladies' room.

"Oh dear," said Posy, looking distressed. "Poor Lyla. And poor Eleanor, too."

Meadow was more to the point. "What on earth did Eleanor think she was doing? At a *quilting* workshop? Like she couldn't just wait for Lyla in the parking lot afterward and rip into her then?"

Miss Sissy said, "Poppycock!" She was so agitated-looking that Savannah quickly rescued Smoke from her possession.

"No harm done to the workshop, Meadow," said Beatrice. "No one's gotten here yet, but now is the time they should start coming in. Here, let me finish distributing those handouts."

They finished getting the room ready and then greeted the new quilters as they arrived. Lyla quickly returned with a big smile for the quilters, and only the brightness of her eyes indicated that she'd recently experienced some strong emotion.

Posy introduced Lyla, and Lyla spoke for a while before demonstrating how to get started with machine quilting. She explained straight-line quilting and demonstrated everything from threading a machine to turning corners and securing the thread. Posy also spoke in her gently excited way about the types of notions and fabrics and other supplies that she had available at the store. Finally, Posy showed them a complete project they could make, and the fabrics they would need to quilt it.

Beatrice murmured to Meadow, "Posy has done such a great job picking out a good first project. These large pieces are going to require a lot fewer seams. It sure makes it easier to be accurate. And the fact they're doing a small project—a baby quilt—makes for a more attainable goal, I think."

"And not only are the pieces Posy chose large, but they're squares. *So* much easier than triangles," said Meadow.

Beatrice agreed. Sometimes she still had trouble with bias edges necessary for triangles.

Soon the women were on the sewing machines, with the Village Quilters standing by, watching them work and leaning in to give advice when needed. Beatrice loved the fabrics on the finished quilts that Posy had on display. The finished baby-girl quilt blocks sported different shades of pink with everything from hearts to flowers with vinelike green stems, little chickens, and to rosy balls. The baby-boy quilt had blocks in color order, with the darkest blues at the top and the lightest toward the bottom. The individual blocks had blue trucks, blue sailboats, and a whimsical blue polka-dot pattern.

The beginning quilters were attentive and seemed enthusiastic, which was the very best outcome one could hope for. They ranged in age from a thin, bespectacled girl in her late teens to a beaming, prematurely white-haired lady in her early sixties, but most of the quilters were in their mid-twenties. There was one couple in the room, and they seemed very quick to catch on and feed off each other's ideas.

Beatrice stood near the teen girl's sewing machine to jump in whenever she had a question. The girl, who had a shy smile, introduced herself as Susan. Although her actions were at first tentative, her eyes brightened as she started catching on, and Beatrice sat down at the machine beside her and worked on the owl quilt she was making for Piper. While they worked, Susan excitedly asked about good patterns for beginners and the most important notions to have starting out. Beatrice loved seeing how quickly she and the other new quilters became engaged in their projects.

There was quite a line at the check-out counter as the quilters, excited by the possibilities of the craft, bought notions and fabric. So, despite its beginning, the day was definitely a success.

Meadow and Beatrice helped clean up the back room while Posy manned the check-out counter and Lyla helped advise the new quilters on purchases. Meadow said in an aside to Beatrice, as they gathered up trash and took quilts off the holders, "Whew. That turned out better than I thought it would. When Eleanor showed up and started throwing accusations around, I thought the quilting workshop was going to be a total disaster."

"At least none of it took place in front of the new quilters," said Beatrice. "And Lyla handled it really well, I thought." She paused. "I really need to talk with her again. Eleanor is so sure she's responsible for Trevor's death."

"Well, catch up with her as she's loading her car, or something," said Meadow. "No time like the present."

After they'd taken everything down and put away the sewing machines, Beatrice spotted Lyla about to take her leave. Meadow made a shooing motion at Beatrice as she saw Lyla heading out the door. Beatrice gathered up the quilt she was making for Piper and her pocketbook, and hurried to follow her.

Lyla's car was only a couple down from Beatrice's, which made approaching her a lot easier. Deep in thought, Lyla didn't hear Beatrice calling her name the first time. Finally, she turned, and Beatrice said, "You did a nice job at the workshop. Posy looked so excited that this new group of quilters was so enthused. I overheard a couple of them talking about starting their own guild—a beginner's guild."

Lyla smiled, but the smile didn't quite reach her eyes. "Thanks, Beatrice. I appreciate that." Her eyes unexpectedly filled with tears, and, as she fished for a tissue in her purse, Lyla made a face as if irritated with herself. "Sorry. It's been a long day."

"I'm sorry, too. You did especially well with the workshop, considering you'd just been attacked by Eleanor moments before. You really recovered from the shock of that quickly."

Lyla gave her a more genuine smile now. "Until now, I suppose. Now it's all starting to set in." She gazed absently across the empty parking lot. "Not that Eleanor's take on Trevor's death *was* a shock. It's simply the fact that she was accusing me in a public place, where I was trying to be organized and professional and give a class. *That* was the shock."

Beatrice said carefully, "Showing up where you were trying to be professional—that was more like Trevor, wasn't it?"

Lyla unlocked the passenger's-side door and placed a basket of materials and a quilt that she was carrying onto the seat. She straightened up and looked Beatrice in the eye. "It sure was. Look, I don't know what people in town are saying about me. But here's the truth: I made a mistake. I'm human. Unfortunately, I'm having to pay and pay for that mistake, and I don't see it ending anytime soon."

"You're saying it was a mistake having an affair with Trevor," said Beatrice quietly.

Lyla nodded. "Clearly. Eleanor's right about that part . . . I pursued him. He was funny and smart and was flatteringly attentive to me. After so many years with Julian, I guess that's what attracted me to Trevor—just the attention. But it didn't take long for me to realize that I was jeopardizing a life that was important to me. When I tried to end our relationship, Trevor absolutely flipped."

"Flipped?" asked Beatrice.

"That's right. He wasn't ready for the relationship to be over. He said it was a lifeline for him." Lyla shook her head, as if not comprehending how Trevor could have felt that way.

But Beatrice, remembering what Trevor's situation at home with Eleanor might be like, did understand it.

"He basically started stalking me all over town. Trevor stopped trying to be discreet. And I didn't want Julian to know anything about my . . . indiscretion. Trevor was making that impossible. And Eleanor clearly already knew, because she was looking at me with tremendous hostility whenever she saw me around town. But how *couldn't* she know once Trevor's behavior went haywire?" Lyla was almost musing to herself now, working out what happened as if she'd practically forgotten that Beatrice was there.

"By Trevor's behavior, you mean his drinking?" asked Beatrice.

"His drinking and everything that resulted from it," said Lyla with a nod. "He wasn't going to work, and from what I knew of their financial situation, that wasn't a good idea. I *had* to get him to stop," she said, her fingers tightening on the sides of the purse she still held. "He was going to destroy both of our lives."

"But you had nothing to do with the sleeping pills in his glass," said Beatrice slowly.

Lyla's head jerked up and she stared at Beatrice with alarm. "Is that what people are saying? I know it's what Eleanor is saying, but it's not true." She started speaking faster and said harshly, "The police should be looking at *Eleanor*. She's the one who was bent on revenge. She's the one who felt humiliated by Trevor's behavior." Lyla glanced around to make sure that she and Beatrice were still alone and then said, "You know Eleanor is unstable. I told Ramsay to make sure to talk to her at her home. Trevor's unbalanced behavior tipped her over the edge . . . and she was already unstable, even years ago."

"So you think Eleanor murdered Trevor?" asked Beatrice, raising her eyebrows.

"I'm sure of it," said Lyla hoarsely. "She's a very dangerous woman. Eleanor approached me at the wedding reception—while I was helping guests sign the quilt blocks—and threatened me."

"In what way?"

"She told me to back off from Trevor, and I told her that maybe she needed to rein Trevor in a little, because I was *trying* to back off and couldn't seem to get away from her husband. The next thing I know, Eleanor told me that I'd better leave Trevor alone or else she'd kill me. She opened her purse, and there was a large knife right there in her pocketbook." Lyla shivered.

"A knife? But you didn't see any loose pills or a pill container or anything like that?" asked Beatrice.

"Beatrice, I can promise you, I only had eyes for that knife. It was an ugly weapon, let me assure you. All I wanted was for Eleanor and Trevor to leave me alone. After Eleanor walked off, I was standing there at the guest table, helping guests sign the blocks, and all I was doing was thinking about how I could get out of my situation." Her eyes became sad. "And then the next thing I knew, Trevor was dead."

Beatrice said softly, "When you and I were standing over Trevor's body, I heard you say, 'Why couldn't we have loved each other at the same time.'"

Lyla made a sound that was halfway between a laugh and a groan. "That's the irony of it all. First, I was chasing Trevor and he wasn't really all that into me. The next thing I know, I'm coming to my senses, and then Trevor is chasing *me*. Life is unfair sometimes."

Beatrice tried to move the conversation back to the murder before the rest of the Village Quilters joined them outside. "So, you think that Eleanor slipped the sleeping pills into Trevor's drink at some point during the reception—and that now she's trying to make you take the blame."

Lyla said, "Doesn't it make perfect sense? Eleanor had the opportunity to tamper with Trevor's drink. She was furious with Trevor—don't let her fool you if she acts like she wasn't. She was bent on revenge, believe me. It gives her a tremendous motive. And then she gets sort of a bonus out of it, because if I go to jail for the crime. And she gets rid of me, too. Besides, we already know she was homicidal, since she was carrying a knife around at a wedding, for heaven's sake. And she's in a pretty fragile mental state, too."

Lyla sighed and looked at her watch. "Sorry, Beatrice, but I've really got to run. I'm getting a headache, and I think it's because I really haven't had anything to eat. Thanks for your support today, and, please, if you hear rumors about me—and I'm sure you will—if you could correct whatever lies are circulating, I'd appreciate it."

As Lyla got in her car and drove away, Beatrice considered Lyla's allegations against Eleanor. Yes, Eleanor was unstable, as evidenced by the huge stacks of hoarded goods at her home. Yes, she was clearly furious with Lyla and might have had similar feelings against Trevor. But would Eleanor have killed her husband and set up Lyla as the killer? She'd have to pay another visit to Eleanor's house to see if she'd talk about threatening Lyla at the wedding.

Chapter Eleven

The next morning, Beatrice had just gotten dressed and was on the point of taking Noo-noo for a stroll when the phone rang.

It was Harper, and she sounded especially cheerful this morning. Actually, it sounded more like Harper was trying to fake cheerfulness. "Beatrice? Hi. It's me, Harper. I was thinking that I'd love to catch up with you over coffee." Some hesitation, and then Harper's voice didn't sound quite as cheerful. "Unless— Well, I know you're probably busy."

"Oh no, I'd love to have coffee and a visit," said Beatrice.

"Great! Um . . . we could meet at the coffee shop downtown. Or, well, there's a breakfast place over on the state highway—have you been there? It's pretty good, although it would be more of a drive." Harper sounded very unlike her usual confident self. "Or we could meet somewhere else, if you want. There's the doughnut shop."

Beatrice said quickly, "Why don't you just drop by here? I've got a good French-roast coffee that I can perk for us. If you don't mind the fact that the newspaper is all over the living room, I'd love to have you come by."

"Perfect." Harper's voice sounded relieved. "I'll be there in a few minutes."

Beatrice made another pot of coffee and set out the coffee cups, half-and-half, and sugars. "I promise we'll walk in a little while," she told Noo-noo. The corgi seemed to understand, because soon she gave up her post at the front door and curled contently near Beatrice on the floor of the kitchen.

The knock at the door sent Noo-noo into startled barking. When she saw Harper, though, she apparently judged her as nonthreatening and immediately flopped over on her back to ask for a tummy rub.

Harper laughed and crouched over to rub the corgi's belly. "Quite the guard dog you have here, Beatrice."

"Oh, Noo-noo's talents lie in being a *watch*dog. She watches and barks. The guarding? It's not really her forte."

The two women settled into the living room. Noo-noo was so impressed with her new friend that she lay on top of Harper's feet.

Beatrice could see that Harper was reticent to talk about whatever was on her mind, so she asked how the house was coming along and filled Harper in on the workshop. Harper looked directly at Beatrice and nodded at intervals, but Beatrice could tell that her mind was miles away.

Finally, at a break in the conversation, Harper said, "It's been so nice visiting with you, Beatrice. I've been in such a state the past couple of days, and I was really looking for some perspective. I spoke with Wyatt briefly, and he suggested that I might want to talk things over with you. He said that you were such a good listener and so levelheaded and thoughtful. I decided I'd run this problem by you. You can tell me whether I'm off in left field or not."

Beatrice nodded encouragingly at her. Harper took a deep breath and continued. "Daniel has been acting kind of funny since that night when we had supper and saw Trevor arguing with that other man. I figured at first that it simply upset him that he had to remove Trevor as best man. Daniel was so preoccupied after that night at the restaurant. He's always been really good about texting me back or returning my calls, but after that?" Harper shrugged a slim shoulder.

Beatrice said, "Why do you think he became so removed after that?"

"I didn't have a lot of time to think about it, honestly. We were so close to the wedding date then, and I was frantically busy. I think part of me wondered if Daniel was sad about losing his bachelor status after so many years. You know?" Harper gave a short laugh.

"And now you've had more time to think about it," guessed Beatrice.

"Right." Harper took a sip of her coffee and seemed to be considering her words carefully. "I don't know, Beatrice. Sometimes it seems that Daniel is holding something back from me. Of course, I know he's a very private person. I understand that. I can be private, too.

But I'm his *wife*. I thought he might open up to me more after we were married—or, at least, I hoped that he would."

Beatrice frowned. "Is there a particular subject that he usually shuts you out of? Like his childhood or friendships or work?"

Harper nodded. "His mother. Or his family, I guess I should say. Whenever I start asking questions, it's like a door closes shut. It's immediate."

"What kinds of questions are you asking? Are they very personal?" asked Beatrice.

"Not at all. Very general questions. You know, just making conversation: 'How old was your mother when you were born?' Things like that." Noo-noo, who seemed to sense their guest's pain, stood up so that she could lean against Harper's leg in a show of solidarity. Harper absently rubbed the corgi.

"As I recall, Daniel's mother lives locally, doesn't she? I think I met her for a few minutes at the wedding."

Harper said, "Yes, she lives in Mountain Vistas retirement home, outside of Dappled Hills. I've met her several times and she seems very nice, but rather reserved. I could tell that Daniel dotes on her . . . Well, a lot of mother-son relationships are like that. He's obviously very protective of her, and that's great. But I think he's hiding something. I hate to say that," she said quickly. "It's just that he closes up at her name, and then for him to have been acting so oddly after that night he talked to Trevor—it's almost as if those two things are connected."

Beatrice said slowly, "Do you think Trevor might

have known something about Daniel? Or his mother? Something that maybe Daniel didn't want to get out?"

"Yes," said Harper quickly, sounding relieved. "That's exactly what I was wondering. At first I told myself that I must be imagining things, that it was only the stress of the wedding getting to me. But the more I thought about it all, the more I wondered. I know Trevor was in debt. I know he was making bad choices. What if he knew something about Daniel—even some information from long ago—and was using it as leverage to get money from Daniel? What if . . ." But Harper broke off, clutching her coffee cup until her knuckles turned white.

Harper's hands started shaking, and she carefully placed the coffee cup on Beatrice's coffee table. "I know this must sound crazy to you, Beatrice. Trevor was having problems, but what I'm talking about is criminal. It's quite a leap to getting into criminal behavior, even if you are in debt."

Beatrice shook her head. "Daniel may not have told you that he and I met up when we were out walking the dogs. I told him that I'd learned that Trevor was extorting money from the mystery man that I'd seen at the wedding and the funeral. Remember? I thought he resembled the man that we saw arguing with Trevor that night at supper."

"Was that who it was?" asked Harper. The fine lines etched on the sides of her eyes stood out in sharp relief against her features, pale from the stress.

"It was," said Beatrice. She paused and then added, "The thing was, Daniel didn't seem very surprised to hear about it. He said that Trevor had mentioned that he knew something about Patrick that would cause Patrick Finley to lose his medical license. And he didn't seem at all surprised about the blackmail."

Harper briefly closed her eyes. "Maybe the reason he wasn't surprised is because Trevor was trying to pull the same trick on him." Her expression grew more calculated. "So, this Patrick was at the reception, too. Maybe he was the one who murdered Trevor. It would make sense. Why else would he have been there?"

Beatrice gave a small shrug. "It could be that he was there to persuade Trevor to stop blackmailing him. Maybe Trevor was avoiding him, and he was simply looking for a time to be able to connect with him in person. It seemed like he was trying to talk to Trevor at that restaurant, but he was too far gone to make any sense that night. Or, yes, maybe Patrick was behind Trevor's death. That would certainly have eliminated the blackmail."

Harper said in a hollow voice, "Or maybe Daniel was behind his death. That would have solved Daniel's problem, too." She covered her face with her hands.

"Have you asked Daniel about this?" asked Beatrice. "Have you pointed out that you know he's keeping things from you and you're worried about him?"

"Beatrice, I'd love to have that conversation with him, but I feel like our marriage is so young . . . I don't want him to feel that I don't trust him." Harper sighed. "It sounds like I really *don't* trust him, but I certainly don't want him to get that impression. It's simply so early in our marriage to have the issue of trust looming over us."

"Would you like me to talk with him?" asked Beatrice. "I wouldn't even have to mention you at all. I could say that I'd gotten the feeling that Daniel might be holding something back. Honestly, I'm not sure *what* I'm going to say, but I can definitely tread softly there."

"Maybe the next time you run into him?" asked Harper, eyes worried. "I don't want him to feel as if you made a special trip over to ask him about it. That will seem like an interrogation, I think."

"I'll wait until we accidentally meet up, then. And, Harper? Try not to worry. I'm sure there's a very logical explanation for this. Daniel is, after all, a lawyer. Maybe Trevor did try to see if he could somehow pressure Daniel for money. Maybe Daniel blew him off and didn't want to bring the episode to the police because he felt it might make him look bad."

"And he *already* looks bad because he dumped Trevor as his best man," added Harper.

"Right. So he wouldn't want to appear any more suspicious. Besides, think about it: it would have been very tough for him to pull this off at his own wedding. I'm not going to say that it *couldn't* happen, just that it would be a real feat." Beatrice smiled at Harper, and slowly she smiled back in return.

Beatrice wished she could only convince herself.

After Harper left, Beatrice was mulling over Daniel's possible involvement in Trevor's death when there was another knock at her front door. Noo-noo cocked her head to one side in surprise, which was mirrored by Beatrice. Had Harper left something behind? Beatrice quickly scanned the room, seeing nothing, as she walked to the door.

It was Meadow, wearing binoculars and a camera

around her neck and a dark, un-Meadow-like top and pants. "Ready to spy on my doctor?" she asked. Then Meadow frowned and looked at Beatrice's white button-down and khaki pants in dismay. "Do you call that the kind of outfit that an undercover operative would wear?"

Beatrice groaned. "Is it Friday already? I've been los-ing track of the days. I could have sworn today was Thursday. And then Harper and I had coffee together, and I guess I got distracted and never looked at my calendar." She blinked at Meadow. "Meadow, I don't think that's the kind of operation we were talking about, was it? We're not trying to be private eyes catch-ing Dr. Finley in any wrongdoing or illicit relationship. We're just hanging out near his car in the community-center parking lot, right? So we can ask him questions when he finishes playing racquetball."

"You're correct, Beatrice, but I think it's very import-ant that we get into the mind-set of a stakeout. Having all the right equipment and dressing the part will help us feel more confident and ultimately obtain more in-formation from the good doctor. Who may not *be* a good doctor." Meadow looked at her bulky wristwatch. "By my calculations, though, we need to be leaving . . . now."

Beatrice picked up her pocketbook and gave a rather sad glance into the kitchen. "I never did have a chance to eat breakfast."

"What? Beatrice, that's the most important meal of the day. You know that," said Meadow, waving her hands around.

"Well, my morning sort of got hijacked," said Be-atrice dryly.

"Lucky for you," said Meadow archly, "that this stakeout happens to be the highlight of my week. So I put a lot of thought and planning into it. I packed us a picnic basket full of breakfast foods and other goodies, in case we wanted a snack. Oh, I packed thermoses of coffee and lemonade, too."

Meadow grinned with pride and took a bow as Beatrice applauded her.

"Sounds like the morning will be a success even if we *don't* see Patrick Finley's car in the parking lot," said Beatrice, smiling at Meadow.

But they found, as they pulled into the community-center parking lot, that a Mercedes with the license plate DOCTOR#1 was indeed parked outside the recreation building. Meadow didn't even have to use her binoculars to spot it.

Meadow's voice was smug. "See? How easy is this? Like taking candy from a baby. So let's hang out in the van, eat some muffins and breakfast pastries, and wait for him to finish exercising. I've even got *bacon*, Beatrice. We're living the high life here."

Meadow was never one to skimp on food. She had filled the basket with egg-salad sandwiches, muffins, pastries, fruit, croissants, and the promised bacon. Beatrice and Meadow could have probably survived in the community-center parking lot for at least a week.

"So, how exactly are we planning to carry this off?" asked Beatrice slowly as she helped herself to some of the mixed fruit. "If we go running toward him, we're going to look like investigative reporters attempting gonzo journalism or something."

"Oh, I don't think so," demurred Meadow. "It'll just

be like we're so eager to get into the community center and start exercising that we can't contain ourselves."

"I think we should make it seem like a chance encounter," said Beatrice, fishing out a fork from the huge picnic basket. "Then maybe I can look thoughtful and say, 'Didn't I see you at Harper and Daniel's wedding reception?'"

"You *always* look thoughtful, Beatrice, so that's not going to be a stretch for you. Then I can follow up quickly and say, 'I think I spotted you at the funeral, too, Doctor Finley,'" said Meadow.

"Which means a very slow intro to our questioning," said Beatrice, staring absently out the windshield in the direction of the community-center entrance.

"To keep him from being suspicious of our motives. Like you were saying."

Beatrice said, "The only problem is that he's going to be in a hurry, won't he? He's been playing racquetball. He's likely going to be pretty sweaty and ready to hit the showers before he takes patients in the afternoon. Much as I hate to say it, we're probably going to have to take the direct approach."

Meadow grinned. "Where I explain that you're helping Ramsay with his inquiries? I've always wanted to say that. It makes both of us sound official. You're the detective, and I'm your loyal sidekick."

"I suppose that's what we should do. There aren't a lot of good options. But no running at him. I think that will scare the man to death," said Beatrice.

Of course, it was at the moment when Beatrice had her mouth completely full of blueberry muffin that

Meadow plastered herself across the window and said, "He's here! He's coming out."

Meadow, naturally, completely forgot their no-running plan and was immediately out of the van and trotting toward the sweaty Patrick Finley. Beatrice frantically grabbed her thermos of lemonade in an attempt to quickly wash down the blueberry muffin. Unfortunately, the lemonade set off a coughing fit, which took a minute to clear. Eyes watering from the coughing and feeling as if she were covered in muffin crumbs, Beatrice hurried to join Meadow, wondering what Meadow might be telling the doctor and how far away it veered from their planned script.

Meadow filled her in. "I was just telling Doctor Finley that you were a superb investigator, Beatrice. Hardworking and astute, and really much more into police work than my policeman husband. And that you had a few questions for the doctor and that I knew where to find him."

Patrick Finley was wearing a white T-shirt and blue workout shorts. Despite this weekly exercise, he had a figure that was trending toward stout. His shaggy hair was plastered to his head from perspiration, except for the bit that was standing on end from where he'd pushed it out of his face. His deep-set eyes, which already had a tendency to appear concerned, regarded them warily.

Beatrice decided not to extend her hand for a handshake. She cleared her throat, hoping the coughing fit wouldn't return. "I'm sure you're probably needing to get ready for work, so I'll keep this short. I've seen you several times lately, although I didn't know who you were until Meadow identified you. You were arguing with Trevor Garber the night that I was out to dinner with friends of mine."

Patrick interrupted. "Trevor *Garber* was arguing. *I* was being very even-keeled and trying to make him see my point of view." He swatted the air a few times with his racket, as if swatting away annoying flies.

"Obviously, your discussion with him ended poorly, because Trevor was incapacitated by that point. But you continued trying to see him, didn't you?"

Patrick said stiffly, "Trevor was a colleague. All the doctors on staff were very concerned by his behavior. I was one of the doctors who cared enough to follow up—that's all."

"I don't think so," said Beatrice. "Why would you have followed up at a stranger's wedding, for instance? Surely that seems like an odd place and time."

Patrick frowned and studied his tennis shoe with rapt attention. "I don't know what you're talking about."

"I saw you at my friends' wedding. Harper and Daniel were also friends of Trevor's—in fact, he was supposed to be Daniel's best man until Trevor's erratic behavior made Daniel change course. But you were there at the reception, standing outside the tent and looking in from the shadows," said Beatrice.

Patrick drawled, "That's rather fanciful of you, isn't it? It all sounds very mysterious. I can tell you that I most certainly wasn't at . . . whoever's wedding. I'm not much of a fan of weddings in general and surely wouldn't attend one when I wasn't even invited. It's hard enough to get me to attend a wedding that I'm *supposed* to go to."

Beatrice gave him a piercing look. "And you were at Trevor's funeral, too."

"Naturally. To pay my respects to Eleanor. And because Trevor was a colleague . . . formerly a respected one." Patrick looked longingly at his Mercedes.

Meadow opened her eyes wide and made a *get on with it* gesture with her hand.

Beatrice took a deep breath. It was time to prevaricate to try to get some real answers. "There are two people who can identify you as having been at that wedding."

"Then those are two people who are wrong," said Patrick simply.

"One of them is Eleanor Garber. She certainly knew you well enough to correctly be able to identify you, didn't she?" asked Beatrice.

Patrick made a choking sound, and a momentary rage stained his cheeks red. "What?" His voice was furious. Beatrice could see that he was working hard to control his temper. Patrick took a few deep breaths and released them after a short interval. It had the effect of making him sound like a locomotive.

Finally, he calmed down enough to respond. "Let's say that I *was* there. At that wedding of those people that I didn't even know. What possible reason would I have to kill Trevor?" As he spoke in an angry whisper, his gaze darted around the parking lot, making sure that no one could overhear their conversation. Satisfied, he whispered again, "What motive could I possibly have?"

"Fear," said Beatrice.

His stunned expression told Beatrice that she had stumbled onto the correct answer. Some of the wind had definitely come out of Patrick's sails at the word, and he slumped ever so slightly. "What do you mean?" he asked, without looking Beatrice in the eyes. But by his voice, Beatrice could tell that he knew exactly what she meant.

Meadow nodded encouragingly at her.

"I mean that Trevor Garber knew something about you. And Trevor was in a dangerous place. Although he had been a respected doctor, he'd abruptly strayed off course and started making a series of bad decisions: an affair, stalking the woman after she'd broken up with him, drinking too much, not going to work. And blackmail."

Patrick's face, still flushed from exercise, went white underneath.

"Trevor knew that you'd made a terrible mistake during surgery. You and he had been drinking together. He was the anesthesiologist in the operating room, and you botched a surgery because you weren't clear-headed enough to have operated on the patient. Trevor saw what happened and figured it would be a great way to use leverage to force you to pay him hush money. Trevor really needed the money. He and Eleanor had a lot of debt. Blackmail became a logical means to an end for him."

Patrick shook his head. "You'll never, never be able to prove it. If it *were* true, which it's not, then Trevor was the only witness to any of the behavior you've mentioned. And Trevor, of course, isn't around to tell what he saw."

"Conveniently," said Meadow succinctly.

"Look, I'm not going to admit to anything," said Patrick. He pulled out his car keys and hit the Unlock button for the Mercedes, still casting it longing looks. "But I can tell you one thing: You're way off track here. There are other people with more motive than I have. Lyla Wales, for instance—she was having an affair with Trevor, and he wouldn't leave her alone after she tried ending it. And I even saw Eleanor around Trevor's drink."

Beatrice raised her eyebrows. "Eleanor around Trevor's drink? At a wedding reception you deny attending."

Patrick shrugged, looking flustered. "Okay, maybe I was there. But I had other reasons, all right? Maybe I still wanted to talk to Trevor about his behavior—wanted to persuade him to clean up his act and get back to work. You know?"

Chapter Twelve

"He did it," pronounced Meadow as she drove back to Beatrice's house. "Sure as anything. Pass me one of those deviled eggs."

Beatrice absently handed over an egg and then ate one herself. "What makes you think he's the murderer?"

Meadow finished chewing and then said, "Trevor obviously was blackmailing him. And he's now admitting he was at the scene of the crime. That's motive and opportunity. And the means? I think any physician could get his hands on some sleeping pills pretty easily, don't you?"

Beatrice nodded. "Probably."

"Besides, I don't want Lyla Wales to have killed Trevor, because she's a quilting sister. And I feel sort of sorry for Eleanor, and I don't want to see her get into any trouble. And Daniel . . . he's Daniel. For your sake, I don't want him to have killed Trevor . . . Daniel being family and all," said Meadow, pulling into Beatrice's driveway. She gave a light tap on her horn, and little corgi ears immediately appeared in the picture window at the front of the cottage. "I just love doing that," she said, grinning at the sight.

"So, your basis for deciding that Patrick Finley is the murderer has to do with the fact that you like the other suspects too much," said Beatrice with a sigh.

"No, not only that. I also admit some natural resentment that I can't schedule office visits with Dr. Finley because he plays racquetball on Friday mornings. That's rather annoying," said Meadow thoughtfully. "Anyway, what's next? Oh, never mind. I know what's next—your date with Wyatt. Tomorrow at lunch, right?"

"Date with Wyatt?" muttered Beatrice.

"At the retirement home. You remember."

"Meadow, that's volunteering. Not a date," said Beatrice. It was really time for her to leave the van. Meadow was getting too exasperating. But there was something about those miniature lemon meringues that kept her in the car, eating.

"It's helping others and helping yourself at the same time, Beatrice. I think that any time you spend with Wyatt, it's a date. Besides, you're eating a meal with him in the dining room there, right? Sounds like a date to me," said Meadow. "Let me know how it goes. And here—I can't eat all this food. Let's put some in a grocery bag for you."

Meadow loaded what looked like enough food to feed Beatrice for the next couple of days into a bag. She said briskly, "Now mull over what I said about Dr. Finley. Women's intuition is a powerful thing, you know. And let me know how the date goes."

Before Beatrice could even formulate an answer, Meadow was already backing out of the driveway, calling "Bye!" through the open passenger's window. Beatrice fished out her keys and patted an excited Noo-noo as she opened the door. "Hi there, girl. It's always very flattering that you're so excited to see me."

She walked into the kitchen and unloaded the bag of food. Beatrice spotted something at the bottom of the bag that made her smile and shake her head. "Meadow didn't forget you, Noo-noo. Look what she stuck in there." It was a bag of dog treats. Sometimes she didn't know whether she wanted to hug Meadow or strangle her.

The Mountain Vistas retirement home was right outside of Dappled Hills. The home was a sprawling, one-story stone structure with courtyards and well-maintained grounds and did indeed, as the name implied, have a beautiful mountain view. It was a lovely day, and Beatrice had walked to the church and then ridden in a van with Wyatt and about five other church members to Mountain Vistas. When Beatrice had sat next to Wyatt in the van, Miss Sissy had given her an onerous glare. Apparently, Beatrice had taken Miss Sissy's usual spot.

"I'm so glad you came," said Wyatt warmly, as they walked into the retirement home together. "I've missed seeing you lately." He shook his head ruefully, "It seems like just when I think things are going to quiet down at the church, they get busy again."

"I've had a lot going on myself," said Beatrice. "I'm glad that we can spend some time together today."

Everyone else in their group was a regular volunteer and seemed immediately to know what they were doing. "Where is everyone helping?" asked Beatrice with a frown. "I sort of thought our visit would be less structured, but the rest of the group is acting like they have a clear-cut duty to perform."

"Jane always calls out bingo for the weekly bingo game. Sally gives manicures to residents at the salon here. Paul enjoys playing cards—the residents are always looking for more players for bridge or canasta. If no one is playing cards, he'll play chess or checkers, too. Trina plays the piano in the dining hall, and usually there's a whole crowd of folks who come over to hear her," said Wyatt. "And Miss Sissy heads immediately to the dining room to 'help' the staff there by sampling the menu for the day."

"What do you usually do?" asked Beatrice. She was feeling rather unqualified at this point. Meadow had mentioned that the volunteers mainly provided an ear for residents, and she was beginning to think that may be all she was capable of doing.

"I like visiting with everyone," said Wyatt, simply. "I go to one of the common areas where residents gather and sit and talk. That's the direction we're walking in now. Sometimes I barely even talk—I just listen while the residents talk. They've got some amazing stories."

"That's what I'll do, then," said Beatrice, feeling relieved.

"After that, we all meet in the dining room for lunch," said Wyatt. "It makes for a nice visit. Actually, I feel very centered when I leave. Here it's not so much hustle and bustle—the slower pace is welcomed."

The common room was large, with comfortable sofas against the walls and tables with chairs scattered around the room. Residents were visiting with each other, reading, knitting, and playing cards. Beatrice wondered if it might be a good place for Posy to do a quilting workshop in the future.

Beatrice wasn't sure at first exactly how to join in with some of the groups of people, but they quickly introduced themselves and pulled her right into conversation. She did notice a few curious glances as she sat next to Wyatt. Did they look that much like a couple?

The next hour passed quickly. Beatrice was glancing at a clock to see if it was time to head over to the dining room when she spotted Daniel Kemp pushing a wheelchair containing a much older lady. He saw her looking in his direction, and Beatrice could have sworn that a look of consternation passed over his features for a moment before he smiled at Wyatt and her.

"Beatrice and Wyatt! What a nice surprise," he said smoothly. He carefully wheeled his mother toward them. He then absently straightened his already perfectly straight tie. "Mother, you remember Harper's brother, Wyatt. And this is Wyatt's friend, Beatrice."

His mother smiled a greeting at them. She was a smartly dressed woman in a red suit and gold jewelry. She appeared to be in her late eighties. Beatrice could tell that although her appearance was carefully maintained, Mrs. Kemp appeared very thin and frail.

"Were you on your way to the dining room?" asked Wyatt. "We're heading over there in about twenty minutes."

"We actually had an early lunch," said Daniel with a smile. "Mother tends to be an early bird, so she's ready for lunch when the dining room opens at eleven thirty."

"And now I'm ready for a nap," said Mrs. Kemp with a short laugh. "It's one of the pitfalls of being very old."

Daniel quickly said, "How about if I go ahead and take you back to your room, Mother? That way you can lie down for a while."

"Actually, I'd rather Wyatt take me, if he doesn't mind," said the old lady, raising her eyebrows. "He was so busy at the wedding . . . understandably. I never really got the chance to visit with him then."

"We can all go back to your room and visit," said Daniel with alacrity.

Beatrice was starting to wonder if perhaps Daniel was trying to avoid a one-on-one conversation with her. But considering the fact that she was planning to ask him more questions, perhaps he was being smart.

Mrs. Kemp looked at her son with surprise. "You know my room isn't large enough to host much company. I'll catch up with Beatrice another time. Besides, when everyone is talking, I can't really hear the conversation. No, I'll have a short visit with Wyatt before he goes to the dining hall." Despite her frail appearance, her voice was still strong and commanding. Beatrice saw that Daniel was reluctantly coming to the realization that he'd lost whatever battle he was waging.

"All right, then." He leaned over and gave his mother a kiss on a powdery cheek.

As Wyatt gently wheeled Mrs. Kemp away, Daniel

gave Beatrice a slightly uneasy look. "Well, I should be getting along home, I guess."

"Would you mind waiting with me for a few minutes here in the common area?" asked Beatrice quickly. "I've got some time to kill until Wyatt gets back and we go to lunch."

"Of course I will," said Daniel perfunctorily. He seemed to be the prototype of the perfect gentleman—even when facing a task he didn't want to do.

Beatrice knew that she didn't have much time with him until Wyatt returned. She also may not have much time before one of the residents tried to engage them in conversation, since a few were already curiously looking their way. As they sat down at one of the small tables, she decided to do what she'd done with Patrick Finley: launch quickly into direct questions.

"I wanted to ask you something," said Beatrice, taking a deep breath. "As you know, it's very likely that Patrick Finley, the doctor I was telling you about, was being blackmailed by Trevor. And I have the feeling, Daniel, that there's something you're holding back—something you're not telling anyone about. Was Trevor also blackmailing you, or trying to?"

The color drained out of Daniel's face before it came rushing back in. He glanced around them quickly to ensure no one was able to overhear them before he answered, "How on earth did you get that information?"

Beatrice lifted her hands in appeasement. "It was just a hunch, Daniel. Although it's a hunch that you seem to be confirming."

Daniel stared at her silently for a few moments. Then he said, "It's so crowded in here right now, Beatrice. Can we take a short walk to the courtyard? It will be a lot quieter there. I don't want to raise my voice over all the conversations in here and risk being heard."

They walked quickly out of the common area and down the hallway to a door leading out to a small courtyard with a fountain, beds of impatiens, and a glider-style canopy swing, which they both sat in.

After a moment's pause during which he seemed to be figuring out his words, Daniel said slowly, "What I'm about to tell you needs to go no farther. I'll tell Harper myself—I don't want her to hear it from you." He stopped and gave Beatrice a somewhat combative look. "The truth is that Trevor knew a family secret. It's something that I trusted him with completely. After all, I'd known Trevor since childhood. I'd discovered, upon finding some old letters when I was helping Mother move here, that the man who had raised me as his son was actually not my father at all."

Beatrice nodded. She'd wondered if Daniel's secret had had something to do with Mrs. Kemp. Daniel was clearly so fiercely protective of her. "Did you confront your mother about it?"

Daniel gave a short laugh. "I don't know if *confront* is the right word. But I did ask her about it. I couldn't help myself. I'd always thought I'd resembled my mother much more than the man I knew as my father, but in the letter that I'd found, there was a picture of a man I didn't recognize. And I looked exactly like him."

"What did your mother say when you asked her about it?" asked Beatrice as they gently swung on the glider.

"Mother said she'd made a mistake. She'd gone

away one weekend to a class reunion a couple of weeks before my father and she married. An old boyfriend of hers from school was at the reunion. After that weekend, she never saw him again, although he'd given her that letter and a picture of himself before she'd left to return home." Daniel looked absently across the courtyard.

"But you were born nine months later," said Beatrice.

Daniel nodded. "Mother said that the man I knew as my father never knew the truth. She had a good life with him, and we were happy together. Mother kept the secret. And now, at the end of her life and when she's so frail, I'm trying to keep the secret, too. To have this get out in connection with a murder investigation when she's worked hard to keep my parentage under wraps . . ." He shook his head.

"How did Trevor find out?" asked Beatrice.

Daniel rubbed his temples with the heels of his palms, as if his head hurt. "I stupidly confided in him. It was when I'd just moved back to Dappled Hills— long before Trevor started acting oddly and before I started dating Harper. I had no one else that I felt I could talk to. Mother specifically asked that I not tell Harper—she didn't want Harper to think any less of her, although I assured Mother that Harper wouldn't. I did respect her wishes on that, although now I feel I don't have any choice but to tell Harper, and then ask Harper not to let on to Mother that she knows." He sighed. "I was out one evening with Trevor after work, having a drink. I told him that I'd just discovered that the man who'd raised me as his son was not actually my father."

"What was Trevor's reaction?" asked Beatrice.

"Concern. And he told me all the right things—that the man who raised me *fathered* me, supported me, encouraged me. Which was the only thing that mattered. And he was right."

Beatrice said, "But at some point, Trevor must have changed his message."

"That's right. Well, as soon as he started acting so erratic and out of character, I was immediately sorry that I'd told him anything at all. But it never occurred to me that he would use my secret against me. That's the thing about living in a small town—it's so easy for any gossip to make the rounds. The night we saw Trevor at that restaurant, I drove him back, and he started taunting me about my father. And then he asked me for money to keep quiet about it." Daniel's mouth tightened in anger.

"What did you tell him?" asked Beatrice, gently swinging.

"I decided to ignore the fact that he was trying to blackmail me. Instead I tried to appeal to the real Trevor, underneath. I reminded him that he'd spent lots of time at my house as a kid. My mother probably saw Trevor even more than *his* mother had. I told him I couldn't imagine that he would deliberately hurt her by spreading the story all over town, especially in her frail condition. I was reproachful, too, telling him that he wasn't acting like a real friend to me," said Daniel.

"How did he respond to that?"

Daniel sighed. "You remember how he was. He was so intoxicated that night that it was amazing he could even think to blackmail me. It was probably the alcohol that made him laugh after I finished my plea. I think it must have been. But whatever it was, I'd had enough. Here I was trying to lay our personal history out on the line, and he was laughing. That was the moment where I told Trevor that I didn't want him to be my best man. By that time, I'd pulled into his driveway and I was ready to help him into his house and wash my hands of him."

"What did Trevor say in response?" asked Beatrice.

"He got very quiet suddenly. I think he was shocked, actually. It had clearly been a point of pride to him that he'd been asked to serve as my best man. And then to have that duty removed from him?" Daniel shook his head. "He must have really been intoxicated to think that I'd allow him to remain my best man, under the circumstances."

"Did he say anything else before you left?" asked Beatrice.

"He did." Daniel closed his eyes briefly. "He said that if I didn't want him to spread the story about my father all over town, I'd better pay up. And then he asked for more money than he had a few minutes before."

Beatrice took a deep breath. "Have you told Ramsay about this?"

"No," said Daniel quickly, "And I have no intention of doing so."

Beatrice thought for a moment. "But Eleanor said that Trevor was planning on reforming. So at some point, he must have changed his mind."

"Maybe he'd just mentioned blackmailing again as a way of getting back at me for removing him as best man." Daniel shrugged. "I don't know. I know only that that's what he told me."

Beatrice said, "I'm curious why you didn't uninvite him to the wedding, as well. After all, at that point, your relationship must have seemed pretty bleak."

Daniel said, "It did seem bleak. I called Harper after I got back home and told her that I didn't even want to see Trevor at our wedding—that he should have no part in such a happy celebration. Harper was surprised. She'd seen Trevor's bad behavior, but she knew nothing about the blackmail. It must have looked as if I were overreacting. Harper told me that I'd regret it if I uninvited him. Besides, she said, she'd like Eleanor to be there. So I kept them on the guest list."

Beatrice said slowly, "And Trevor came to the wedding and behaved very well throughout the ceremony and reception. He didn't drink any alcohol or behave badly. Eleanor swore he'd promised to improve. So maybe he was wanting to apologize to you at the reception? I know you did talk there."

Daniel's eyes were sad. "He didn't come out and apologize, per se, but you could tell he was sorry. And *I* was sorry. That wasn't how I'd wanted our relationship to turn out. Of course, I couldn't really spend much time with Trevor, either—as the groom, I had guests to greet, pictures to take, guests to thank, cake to cut . . . It was a busy evening. But I did have a chance to thank him for coming and to tell him I hoped our friendship would soon return to normal."

Daniel was busy at the reception, no doubt about it.

But Beatrice did remember him spending time at Trevor's table. And it wasn't only for a minute, either.

He looked at his watch. "Now I really should go. And you'll need to meet Wyatt in the dining room. I'll see you soon, Beatrice."

As he hurried away, giving a small wave as he left, Beatrice couldn't help but wonder if Daniel hadn't gotten the memo about Trevor's plan to reform in time—and had proactively decided to stop the blackmail himself.

Chapter Thirteen

Daniel had given Beatrice a lot to think about, and she felt rather weighed down as she walked back along the long hallway. Then she spotted Wyatt, listening intently to a resident. He looked up with a quick smile as he saw her. She smiled back, and suddenly all she could think about was him.

They walked into the sunny dining room together. There were flowers on every white tablecloth-covered table and a piano in the corner, which a sprightly resident with an erect bearing was playing with enthusiasm. Beatrice and Wyatt stood in a long cafeteria line, holding blue trays as they waited for their roasted vegetables and spiral-cut ham. "I'm so glad you could be here today," he murmured to her.

And once again she had the feeling of all the worrying thoughts and the pressure drop from her. The only thing that remained was the two of them spending time together . . . even if it was while they were volunteering their time or delving into a mystery.

Before she could answer Wyatt, she saw a wispy woman who appeared to be in her eighties giving her a wink and a thumbs-up. It was all Beatrice could do not to giggle like a schoolgirl in response. Instead she said, a little breathlessly, "I am, too."

She and Wyatt sat at a table for four. A gentleman who was particularly hard of hearing sat with them. After Beatrice and Wyatt made several attempts at conversation, he waved at his ears, shrugged, and focused all of his attention on his plate. The lady who'd been vigorously playing a complex and lively piano piece settled into slow, gentle piano jazz. The ham and vegetables were much more flavorful than Beatrice had anticipated and she felt almost as if she and Wyatt were at a restaurant.

"What quilt are you working on now?" asked Wyatt. "Did you finish the owl quilt you were making for Piper?"

"Almost. Then I'm going to try something new—a kaleidoscope pattern," said Beatrice.

Wyatt raised his eyebrows. "That certainly doesn't sound easy. I'd love to see it when you're done. Maybe it's time for another quilt show at the church. I'll have to check with Meadow to see if she's interested."

Beatrice smiled. A man who appreciated her craft, a tasty lunch, and jazz music. Who could ask for more? She felt herself relax, muscles loosening for the first time in days.

After lunch, they headed back to Dappled Hills Presbyterian in the van. Now Beatrice was preparing to walk home from the church.

"Want a ride?" asked Miss Sissy. She pointed an arthritic finger in the direction of her ancient Lincoln.

Beatrice repressed a shudder. Miss Sissy saw no difference between the road and the sidewalk. In fact, she usually chose the sidewalk to drive on because there was less traffic there. "No, thanks, Miss Sissy. I could use the exercise."

"Do you want me to give you a lift?" asked Wyatt under his breath, as Miss Sissy climbed into her car and drove away after a series of backfires. Beatrice realized that although she'd tried to be talkative during lunch and the ride back to the church, she'd had a lot on her mind after her talk with Daniel. And she was conflicted about whether she should share it with Wyatt. She finally decided that she shouldn't fill Wyatt in until at least Daniel had time to talk with Harper.

"Oh no. It's just right down the road."

"Then let me walk with you. After the huge lunch we had at Mountain Vistas, I think I could use a little walking," said Wyatt, patting his stomach.

There was a spring breeze blowing around them as they walked, and Beatrice gave a small shiver. Wyatt immediately removed his light jacket and put it around Beatrice's shoulders. She smiled at him, and he reached for her hand. In a soft voice he said, "I'm happy we were able to spend some time together today." He hesitated before saying, "Although I love my work with the church, it sometimes pulls me in many different directions. It doesn't mean that while I'm being pulled off, I wouldn't rather be spending time with you."

Beatrice gave his hand a squeeze, and they walked to her house in comfortable quiet.

*   *   *

The busy day tired Beatrice more than she'd thought. She ate a light supper of tomato soup before turning in before ten o'clock. Beatrice slept soundly until gruff barking from Noo-noo sometime before dawn startled her awake.

Beatrice frowned. Noo-noo usually only barked if there were people knocking on the door. She listened hard, but couldn't hear any unusual sounds. And then Noo-noo gave another gruff bark.

That was enough for Beatrice. The corgi's ears were so large, she trusted that her dog was hearing something that Beatrice's pitiful human ears couldn't. She pulled on her bathrobe from the foot of the bed and stuck her feet into a pair of fluffy slippers. Beatrice paused long enough in the living room to grab a fireplace poker from the hearth and then cautiously moved toward the front door.

Peering out the window, all she saw was the dim light of the dawn struggling against cloud cover. Then she looked down and saw a large, wriggling black object. Meadow's Boris.

With a sigh she opened the door. "Boris, what are you doing here?" she scolded the animal. "It's too early to visit."

Boris grinned joyfully at Beatrice, sure that his presence was a delightful surprise. He touched noses with Noo-noo, who gave Boris a disdainful look and backed away. And then Beatrice saw Boris had apparently been swimming in a nearby creek. A second, closer inspection revealed that it was mud, not water, covering Boris.

"Boris!" said Beatrice with exasperation. She couldn't

let the dog back outside or he'd run off again. But she didn't want the red mud all over her floors and throw rugs, either. "Sit, Boris!" she said sternly. "Sit!"

Boris continued grinning up at her. Beatrice very much doubted Meadow's assertion that Boris was part corgi. If Boris had had an ounce of corgi in him, he'd be sitting with alacrity by now.

Beatrice hurried into the kitchen and pulled open a drawer with folded cleaning rags inside. She took out three and then got another. Boris had, naturally, followed her from the doorway and was finally sitting, tail slapping the floor as he wagged it. Beatrice took out a bucket, filled it halfway with water, and got to work scrubbing the mud off Boris.

At least he lay still and the job didn't take as long as Beatrice had thought it would. Although she somehow still managed to get muddy red clay all over her robe, the hem of her nightgown, and parts of her slippers.

She patted him down with a dry towel. "All right, Boris. I'm not sure Meadow is up yet, so why don't you just hang out here for a while?" Beatrice, stiff from having crouched on the floor for so long, stood with a bit more difficulty than she'd expected. She sent Meadow a text message so that once she woke up, she'd know where Boris was. Then she mopped up the muddy paw prints, changed clothes, and started a load of laundry.

Thirty minutes later, Meadow appeared. Beatrice wordlessly handed her a cup of coffee as Meadow walked through the door. Meadow looked wild, and was wearing startling yellow pajamas that made her look like a canary. Her gray braid was messy, with most of the strands working their way out. She immediately spotted the mop and bucket and the sparkling-clean Boris and said, "What a bad dog! We don't visit neighbors before dawn—and definitely not when we're filthy."

"How do you suppose he got out, Meadow?" asked Beatrice.

"I haven't the foggiest idea." Meadow gave Boris a look of reluctant admiration. "But he's such a smart dog that I'm not all that surprised. He escapes on a regular basis. It's quite astounding." She pointed over to the living room. "Is it okay if we visit for a while?"

Meadow sat on the cushy sofa, and Beatrice sat in the overstuffed gingham armchair next to her. Through the large window in the back of the room, Beatrice saw that the sun was coming up and shining bands of light across Beatrice's backyard, illuminating the gardenia bushes, azaleas, and trees. Cardinals, chickadees, and Carolina wrens were at the feeders. This was, actually, her favorite time of the day.

Meadow took a large sip of her coffee and leaned back into the softness of the sofa. "Now, *this* is a good start to a morning. Not like having to clean up a muddy dog and muddy floor. Sorry about that, Beatrice. But I'm glad I'm here because I wanted to ask you how everything went with Wyatt yesterday at the retirement home. Did you get to spend some quality time together?"

Beatrice gave a rueful smile. When Meadow was stuck on a topic, she was *stuck* on it. "We did. It was a nice day. I think Miss Sissy's nose was a little out of joint that I took her spot on the church van, but, other than that, everything was good." Except, maybe, for the fact that she'd discovered Wyatt's brother-in-law's secret. That wasn't all that good.

"See, I think you're holding out on me. Something happened. Maybe, judging from that look in your eyes, something that wasn't so great. And I don't need to hear the scoop on Miss Sissy, for heaven's sake. So, fill me in." Meadow used her most commanding voice.

"Wyatt and I spent time together. We visited with residents there. We ate lunch in the dining room. And he walked me back home afterward. So we had a very pleasant day together. And, yes, something did happen. Something related to the case. But I don't feel right about disclosing it now. That's all." Beatrice gave a small shrug, as if that was all she had to say. She knew Meadow wasn't going to let it drop at that, however.

"You can't just leave me hanging like that," said Meadow reproachfully. "I'm your sidekick."

Beatrice wasn't convinced.

Meadow paused. "All right. Well, at least tell me who it's regarding and what it's about, even if you don't give me any details."

Beatrice considered this. "All right. But not a word to anyone."

"I *never* gossip."

Beatrice rolled her eyes.

"Revision: I never gossip during murder investigations. I wouldn't—it would go against the sidekick code of honor," said Meadow, crossing her heart with her finger.

"I didn't realize that sidekicks had a code of honor," said Beatrice with a smile.

Meadow said breezily, "Oh goodness. We're very advanced as an organization. Even unionized."

"Okay. Well, basically, when Wyatt and I were volunteering at the retirement home, we saw Daniel there with Mrs. Kemp in one of the common areas. He looked alarmed at seeing us, actually," said Beatrice.

Meadow's eyes opened wide. "Did you have an opportunity to speak to him?"

"I did. We'd finished visiting with the residents there and were about to head to the dining room for lunch. You know how Trevor needed money and was attempting to blackmail your doctor, Patrick Finley? He was also apparently trying to extort money from Daniel," said Beatrice.

Meadow released her pent-up breath. "Oh no. That's what I was hoping *wouldn't* happen. That means that Daniel had more of a motive than we thought. We were thinking he was simply angry at Trevor for his crazy behavior. It didn't seem like he had that much reason to kill Trevor—not like Eleanor or Patrick or Lyla, anyway. Now it looks a lot more likely. And who would suspect the groom?" Looking despondent, she collapsed back into the cushy depths of the sofa. "And I like Harper so much. She is going to be your sister-in-law."

Beatrice's head was starting to hurt. She rubbed it with a few fingers. "I was sorry to hear it, for sure. Although I'd suspected that something like that was possible, I was upset to have it confirmed. But, Meadow, it doesn't mean that Daniel *did* murder Trevor. Think about it: Trevor was a very good friend of Daniel's. And it was Daniel's wedding, after all. He was in the spotlight. He'd have to have been pretty brazen to slip sleeping pills into his former best man's drink during his own wedding reception."

"Or desperate," pointed out Meadow, glumly. "Besides, he's a lawyer, and they're brimming with self-confidence. And he hangs out with criminals all day."

Beatrice gave a spluttering laugh. "In the context of a trial, maybe. It's not like he's hanging out with bad guys on street corners."

"Whatever. It all seems very grim suddenly."

Beatrice took a thoughtful sip of her coffee. "Let's think of it this way. As you mentioned, there were other people who were more likely to have killed Trevor."

"Until now."

Beatrice ignored her and kept going. "Your physician, for instance. Patrick Finley was being blackmailed by Trevor Garber for something that could end his livelihood. That's pretty major. I'm not going into details about what Daniel was being blackmailed for, but I can promise you that it was nothing in the same league."

Meadow looked somewhat more cheerful.

"Besides, Patrick wasn't supposed to even be at the wedding at all. Daniel and Harper didn't know him. So it seems rather more suspicious that he was lurking around the tent," said Beatrice.

"He claims he was lurking around the tent to wait for an opportunity to reason with Trevor, right?" asked Meadow. "That's how he explained it, anyway. And it kind of makes sense, if you think about it. Dr. Finley probably figured that Trevor would be on his best behavior during a wedding."

"Wonder how Patrick even knew about the wedding?" asked Beatrice. "Considering he wasn't invited at all."

Boris, sound asleep on the floor, started having a nightmare, and Meadow patted him reassuringly. "Trevor probably told him about the wedding, maybe even when they were out at the restaurant that night. Or maybe he made a note of it when the engagement announcement was in the paper. Patrick might have figured that Trevor, as best man, would be of sound enough mind to reason with. That maybe Trevor took the position seriously enough that he wouldn't be completely intoxicated at the wedding, and Patrick could reason with him. Maybe he tried to catch Trevor at home several times and Trevor was in no condition to speak to him then. And we know that Trevor wasn't really going into work any longer, so he couldn't speak to him then."

Beatrice said, "I thought you were convinced that Patrick Finley did it. Now you're backpedaling."

"Only because you presented such compelling evidence and motive against Daniel," said Meadow.

"I know you're not crazy about Eleanor and Lyla as suspects, but they've also got plenty of motive," reminded Beatrice. "Eleanor desperately needed money, for one. And, apparently, there was a nice insurance policy on Trevor that's going to help her with some of her financial problems."

"They've been married for ages and have grown children. Do you think Eleanor would really kill her husband for money?" asked Meadow doubtfully. "I know she seemed somewhat unstable when we visited her. At least, her house indicated that she might be unstable."

"Money is usually a pretty strong motivator," said Beatrice. "Besides, there's also the fact that her husband's affair was going to become public knowledge in Dappled Hills. Trevor was practically stalking Lyla, and seemed to be getting less and less interested in being covert about it."

Meadow nodded. "That's right. He was making scenes, wasn't he? Which is exactly the way people in small towns find out about stuff. It would have made living in Dappled Hills uncomfortable for Eleanor for a while, for sure. So, okay, Eleanor is still a strong suspect, although I feel sorry for her and would hate for her to be responsible for all this. And I guess this leads us to Lyla. You know I feel as if Lyla is a quilting sister of ours and would hate to see her get dragged into this."

Beatrice raised her eyebrows and set down her empty cup on the coffee table. "Lyla, quilter or not, is hardly a victim in all of this. It sounds as if she was the one who pursued Trevor to begin with."

"I'd forgotten that. And at first he wasn't interested. Then he became *too* interested." Meadow looked into her own empty coffee cup. "I'm going to need to have more of this to be able to make sense of this case." She got up and headed to the kitchen for a minute before returning with another steaming cup of coffee.

Beatrice said, "That's right. Lyla was the instigator and Trevor the reluctant one at first, before it all totally flip-flopped." She hesitated. "One thing that I haven't told you about is that when Lyla and I were crouched over Trevor's body at the wedding reception, I heard Lyla ask, 'Why couldn't we have loved each other at the same time?'"

"Really?" Then Meadow frowned at Beatrice and wagged a finger at her. "You've been holding out on me."

"I didn't tell you because it seemed really personal at the time. Lyla was right over Trevor's dead body. It was sort of an emotional moment that I wanted time to unpack. But you are my sidekick, after all." Beatrice gave her a smile.

"So, she still felt tender about Trevor," mulled Meadow. She took a sip of coffee, and then another couple of sips, as if trying to quickly fuel her brain. "But she was also desperate to get rid of him, too. It must have felt as if her husband was on the brink of knowing, what with Trevor pounding on their door at all hours to see Lyla. He was even bothering her at work, and she could have lost her job over personal issues that were taking over work time."

"Maybe she felt conflicted. On the one hand, she still cared about Trevor on some level. But on the other, she desperately wanted to get rid of him. Once he was dead, she really could have mourned that relationship. Or she could have killed him herself. She certainly passed by Trevor's table. Lyla wouldn't have known that Trevor was trying to reform. She was probably worried that he was going to make another scene," said Beatrice.

Meadow blew out a loud sigh. "You know, it would be a whole lot easier if people would stop trying to cover stuff up and would actually start telling you the truth. Instead, they're blaming other people. We've got Patrick trying to blame Lyla or Eleanor or anyone but himself, Eleanor convinced that it's Lyla, Lyla convinced that it's Eleanor. And Daniel . . . who does he think is responsible?"

"He didn't really say, but I'd guess that he'd push us to look harder at Patrick Finley, since he knew Trevor had leverage on him." Beatrice felt Noo-noo put her head on Beatrice's leg in reassurance, and knew that her voice must have sounded concerned as she was working through the case. Beatrice got up from the chair and sat on the floor with Noo-noo, patting her.

Meadow said abruptly, "You know what we should do? Take a walk with Boris and Noo-noo. I'm falling down on my exercise goal because I'm so busy pushing you in Wyatt's direction that I haven't considered how that's going to cut back on our time together. Especially exercise time!" Meadow leaned over and offered Beatrice a hand off the floor.

Beatrice groaned as Meadow pulled her up with a yank. "I don't know, Meadow. Remember what happened last time? I think Noo-noo and I have only recently recovered from our last walk. Noo-noo hasn't even stared meaningfully at the leash lately." She looked Meadow up and down. "Besides, I hate to point this out, but you're not even dressed."

"Oh, I can dash in and change when we pass by my house. But I know what you mean about the last walk we had. Let's leave the dogs out of it. I'll drop Boris off when I get changed, and we can continue on without them. I feel like my mind is going in a million different directions, mulling over the case, and maybe some fresh air will provide me some clarity."

Fifteen minutes later, Boris was carefully shut inside Meadow's house, and Meadow was wearing yellow track pants and a deep orange top. At least, figured Beatrice, they weren't likely to be hit by a car. A motorist could spot Meadow from a mile away.

"What direction should we walk in?" asked Beatrice. "Are you wanting to head toward town or through the neighborhoods?"

"Let's go toward Eleanor's house," said Meadow. "Maybe she'll even be out in the yard or something. Maybe she keeps her yard up because she's trying to escape from all the stuff in her house. Anyway, it's a gorgeous spring morning, so maybe we'll see her."

It was beautiful outside. There had been rain the night before, and the ground was still moist. Robins hopped through the grass on the sides of the road, looking for an early-morning meal. The air felt crisp. It was the kind of morning where you felt anything was possible.

"I'd like to see Eleanor and make sure she's all right," said Beatrice. "She made quite a scene at the Patchwork Cottage. I'm worried that she's really working herself up about Lyla."

Meadow gave a short laugh. "Maybe we should be worried about *Lyla*. She's the one whose life appeared to be in danger. Eleanor sure was mad." She squinted ahead of them. "Okay, it's hard to see through that bit of low-lying fog, but is that Miss Sissy up ahead?"

Sure enough, the old woman was making her way along the side of the road with that odd, galloping gait of hers. She was gripping a wooden cane with one hand and a plastic bag in the other. Beatrice surmised that the cane was to offer some sort of protection, since Miss Sissy seemed too spry today to need any support. "Hi, Miss Sissy!" called Meadow in a cheerful voice.

The old woman immediately scowled and eyed Meadow and Beatrice suspiciously, clutching the plastic bag she was carrying closer to her, as if the two women might snatch it away.

This, of course, had the effect of making Meadow even more curious. "What have you got in the bag, Miss Sissy?"

"A gift," she said gruffly. And then she added, in case Meadow and Beatrice were in any doubt, "But not for you!"

"May I see it?" asked Beatrice. "I won't touch it if you don't want me to."

Miss Sissy hesitated, and then took the handles of the plastic bag off her skinny arm. She opened the bag and pulled out a quilted mat of fabric with gold tassels on the end. The mat appeared to be stuffed with batting and sported pictures of whimsical cats in a variety of playful poses.

Beatrice said, "It's really cute, Miss Sissy." She didn't want to admit that she had no idea what the item was. It wasn't stuffed enough to function as a throw pillow, and it was too big to be a trivet or potholder.

Meadow, however, had no such reservations. "What is it, Miss Sissy?"

Miss Sissy glowered at Meadow. "A cat mat." Meadow still squinted uncomprehendingly, and Miss Sissy repeated herself, louder this time, as if Meadow were going deaf. "A cat mat! For Smoke to sleep on."

"Ohhh, I see. A bed for Smoke. Well, it sure is cute. Can it go in the washer?" asked Meadow with some concern. "These pet beds get dirty, you know. I have to throw Boris's in the washer every couple of days."

"Course it can." Miss Sissy brandished the cat mat at Meadow, as if daring her to contradict.

Beatrice watched as the old woman quickly bundled up the mat and lay it gently back in the bag. "Aren't you heading in the wrong direction if you're giving the mat to Smoke?" she asked.

Miss Sissy's face fell. "Wasn't home. No one was home. Smoke meowed at me through the window." There was a look of longing in her eyes.

"Oh," said Meadow. "Well, Georgia leaves the house very early to go teach school. And Savannah . . . maybe she went out for breakfast. She's an accountant, and I've seen her in the coffeehouse in downtown in the mornings, working. You could have left the bag hanging on their front doorknob, you know. Savannah will probably be home in an hour or so."

Miss Sissy gave Meadow a black look. "Might get ruined. If it rained."

"It's a quilt! It would be fine. And it's a beautiful day!" Meadow made a sweeping gesture with her arm, as if to encompass all of nature.

Beatrice suspected the real reason that the old woman didn't want to leave the cat mat involved the fact that she'd lose an opportunity to play with Smoke if she did. From what she'd seen at the quilting workshop, Miss Sissy appeared as if she might easily become attached to the little cat.

"Need to go," muttered Miss Sissy. She peered at Meadow again. "Savannah will be there in an hour?"

"Maybe. It would help if you called her before you walked over." Meadow paused. "You do have a phone, don't you?"

It was a reasonable question, considering the fact that Miss Sissy had given the evil eye to Posy's cordless phone at the Patchwork Cottage, calling it an instrument of the devil.

"Yes!" Miss Sissy eyed her disdainfully.

"Okay, so give her a call before you walk over. It might save you a trip," said Meadow.

They watched the old woman walk away, muttering to herself as she went. Probably dire imprecations directed at Meadow and Beatrice's nosiness.

Chapter Fourteen

"Wow, she was in a funny mood. Even funny for Miss Sissy," said Meadow.

They started walking again. Beatrice said, "I think Savannah better make sure that Miss Sissy doesn't kidnap Smoke during the visit. She sure does like that little cat."

Meadow's eyebrows shot up. "You don't think Miss Sissy wants a cat of her own, do you? Miss Sissy can barely even take care of herself. Besides, she has a hobby that takes up most of her time."

"Quilting is a great hobby, but it doesn't exactly measure up to owning a pet," said Beatrice thoughtfully. "Although I know what you mean. Miss Sissy isn't exactly completely compos mentis."

"And what would happen if she got worse somehow? Who would take care of the cat?" asked Meadow. She gave Beatrice a meaningful look.

"Oh no. No, I don't think I want to take on more pet

ownership right now. I've had a bunch of pets in my day, but now I'm ready for a break. Noo-noo is definitely enough. I've only just unloaded Smoke on Savannah, remember?" said Beatrice. "Maybe Boris would like a little brother."

"Boris?" Meadow made a face. "I have a feeling that Boris would get pretty jealous. And he's not crazy about cats, anyway. Didn't you tell me that Noo-noo wasn't happy about Smoke when he was staying with you?"

"Her brown eyes were green with envy," said Beatrice.

They chatted about other things for a few minutes as they walked. Then Meadow said, "There's Eleanor's house, but I don't see her outside, unless she's in the side yard or around the back. Let's walk slowly and maybe we can spot her."

Beatrice said, "All I see is her neighbor. He's looking rather suspiciously at us, too." The neighbor was a short, rather stout man of about sixty-five years, and wore a baseball cap. He was dressed for the yard in a navy T-shirt that had seen better days and a disreputable-looking pair of blue jeans. He squinted in their direction, a grumpy look on his face. Beatrice frowned. "Didn't Ramsay say that he had to make a call at the neighbor's house recently? Something about the neighbor and Trevor arguing, wasn't it?"

"You've got me. I usually zone out when Ramsay starts talking shop. Although it's interesting when *you* talk shop. Who knows why that's the case?" said Meadow.

They drew closer to the man, who said, "Sorry for

the scowl. I was just making sure you weren't that crazy old woman coming back."

Beatrice and Meadow looked at each other. "Miss Sissy, you mean?" asked Beatrice.

"Whoever she is." The man shuddered. "She's scary. Acted like she thought I was going to steal her bag away from her. I walked up to the curb to lay down some cut branches, and she started chasing me and waving that big cane."

"Sounds likely," said Beatrice with a smile.

"She's harmless, by the way," said Meadow in a re-assuring voice.

"Except if she's driving," corrected Beatrice. "Then you have to dodge out of her path, even if you're on the sidewalk."

"She should be locked up," muttered the man. "I'm Bertie, by the way."

He stuck out a callused hand, and they shook it. He continued. "I tell you what: This neighborhood is get-ting too weird for me. I thought this would be a nice place to retire, but stuff keeps happening." He nodded his head in the direction of Eleanor's house. "Case in point: a murder next door."

"Well, not exactly next *door*," said Meadow. "It hap-pened on the church grounds."

"I stand corrected," said the man. "I should have said that my *neighbor* next door was murdered." He rolled his eyes and leaned on his rake, as if conversa-tion with Meadow was exhausting. Beatrice really couldn't blame him.

Beatrice asked carefully, "How did you and your neighbor get along?"

"Not particularly well," said Bertie succinctly. "He was an okay guy at first. He was busy, you know. I really didn't see him much because he was working a lot and working odd hours. A doctor, I think. I'd see his wife, though, Eleanor. She works out in the yard a lot, and so do I. Although she's not the friendliest person in the world. She'll say hi and then she's wanting to pretend you're not even there."

Meadow said loyally, "Eleanor is introverted, that's all."

"You said that your neighbor, Trevor, was an okay guy *at first*. When did that change?" asked Beatrice.

"When he started acting up. He was coming in at odd hours. He did that sometimes with his work, but then he was coming in wearing scrubs. This was more like he was wearing junky clothes and acting drunk, setting off his car alarm by accident at three in the morning—that kind of thing. He starts arguing with me over stuff with the yard, like my tree's leaves were blowing over into his yard and making a mess for him to rake up. He wasn't acting like he usually did," said Bertie.

"But you don't have any thoughts on what happened to him, do you? I mean, I know you weren't at the wedding reception where the murder occurred, but you haven't observed anything as a neighbor that makes you feel you know who might have killed him?" asked Beatrice.

"Oh, I've observed things, all right." Bertie puffed up a bit, looking smug.

Beatrice said, "What kinds of things?"

"Arguments. I don't know who killed Trevor. I'll

state that for the record. Don't want anyone suing me for slander, right? But I will say that he really got into some yelling matches lately. Can't say I blame the people—Trevor wasn't easy to get along with." Bertie stopped leaning on his rake and took a few swipes at some of the grass clippings he was corralling into a pile.

Bertie continued. "He was arguing with his wife a lot. She'd try to convince him to head off to work, and he'd be unshaven and wearing a sweat suit and clearly not planning on going to the hospital." He gave a delicate cough. "Apparently, they were having some money issues, and his wife was reminding him of that a lot when she was telling him to get ready for work."

Beatrice nodded. "Anyone else?"

"Sure. Let's see. There was also that guy in the suit. He was by here a few weeks ago and had a real fight with Trevor in the driveway. Tall, lean, was wearing glasses. Looked real serious, but he wasn't reserved at all when he was yelling at Trevor. And Trevor was falling-down drunk in the yard and trying to yell back, but not making any sense."

Beatrice and Meadow exchanged looks. That must be Daniel. And he hadn't had the civil conversation with Trevor that Beatrice had heard about; he'd been clearly very angry.

Bertie seemed ready to finish up his yard work, so Beatrice and Meadow continued on their walk. Eleanor never did make an appearance, despite Meadow's loitering as long as possible in front of her house. They strolled farther through the neighborhood before finally turning around and heading back.

"Well, at least we fit in our exercise. What else are you planning on doing today?" asked Meadow as she stood at the top of her driveway at the end of their walk.

"I was thinking that I'd head over to the Patchwork Cottage for a while," said Beatrice. "That's usually the best place to get caught up on what's going on around town. And, besides, I thought I might pick up a couple of things there for my next quilt, after I finish the one for Piper."

"Let me know how things are in the shop today. I'm hoping the place is hopping after that workshop," said Meadow.

Actually, Posy's shop *was* hopping. When Beatrice walked in, she saw two of the quilters from the workshop—and it didn't seem to be their first time back. One of the shoppers had even brought two friends along, and they were planning to start their own guild in Lenoir. Posy had a spring in her step as she hurried about the store, making recommendations and checking customers out. She waved at Beatrice, and Beatrice grinned at her.

While Posy was checking out the last customers, Beatrice shopped for fabric for her next project: a kaleidoscope quilt. She'd understood that it was tricky to get just the right fabric for the quilt, but she was ready for a challenge after the simpler, machine-quilted owl quilt she was finishing up for Piper. Beatrice knew she needed a medium-to-large print with enough of a light-colored background to keep from losing the design within each block. She chose fabric with geometric shapes in vibrant shades of lavender, turquoise, and plum.

Posy joined her after her customers had left. "That fabric will make a beautiful quilt."

"I hope so. But it's a really difficult one for me to take on. I'll probably be spending a lot of time at the Patchwork Cottage, getting help. And it looks like you've got some other customers doing the same! I noticed a couple of faces from the new quilter's workshop," said Beatrice.

Posy smiled happily. "It's turned out really well. And the nice thing is that some of them have introduced their friends to quilting, too. It's been very busy here at the shop. I've got some other ideas, too, for community outreach. At the spring festival, I'm having a sort of quilting 'petting zoo.' Lyla is going to help me set it up."

Each year the town of Dappled Hills sponsored the festival, and it had become a highlight for the community. It was held in the old fairgrounds on the other side of Dappled Hills. The property itself was nicely flat but surrounded by mountains and had a nice view of the forested valley below from the height of the Ferris wheel. The local children enjoyed the rides and the hands-on mountain crafts like pottery making. The adults enjoyed the fellowship, juried craft exhibitions, and fair food.

Beatrice raised her eyebrows. "So the 'petting zoo' will be a way for people to try out quilting for a few minutes?"

"Right. Because I think there's this idea that it's too difficult to take on and it might be scaring away younger quilters. And it *can* be really difficult, but it can also be very easy, depending on which pattern you're choosing and if you're machine quilting. It's the kind of hobby that you can grow with," said Posy. She spoke faster than usual in her excitement.

Beatrice said, "So, you'll have a booth at the festival with a sewing machine in it?"

"That's right. The booths all have outlets, so I can have a couple of sewing machines and quilts in different stages of completion. Meadow and Savannah are going to help me out, too," said Posy. She gave Beatrice a smile. "I'm thinking you're going to be attending the spring festival with Wyatt, aren't you?"

Beatrice nodded. "That's the plan, although the church does have a booth at the festival. The women of the church are having a bake sale to benefit local children's charities. But he's not obligated to do anything but the cleanup after it's over. So, we're really looking forward to it."

"Beatrice, I feel like we haven't caught up for ages. Would you like to come to my house tonight to have supper with Cork and me? We're not planning anything special, just a veggie night. I'm making some roasted red potatoes, lima beans, and a salad, and I've got some delicious strawberries from the farmers' market that I thought we might slice up. And a bottle of wine," she added with a laugh. "Since Cork thinks a meal is uncivilized without one."

"A natural sentiment from a man who owns a wine shop," said Beatrice. "And one that I have to agree with him on. I'd love to."

A bell chimed as the door opened and Savannah walked in. As usual, she was wearing a rather severe outfit: an ankle-length skirt and a long-sleeved floral blouse. But her hair, usually pulled back tightly into a bun, was gathered less tightly, giving her an overall softer look. "Hi, y'all," she said. "Thought I might pop my head in to say hello for a few minutes."

Beatrice said quickly, "You've just left work, then? You haven't seen Miss Sissy, have you?"

Savannah frowned. "No. Was I supposed to?" Then she sighed. "This is about Smoke, isn't it? I could tell Miss Sissy was getting attached to him."

Posy said in a sympathetic voice, "I remember at the workshop you could hardly pull Smoke away from Miss Sissy."

"I'm sure Miss Sissy has got to feel lonely sometimes," said Beatrice. "I was wondering if a pet might do her some good. But I don't think she could take care of one all the time, either."

Savannah reached up a hand to clutch at her high collar. "You don't mean that I should share Smoke with Miss Sissy, do you? Because I don't think I could possibly consider that. I barely see enough of Smoke as it is."

"No, no. I don't think you should share Smoke—he's your cat and you're crazy about him, I know. Maybe we could think on it," said Beatrice.

Posy said slowly, "I was thinking, after seeing everyone's reaction to Smoke at the workshop, that it might be fun to have a cat for the shop. A kitten probably wouldn't work as well, because I'd have to keep too close an eye on it. But a lazy, grown-up cat—maybe one we could find at the shelter might be fun. Then Miss Sissy could take the cat home with her some days and bring the cat here, too, to spend time at the shop."

Beatrice smiled at Posy. "That's really generous of you. It's not as if you don't have enough going on with the store and all the new customers. And then going home to spend time with Cork and cook supper . . . it's a lot."

"Well, a shop cat would be something the customers would enjoy, too. Maybe they'd linger longer in the store if they had a kitty to visit. And if I could split the responsibility for a while, that would be nice, too," said Posy.

Savannah said, "I'm surprised you haven't had a cat before now. I know you love them."

"Oh, I do," said Posy. "I guess I've just never gotten around to it, or maybe it hasn't been the right time."

Beatrice said, "And I think you've always felt like Miss Sissy sort of *was* the Patchwork Cottage cat. At least, she's spent so much time napping here that it could be easy to make that mistake."

"That's certainly true. Although I do love having her here. She keeps the place lively. So, a cat. If y'all could keep a lookout for one, I'd sure appreciate it. Otherwise, I'll find a day to take Miss Sissy down to the animal shelter and we'll pick out a cat there," said Posy.

Savannah glanced down at the fabric that Beatrice was still holding. "I really love those colors. What kind of quilt are you doing?"

"A kaleidoscope pattern," said Beatrice.

Savannah beamed at her. "One of my favorite kinds!"

"Savannah does so well with those geometrics," said Posy. The truth was that Savannah was an excellent quilter, and was very fond of precise geometric patterns, which greatly appealed to her sense of order.

"Will you put one of your quilts in the juried show at the spring festival?"

"I sure will. I've had a very good reception from judges for my quilts in past years," said Savannah proudly.

"You certainly have," said Posy with a smile. "I think you placed last year, didn't you?"

"I did." Savannah smiled at the memory and then said, "What we really need to do is persuade June Bug to enter something in the show. She's still so insecure about her quilting."

Posy nodded. "Very true, even though she's certainly been getting recognition for her quilts. I feel that if she can get more awards and attention, she might start feeling even more confident about experimenting."

Savannah peered at her watch. "I suppose I should be getting back, if Miss Sissy is waiting for me." She sighed. "The last time she came to visit, she stayed for hours, playing with Smoke. The poor kitty slept for days afterward."

"She does have a present for him," said Beatrice. "I think you'll like it. She almost didn't even let me see the gift, she was so fiercely protective of it."

Savannah brightened. "Really?"

And in a moment, she'd hurried out the door to head home.

Beatrice snapped her fingers. "I need to go home, too, before I meet you for supper. But I know what I wanted to ask you. Posy, I was wondering if you knew of any tricks to keep my sewing machine's foot pedal from sliding. It keeps trying to escape, and I feel like I'm chasing it all day."

Posy said, "Lyla shared a good tip with me the other day. She said to use a nonslip silicone pot holder—the pedal will stay exactly where you want it to. She said it was one of her favorite quilting secrets."

"I think I have one of those at home," said Beatrice thoughtfully. "I didn't really like it as a pot holder, but it would be the perfect size to use under the foot pedal. Thanks."

"These tips make life a lot easier for us quilters," said Posy. She paused thoughtfully. "Maybe it would be fun to put up a bulletin board in the shop with paper blocks on it. Quilters could write down their favorite tips to share them with others."

"You're just full of ideas today, Posy," said Beatrice. They headed over to the register, and Posy checked out her fabric.

"See you at six thirty?" asked Posy.

"I'll be there."

Posy was an excellent cook, and her simple supper was more like a feast. Her husband, Cork, who always seemed a bit severe, with his dour expression and bald head, was actually a lot of fun to spend time with. They'd eaten outside in Posy's tidy backyard, Cork entertaining them over a bottle of wine by telling stories of unusual customers he'd had over the years. As the sun went down, the birds were still flying to the feeders on the edges of the yard and singing from the rhododendrons and birch trees. After spending so much time thinking about Trevor Garber's murder, it was a pleasant break to while away a couple of hours with good friends, great food, and engaging conversation.

When it had grown dark outside, Beatrice helped clear their plates and glasses from the table and bring them inside Posy and Cork's small ranch house.

"I should be getting back home," she said a bit reluctantly. "Noo-noo will be wondering where I am."

"Next time let's make it a couples' dinner," suggested Posy warmly. "We'd love to have Wyatt over here, wouldn't we, Cork?"

Cork nodded. "It would be a pleasure to have him over. As it was hosting you, Beatrice. Somehow, lately, it seems like we only ever have Miss Sissy over here." He made a face. "And she invites herself, comes in the middle of supper, and then spends much of the time hissing at me."

"Oh, Cork, you know you love having Miss Sissy over. She only hisses when she thinks you're being unfriendly. Besides, if it weren't for Miss Sissy, where else would you get so many colorful stories to tell your customers?"

Cork shook his head in denial, but reached over and gave Posy a fond hug. "We'll set up that supper. Good to see you, Beatrice."

On the short drive home, Beatrice thought again how fortunate she was to have such good friends. It had been an adjustment moving from Atlanta to Dappled Hills, but she was so glad she had. Life here was in many ways so much easier, with a slower pace. Friendships seemed to grow faster and stronger here.

Beatrice pulled into her driveway and gathered her

purse from the passenger's side. She looked for her phone, frowning. She patted the pocket of her slacks and turned on the car's interior lights to see if her phone had slid off the seat or if she were sitting on it. Then she rifled through her pocketbook. No phone. Beatrice sighed. She must have either left it at Posy's house or at the Patchwork Cottage earlier in the afternoon. Beatrice tried to remember when she'd last checked it or used it, and couldn't. She'd just call around tomorrow on the house phone and see if she could find it.

Beatrice got out of her car and walked up to her front door, fumbling with the keys as she tried to remember where she might have put her phone. As she was putting her key in the lock, she gave a startled cry as someone jabbed what felt like the steel barrel of a gun into her back.

Chapter Fifteen

Beatrice's scream alerted Noo-noo, who started frantically barking inside the house. Now a gruff voice that she couldn't place and could barely hear over the barking said, "Get inside!"

With shaking hands, Beatrice tried again to insert the key into the lock. Then, suddenly feeling much calmer, she took a deep breath and purposely dropped the keys to the ground with a startled exclamation. The intruder jammed the gun harder into her back, which she took as a cue to pick up the keys. As she started to bend over, she made a backward kick with her right leg and slammed her foot into the intruder's shin.

The intruder cried out in pain, crouching over the hurt leg. Beatrice used the opportunity to swiftly grab the keys, shove the house key into the lock with shaking hands, push open her front door, and lock it behind her. She ran into the kitchen to grab the house phone and dialed the Downeys' number as quickly as she could.

Beatrice peered out the kitchen window, concealing herself as much as possible by looking out the side. She saw no one. Ramsay answered the phone, and Beatrice said breathlessly, "It's Beatrice. Someone with a gun is here at my house and surprised me at my front door."

"I'll be there in a second," said Ramsay grimly.

Beatrice could hear Meadow talking anxiously to Ramsay in the background and said quickly, "Meadow worries too much about me as it is. You can tell her about this, but please don't mention the gun." Then she hung up.

There was a knock at her front door, and Beatrice froze. Unless Ramsay had the secret power of teleportation, she doubted that he could have arrived at her door that quickly. But would an attacker knock?

Beatrice hurried to the door and peered out the side window. Exhaling in relief, she saw Piper there. She quickly opened the door, "Come in! Hurry!"

"Mama, what's wrong? What is it?" But she darted inside as instructed.

Beatrice locked the door behind her. "There was someone out there a few minutes ago." She paused. She hated to worry Piper with the details. "They . . . tried to force me into the house . . . I guess they were trying to intimidate me." She filled Piper in quickly.

Piper gaped at her. "What? Mama! How terrifying for you." Piper gave her mother a long, tight hug. Then she pulled back slightly, searching her mother's face in concern. "Let's get you to the sofa. You're trembling. I'll pour you a glass of wine."

"And Ramsay's on his way." Another sharp rap at the door, and Piper glanced out before opening it to a stern Ramsay.

Meadow had come, too, but this time she was unusually quiet as she heard Beatrice once again explain what had happened. Meadow gave Beatrice a tight squeeze and then gave Piper one, too . . . just because she was crazy about Piper. Beatrice carefully left out mention of the gun so as not to alarm Meadow. Otherwise, Meadow might try to foist Boris on her for protection. As it was, she kept shaking her head, as if she couldn't believe such a thing could happen in Dappled Hills.

"The whole reason I'm here," said Piper slowly, "is because you didn't answer your cell phone. Or the house phone, either."

"I think I left my cell phone at the Patchwork Cottage. And I would have been at supper with Posy and Cork when you called the house phone," said Beatrice. She shivered uncontrollably. "I'm so thankful you didn't come over a few minutes earlier and encounter that intruder."

Ramsay said, "Beatrice, you're sure you didn't see or hear anything that could give us a clue who was behind this? Did you have the impression that it was a short or tall person behind you? Or whether it was a man or woman speaking?"

Beatrice shook her head in frustration. "That's the thing. I had no impressions at all. The intruder was careful not to give anything away, I guess in case I'd somehow manage to get away. The voice I heard was gruff and was clearly disguised, and Noo-noo was being a good watchdog and barking up a storm. And I used the moment of injury to get away. I had an impression of someone dressed in black, but that was all. It was dark outside and I didn't see anything else."

"Why do you think the intruder wanted to force you inside the house?" asked Ramsay.

"I'm assuming that he or she was trying to intimidate me," Beatrice swallowed, her throat feeling desperately dry as she realized again how lucky she was.

Ramsay gave her a knowing look that said that he knew it was more than just intimidation if her intruder had brought a gun.

Meadow's eyes opened wide at the thought, shaking her head in disbelief. "What on earth is this town coming to?"

Piper gave her mother a tight hug. "I'm so glad you got away."

Ramsay asked intently, "Do you have any idea what he was after or why he might have wanted to intimidate you, Beatrice? Do you have any information about this case?"

A frown creased Piper's forehead. "You haven't been trying to poke around in this murder, have you? You know how that always worries me, Mama."

"It worries me, too, even though you're good at getting to the bottom of things," said Ramsay.

Meadow shot Beatrice a guilty look.

"I honestly have no idea what made the intruder think I was onto him. Maybe it's the fact that I've been asking questions that's made him nervous." Beatrice fought the uneasy feeling that it was Daniel who'd seemed most upset by her questioning. Who else might be thinking that Beatrice was getting too close to finding out some answers?

Meadow said, "Ramsay, don't you think someone should look after Beatrice tonight? To make sure whoever was here doesn't come back?"

"I really don't need. . . ." started Beatrice.

Piper quickly said, "I'll stay here."

"Piper, there's not even a guest bedroom here!"

"I can sleep on the sofa. I'll be perfectly comfortable on this sofa." Piper gave a small bounce on the sofa to emphasize its softness and complete suitability for sleeping.

"There's absolutely no need . . ."

Meadow brightened. "Boris! We can lend you Boris tonight. Not that Noo-noo isn't a wonderful watchdog, of course, but it seems as if your intruder tonight wasn't as concerned about Noo-noo's potential for ferocity. Boris has size on his side."

"I'd be happy to lend Boris out," said Ramsay with alacrity.

Beatrice decided that a marauding Boris was the last thing she needed that night. Thank heaven she hadn't mentioned the gun to Meadow, or her home would have turned into the Beatrice Coleman Home for Wayward Dogs.

"Listen, everyone. I really, really appreciate your concern. But there's no need to worry. No one is coming back here tonight. This intruder is probably nursing a very sore shin. All I need is some sleep, and tomorrow morning I'll be fine."

They all finally reluctantly left, Ramsay last. He said in an undertone to Beatrice, "You and I know that someone with a gun was probably intending on using it. Intimidation is one thing, but I think this was something else. This person wanted to get rid of you. Please think about what you know and what you may know that you don't know you know."

Beatrice gave him a bemused look, and Ramsay sighed. "I know that didn't make much sense. But you get my drift, right? Let me know if you have any information that could implicate someone. The sooner I make an arrest in this case, the better. Your safety is at stake."

Beatrice swallowed hard and nodded. "And thanks for keeping this under your hat, Ramsay. I appreciate it."

Beatrice slowly got ready to turn in. But she was awake until the wee hours—listening to every creak of the house and small sound outside.

The next morning, Wyatt called her early. "Is it all right if I drop by? I talked to Piper when I was out getting coffee. I'd like to see with my own eyes that you're okay."

A few minutes later, Wyatt was sitting beside her on the sofa, holding one of her hands and studying her with his kind, concerned eyes. "You didn't sleep last night, did you?"

Beatrice smiled at him. "You're much too observant, Wyatt. No, I didn't sleep. I think I had so much adrenaline pumping through me last night that sleep was completely impossible. But I'm fine—I promise. Except that now I'm even more determined that this person should be behind bars."

"I can understand that," said Wyatt. "Of course you'd be angry. It must have been terrifying."

"It was. And I'm not one who deals well with terror," said Beatrice with a sigh. "It's making me most remarkably vengeful." She shook off the unwelcome emotions and said, "Want some coffee? I know you said you had some earlier."

"No, no, I'm fine." Wyatt was still studying her. "I hate the thought that something could have happened to you, Beatrice. Please, please be careful."

She nodded. "Of course I will. I promise. No more fumbling in my pocketbook for lost phones. I'll be aware of my surroundings. I will allow nothing else bad to happen to me, or else Meadow will follow through with her threat to loan me Boris for protection. And now"—she gave Wyatt a beseeching look—"can we move on to more pleasant topics?"

"Like the spring festival?" he asked with a grin. "We're still going together, right?"

"Absolutely. And I plan on beating you at the horse-shoe competition."

"Oh, I see—a challenge! I'll take you up on that, Beatrice. I fancy myself a master at the art of horseshoe throwing." He puffed up his chest.

"It's an art now, hmm? All right. I haven't actually been to this festival before, but I have heard about the horseshoes. But tell me this: is this the kind of event where I need to eat before we go?" asked Beatrice.

Wyatt blinked at her. "Eat before we go?"

"You know. Does it have the typical fair food?" asked Beatrice.

"If you mean cotton candy, fried pickles, and hot dogs, then yes. And they always have the best hot-dog chili I've ever tasted—you definitely don't want to miss out on the hot dogs. So *naturally* you won't want to eat before you go, or you'll completely miss out."

"On the stomachache, you mean?" asked Beatrice wryly.

"Well, if you're determined, at least save room for the boiled peanuts. They're amazing and my personal favorite," said Wyatt.

"I guess I could make boiled peanuts the exception," said Beatrice with a smile. "And you still don't have to help out with the church booth, right?"

"That's right. Except for the fact that I really should support the women of the church and buy a cake, but that's not exactly a hardship. And I'll help them with cleanup after the festival."

"So separate cars," said Beatrice. Then she reluctantly realized that this was exactly the type of activity that Meadow was so insistent that she should help with to spend more time with Wyatt. "Unless you need help with the cleanup. Then we could go in the same car."

Wyatt gave her a quizzical look. "That's nice of you to offer, but you know how the bake-sale booth goes. It should be pretty quick cleanup. We'll load up the unsold cakes and the table and chairs, and that's it. But I appreciate it. You know, if you're looking for a way to help out at the church, there's actually something we do need help with this afternoon." He hesitated. "If you're up to it, of course. You had a fairly harrowing experience last night."

"I'm up to it," said Beatrice quickly. Then she smiled. "So, what have I signed myself up for?"

Wyatt laughed. "You didn't even ask. I could make it some really heinous activity involving polishing the church silver. But, actually, it's not so bad. There's a group that's assembling casseroles to freeze for the funeral and new baby ministries. We had a couple of regulars cancel, so that would be a huge help. I'll be there, too."

Beatrice laughed. "Will you be showing off your cooking skills again? You'll really make me feel inadequate if you do."

"No cooking skills required for this ministry! All the ingredients are in separate zipper bags, and we all put them together in an assembly line. It takes no time, and we end up with a freezer full of food when one of our families needs some extra help," said Wyatt. "We're meeting at the church kitchen at two o'clock."

"Now, *that's* the kind of cooking I think I can handle," said Beatrice. Wyatt squeezed her hand in thanks.

They sat quietly for a few moments, enjoying the peace of the room together. Then Wyatt said in a soft voice, "Beatrice, I can tell you've had something on your mind lately. Other than Trevor's death. You've been lost in your thoughts whenever I've spoken to you. It seemed like it started when we were visiting at the retirement home. Did anything happen then? I know you spoke to Daniel for a while as I visited with Mrs. Kemp."

Beatrice felt the muscles in her neck and shoulders bunch up. The last thing she wanted to do was to give Wyatt something to worry about—especially when there really might not *be* anything to worry about. But by now, Daniel surely should have told Harper about his parentage and Trevor's attempt to extort money from him. Not to tell Wyatt felt somewhat dishonest.

She took a deep breath and told Wyatt what she'd learned from Daniel. That his father hadn't been the man who'd raised him, that he wanted to ensure his mother didn't suffer any discomfort at this stage of her life. That he'd told Trevor as a friend in order to try to work through his feelings—and that Trevor had betrayed his trust by attempting to blackmail him. Wyatt sat very still and listened intently as Beatrice spoke.

Finally, at the end, he remained silent, considering Beatrice's words. "Have you told Ramsay this?" he asked.

"No. Not yet. Daniel wanted to tell Harper first. That's why I didn't tell you earlier—he thought Harper should be the first to know." Beatrice hesitated. "Wyatt, I'm sure that Daniel couldn't have anything to do with Trevor's death. And could you even imagine his attacking me last night? It really seems outside the realm of possibility."

Wyatt's eyes were tired as he gazed at Beatrice. "All of it seems outside the realm of possibility. But the facts show that Daniel did have motive and opportunity. He had something to gain from Trevor's death. And if he thought that his secret—his mother's secret—needed to be protected at this late point in her life, I'm not sure how far he might go. He's very protective of his mother—something that I'd originally seen as a good trait and a sign that he might also be the same for my sister."

"I still don't see him as the murderer. Or, even if I can imagine it, I don't want to. I'm planning on digging further to see what I can do to prove his innocence," said Beatrice.

Wyatt was shaking his head, anxiety creasing his brow. "Beatrice, this person is dangerous, whoever he is. You've already encountered that once. Please don't keep asking questions. We must do the right thing and present the evidence we have to Ramsay, and let him decide how to handle it. Before more deaths occur."

"And I will. But give me a little time before I do, Wyatt. Just a few days . . . until after the festival, maybe. Then I'll let Ramsay know," said Beatrice.

Wyatt slowly nodded. But he didn't look happy about it.

After Wyatt left, Beatrice decided the first order of the day was to find her cell phone. She figured Posy and Cork would have discovered it if she'd left it at their house. So she headed off to the Patchwork Cottage to see if she'd left it there while she'd been visiting with Posy and Savannah.

Posy was once again surrounded by customers, so Beatrice walked straight over to the sofa where she'd sat the day before. Unfortunately, this time Miss Sissy had beat her to the shop and was already boisterously snoring there.

Beatrice glanced around and under the furniture, but didn't see the phone. Miss Sissy was sitting right on top of where she'd been. She softly said, "Miss Sissy?" But the old woman didn't stir. So she gently reached to the side of her to see if the phone had slipped under the sofa cushion.

Beatrice jumped as a wiry hand with a strong grip clamped around her wrist. "Pickpocket!" howled Miss Sissy.

"No, no. I'm looking for my phone," said Beatrice, pulling away with some effort and then rubbing her sore arm. She gave a reassuring smile to several shoppers who looked her way with narrowed eyes.

"Why didn't you say so?" grumbled the old woman. She hopped up off the sofa. Beatrice pulled up the cushion and found her phone underneath.

Beatrice gave a sigh of relief. "Well, it's got a dead battery, but at least I found it. Sorry, Miss Sissy."

Miss Sissy sat down again in a bit of a huff at having her nap disturbed.

Beatrice cleared her throat. She clearly needed to make amends for the interruption. "So, Miss Sissy, did you catch up with Savannah? And give Savannah her cat mat?"

Miss Sissy glared at her. "It wasn't *Savannah's* mat. And I wasn't there to visit Savannah. I was there to see Smoke." She gave Beatrice a fierce look. "Smoke is my friend."

Beatrice nodded. "Of course he is." She sure hoped that Posy was able to find a cat soon, or else Miss Sissy was going to move in with Savannah and Georgia.

The shop's bell rang, and Beatrice turned to see that Georgia was, as a matter of fact, walking into the Patchwork Cottage. There was a sparkle in her eye and a lightness to her step. Beatrice decided that Tony was good for her.

"Hi, Miss Sissy," said Georgia cheerfully. "We sure enjoyed seeing you yesterday. And Smoke loved having some extra playtime."

Miss Sissy preened. "He liked the toy I brought."

"That's right." Georgia turned to Beatrice and gave

her a small wink. "Miss Sissy not only brought a precious cat mat for Smoke, but she also made a cat toy for him with string and a dowel. That is one spoiled kitty."

"How are things going for you, Georgia? I haven't had a chance to catch up with you for a while," said Beatrice.

Georgia blushed. "That's because I've been spending so much time with Tony. Apart from teaching, I mean. Even at the wedding. Sorry I didn't really visit with you then."

"That's all right—it was a busy evening. It sounds like you and Tony are a wonderful couple. I'm so happy for you both," said Beatrice warmly.

Tony, who ran errands and home repairs for Miss Sissy, was one of her favorites. She barked, "Tony is a nice boy!"

Georgia beamed at her. "Yes, indeed he is!"

"Do y'all have any special plans today?" asked Beatrice. Then she frowned. "Don't you have school?"

"Spring break," said Georgia happily. "And we do have plans this afternoon. We're going fishing."

Miss Sissy made a face.

Beatrice wanted to agree with Miss Sissy that fishing was hardly a romantic date, but Georgia seemed so excited about it. Clearly, any activity was romantic if Tony were there. "Well, I'm sure you'll enjoy just being together."

"I'm packing a picnic lunch for the boat, with a bottle of wine for us to share. So it should be a lot of fun. The weather is gorgeous. And then we have the festival coming up, too. It's really going to be a wonderful week."

Miss Sissy nodded. "Festival. Food!" Her eyes gleamed greedily. If there was one thing Miss Sissy loved above all else, it was a good snack.

"Well, I'm not sure how much food we'll be eating at the festival. Tony's won the pie-eating contest for the past few years, and he wants to maintain his title. So maybe I'll have some cotton candy, but we'll have to protect Tony's appetite for the competition." Georgia sounded as serious, as if the competition meant a national tennis title. She gave Beatrice a shy look. "Are you and Wyatt going together to the festival?"

"Yes. But no worries—I'm pretty sure he has no plans to compete in the pie-eating contest." At least, she certainly hoped not. "His talent lies in horseshoes, or that's what I'm led to believe."

Georgia nodded. "Maybe we'll see y'all out there. Have you got any other plans with Wyatt? What kinds of things do you like doing together? Tony and I are always looking out for fun things to do."

What *did* she and Wyatt do together? Unfortunately, not as much as they'd like to. "Well, this afternoon, we're spending time together assembling casseroles at the church," said Beatrice dryly. "And we spent much of the day visiting the Mountain Vistas retirement home last week."

Georgia looked about as impressed with Beatrice's dates as Beatrice and Miss Sissy had at Georgia's fishing date. "Isn't that nice?" she said quickly, in a bright voice.

Chapter Sixteen

Beatrice was walking into the parking lot near the Patchwork Cottage when she again saw Lyla Wales there, carrying a grocery bag, her car parked right next to Beatrice's.

When Beatrice's key's jangled as she pulled them out of her purse, Lyla swung around with a wary look on her face. She relaxed as she saw Beatrice. "Oh, it's you. We meet again, hmm? Sorry at my reaction. I've been having some issues lately." She grimaced.

"Issues?" asked Beatrice, opening her car door.

"I thought you might be Eleanor. She simply won't leave me alone," said Lyla between gritted teeth. "She blames all of her many problems on me. Eleanor follows me to work and sits in the parking lot for an hour or more. Or she'll show up there when it's time for me to head home, and just look menacing. I felt sorry for her at first, but I'm about to have to tell Ramsay about it. Maybe I should get a restraining order or something."

"I can completely understand your feeling that way," said Beatrice. "But maybe it would be a better idea if I ran by and talked to her. I don't know Eleanor all that well, but she seemed receptive to me the last time I visited with her. Maybe I can help her realize that there are better uses for her time. Besides, she probably needs someone to check up on her."

"If you want to," said Lyla with a small shrug. "That's nice of you. I wish I could summon some sympathy for Eleanor, but I simply can't seem to right now. I know she has issues, though."

"I'll try to call on her either this evening or tomorrow. I've got a commitment this afternoon." Beatrice paused for a moment. "Hope you don't mind an off-topic question, Lyla, but could you tell me what you were doing last night?"

"Last night?" Lyla's forehead creased in a frown. "When?"

"Oh, I don't know. Maybe at nine o'clock?"

"Who knows? I was home with Julian. We'd have been watching the news or something. I would have been quilting as I watched. I'm not sure exactly what time that was, but that was basically our whole evening before I turned in. Early." Lyla tilted her head to one side. "Why do you ask?"

"Oh, nothing. Sorry. It's just something I was following up on. Thanks, anyway." Beatrice hopped into her car before Lyla could follow up with any more questioning. But she saw her still standing, watching her as she drove away.

Beatrice blinked as she entered the church kitchen. There were five or six women and a couple of men lined up in stations. Each person had a good amount of a single ingredient in front of them—cheese or ham or cooked pasta. There was a stack of foil casserole containers, too. It looked as if they were planning on making quite a few casseroles, but Beatrice was relieved to see that even though the kitchen was fairly modest, befitting a smaller church, the oven was industrial-sized.

"This is quite an operation!" murmured Beatrice to Wyatt.

"It is, isn't it?" said Wyatt with a smile. "We can make a lot of meals, too. We're not trying to rush the process too much, but we've made as many as twelve casseroles in ninety minutes."

One of the volunteers called out, "A record that's begging to be broken!"

"So, these go to members of the congregation who've lost someone or had a new baby?" asked Beatrice.

"That's right. Although we don't currently have anyone who's in need. What we do is assemble these casseroles, label them with heating directions, and then store them in the freezer to keep until they're needed. You wouldn't think that a small congregation would have much need, but we've found that this is a ministry that is constantly tapped. So we do our best to fill it," said Wyatt.

"Oh, okay. So they don't even need to be baked today—they go in frozen and are baked by the recipients. What are we making today?" asked Beatrice.

"We've got a few different kinds that we're assembling, actually. That way, we can provide several casseroles to one member of the congregation. Today it's . . ." He looked to one of the others to help him out.

An elderly man quickly said, "Tex-Mex chicken casserole, hash brown potato casserole, and cheeseburger casserole."

"I have a feeling I'll be starving by the end of this process," said Beatrice dryly.

"We get really good reviews on the casseroles," said Wyatt with a smile.

Wyatt briefly introduced Beatrice to the rest of the volunteers and handed her a pair of plastic gloves, and they were ready to start.

Beatrice had tried to listen and remember the volunteers' names as Wyatt had listed them, but had gotten hopelessly lost by the end. She kept trying to do better with names, but it was a constant struggle for her. She smiled at the woman standing beside her. "I'm Beatrice Coleman," she said. "I'm sorry—I don't remember what your name was."

The woman was about fifty years old, with black hair laced with silver. She wore a good deal of makeup, but somehow it was a look that suited her. "I'm Denise Finley," she said.

Beatrice started a little. She remembered that Meadow had mentioned that Patrick Finley sometimes volunteered at Dappled Hills Presbyterian. Was this the doctor's wife? "It's good to meet you," she said. "Are you, by any chance, related to Dr. Finley?"

"I'm his wife," she said with a smile.

They got to work assembling the casseroles after Wyatt thanked them all for being there. Beatrice had the frozen hash browns, and carefully layered them into the containers as they were passed her way.

Denise Finley was a chatty worker and spent a long

time asking Beatrice how she was enjoying Dappled Hills. She told Beatrice that she'd lived in Dappled Hills most of her life and had met her husband in college.

Beatrice said, "It seems as though it could be really challenging being married to a physician. Their hours are all over the place, aren't they? Is he on call much?"

Denise nodded as she stirred in a mixture of cream of chicken soup, sour cream, cheese, and onions into the hash brown potatoes. "He is. But that's because he's a surgeon, and you never know when someone might need emergency surgery. He was out last night for a long time, for instance. But I've gotten used to the unpredictability of his life—and mine."

Denise continued talking about various holiday meals and other events in the past that had been interrupted by her husband's erratic schedule, but all that Beatrice could focus on was the fact that Patrick Finley was out during the time that her intruder had shown up. How tied up at the hospital had he been? Could he have gotten away in between surgeries? Had he even gone to the hospital at all? Surely Ramsay was checking on these alibis—whether Lyla had actually been with Julian and whether Patrick had been in an operating room.

There was a pause in conversation, and then Beatrice said, "Your husband probably knew Trevor Garber, too. He was an acquaintance of mine."

Denise pursed her lips in disapproval. "He did know Trevor. I hope I'm not offending you when I say that he and Trevor weren't getting along in the weeks before Trevor's death, however. I always hate to speak ill of the dead, but I guess you probably know that Trevor wasn't exactly acting normally before he died."

"I'd heard that, yes," said Beatrice. "So he and Trevor had a falling-out, then."

"Very abruptly," said Denise. "And Patrick never really said what it resulted from. I got the impression that it had something to do with an incident at work, and Patrick never really talks very much about his work. But it was very odd. Before that point, they spent a good deal of time together—golfing, going out to eat, or having a drink together. Then, one night, he never wanted to speak of Trevor again."

"But he never said exactly why?" asked Beatrice.

"No. Only that Trevor wasn't the same person. I thought it was a shame, because they'd gotten along well in the past," said Denise.

Someone on Denise's other side started asking her about the Sunday-school class they both taught, and Beatrice lost the thread of conversation. But she'd gotten her confirmation that Patrick's break with Trevor was abrupt—just as it would have been if Patrick had been blackmailed (as Daniel was), and that Patrick was conveniently out at the time of Beatrice's intruder.

Although the casserole assembly was an easy project, Beatrice found that her back was hurting her by the end of it. On the upside, they'd made more than a dozen casseroles for church families. And Wyatt and she had spent some time together, as they'd cleaned up the kitchen afterward. On the downside, though, she didn't feel up to visiting Eleanor that evening. She knew sitting down was a bit of a challenge there, and Beatrice wasn't sure that she wanted to stand any longer that day. She decided to check in early in the morning—in fact, she'd make it a double good deed and ask Meadow if she wanted to walk. Meadow was clearly feeling left out with Beatrice's different activities with Wyatt, and this would be a good way to make amends. She called her.

"Tomorrow morning for a walk?" Meadow's smile beamed through the phone. "Oh, we'd love to!"

"We?" asked Beatrice with some concern. She knew *we* didn't include Ramsay, who found exercise rather abhorrent and would much rather sit in a comfy recliner with a good book. So she was very much afraid that *we* included—

"Boris and me, of course. Boris adores the exercise and is so much better for it. Really, he doesn't try to escape nearly as much if he has regular walks," explained Meadow.

"Oh, but I didn't explain one part of the walk," said Beatrice, desperately trying to forgo the Boris part of the activity. She'd have to make the next bit sound as appealing as possible. "You see, we've got a secret mission, too."

"Secret mission?" asked Meadow in her loud voice.

"Shh!" said Beatrice, rolling her eyes. If she really did have a secret mission, it would certainly be blown by now. And, honestly, she wasn't particularly keen on Ramsay knowing about her plans, considering his concern over her safety last night. "Is Ramsay there?"

"No, he's out. What secret mission?"

"I think we need to check in on Eleanor," said Beatrice.

Meadow's voice sounded somewhat deflated. "Is

that all? I mean, I agree with you—she certainly seems kind of ... mentally fragile, and it would be very neighborly of us to check in with her and make sure she's all right."

"Make sure she's all right and maybe carefully, gently question her some more. I ran into Lyla Wales earlier today, and she said that Eleanor has been hounding her. She's followed her to work and sat there in the parking lot. Lyla said that Eleanor clearly blames her for Trevor's death because they were having an affair," said Beatrice. "But it all made me wonder if maybe ..."

"Maybe Eleanor really *does* have some information on the case that we don't know about," said Meadow thoughtfully. "All right. It's a plan. What time do you want to check in?"

"Could we make it early? My day today got completely filled up in no time. Is Eleanor an early riser?"

Meadow said, "She seems to be. I've seen her out in the yard pretty early the times I've walked by. How about eight o'clock? And if we don't see her out in the yard, let's tap on her door. We can tell her we were worried about her, considering that Dappled Hills has become such a hotbed of crime." Meadow heaved a huge sigh.

The next morning wasn't exactly a picture-perfect day for a walk. It was raining steadily at seven forty-five and it was foggy, as well. Beatrice belatedly checked the forecast and saw that the rain was supposed to continue until the afternoon.

The phone rang, and Beatrice picked it up to hear Meadow's voice. "We're still going, aren't we? After you called me, I couldn't get Eleanor off my brain. I even dreamed about her last night. We should definitely check on her."

"We could visit without going on the walk, couldn't we?" asked Beatrice, still looking outside at the rain hitting the windows.

"A little rain won't melt us, right? I've got a rain slicker and boots and a golf umbrella. I won't get a drop on me, anyway," said Meadow. "Don't you have rain gear?"

"I've got a very dainty umbrella that wouldn't even keep Noo-noo dry," said Beatrice glumly.

"Well, put on a raincoat and drive over here. I've got another big golf umbrella I can lend you. That way we can tell Eleanor that we were just walking by her house— being dedicated to our physical exercise as we are—and thought we'd pop our heads in and see how she was doing and if she needed anything," said Meadow.

"And that's less obvious than driving up in a car?"

Meadow said, "I think driving up at eight a.m. is rather ominous, don't you? Like we're about to grill her or something. No, this will be a friendly, spur-of-the-moment visit during our usual walk."

As she took the large umbrella from Meadow minutes later, Beatrice grimly reflected that the walk itself seemed completely bizarre. By then the rain was sheeting down, and she could barely even see Meadow as she walked next to her. The only reason she *could* see her was because Meadow was bedecked in safety-yellow rain gear, from her boots to her long slicker and her hat. In the getup Meadow was wearing, she should technically have been able to be seen from outer space.

And she did seem to be drier than Beatrice, who was wearing an old brown raincoat that was only tea length.

"I don't suppose we'll see Eleanor out gardening," said Meadow loudly, trying to be heard over the wind.

"Not unless she's taken complete leave of her senses," agreed Beatrice. "But this is probably an easier way to finagle a visit with her—she'll take pity on us and bring us in out of the storm."

"Absolutely," said Meadow. "Eleanor loves us."

Further conversation was cut short as the wind and the rain both kicked up a notch. The two women battled the squall, fighting their way up Eleanor's driveway.

"Thank goodness we're here," muttered Beatrice.

"We're good friends," said Meadow smugly.

Beatrice and Meadow huddled on the covered front porch, although they weren't receiving much protection from the elements even there, with the wind blowing the rain sideways. Beatrice rang the doorbell, and the two women waited.

After ten seconds had passed, Beatrice thumped loudly on the door.

Meadow gave her a reproachful look. "Beatrice, she's probably going to think we're home invaders or something. That was quite a knock on the door."

"I can't help it—I'm desperate to get out of this rainstorm." Beatrice gave another resounding knock on the front door.

Meadow said in her stage whisper, "It probably takes her a long time to navigate those piles of things to even get to the door. Or maybe she's in the shower. Or decided to sleep in this morning."

Beatrice tried the handle and the door opened. "Maybe so, but why would she sleep in or take a shower with the door unlocked?"

Meadow shrugged. "It's a small town, and old habits die hard. Ramsay says he's constantly having to remind residents to keep their doors locked. Folks who've lived here all their lives don't remember."

Beatrice frowned. "Just the same. We're here to check in on Eleanor, and we should check in. Let's stick our heads in and call and see if she hears us, or if we hear water running or something like that."

She cautiously opened the door, poked her head through the crack, and called out, "Eleanor? It's Beatrice and Meadow. We thought we'd drop by to say hi." She paused and listened hard. Then she called again, "Eleanor?"

"Do you hear water running? Or snoring? Or a loud TV drowning us out?" asked Meadow, looking worried. "Or anything?"

"Nothing," said Beatrice grimly. "I'm going inside."

Beatrice pushed the door open and stepped in. As before, there were piles and piles of newspapers, catalogs, and unopened boxes of kitchen gadgets, etc. But unlike before, there seemed to be a bit more organization. As Beatrice looked closer, she saw that it looked as if Eleanor had been sorting her piles into three distinct piles; she'd even labeled the three piles with a piece of paper. There was a give-away pile, a throw away pile (complete with large black garbage bags), and a keep pile.

Several cats perched on the tops of piles and looked down at them with varying degrees of disdain.

Meadow studied the piles as she came in behind Beatrice. "It's a pity that the keep pile is so large. Maybe she'll reconsider some of those things later."

"Maybe. Right now I'm more concerned about finding her. Especially considering what happened to me a couple of nights ago." Beatrice moved through the living room and dining room into the kitchen. Then she swiftly climbed the stairs, which were miraculously uncluttered, and checked the upstairs, but didn't Eleanor. "We'd better check the garage. Maybe she's out."

"But it's so early!" Meadow said.

"*We're* out, though. And Lyla is probably out, too," said Beatrice in a whisper. "Which may be what Eleanor is out doing—following her around. Let's see."

Beatrice opened the garage door and peered in. There was no car there. She relaxed. "Okay, so I guess Eleanor is really lax about keeping her door locked. Although I do think that's pretty odd, considering her husband just got murdered."

The garage door started going up, and Beatrice and Meadow gaped at each other. "We're going to scare her to death if we're in here as she's coming in," said Beatrice. "Should we go back out through the front door and knock again?"

"In that monsoon?" scoffed Meadow. "You can if you want to, but I think I'll stay here for a while, until the rain tapers off."

They could hear the rain still pounding outside the windows of the kitchen. Beatrice said, "All right, but I'm calling out to her as soon as she opens her door. I don't want to give her a heart attack."

"Eleanor will be delighted to see us!" said Meadow.

The car pulled into the garage, windshield wipers still swishing aggressively from side to side. Beatrice waved from the open door into the house, but with Eleanor's headlights on, she couldn't see if she'd noticed she was there.

Eleanor opened her car door, seemingly lost in thought. She jumped violently when Beatrice said, "Eleanor? It's Beatrice and Meadow."

Chapter Seventeen

"What . . . what are you doing here?" Eleanor was more than just surprised. She was trembling all over.

"I'm so sorry—I was trying not to scare you. Meadow and I were on a walk," said Beatrice sheepishly. It seemed even more absurd as a peal of thunder rang out on cue. "We wanted to stop by to see how you were doing."

Meadow assertively stepped in. "But you didn't answer our knocks or the doorbell. So Beatrice tried the front door, and it opened. We wanted to make sure you were all right, considering . . . uh . . . recent events," she finished delicately.

Eleanor didn't quite meet their gaze. "Well. That's very sweet of you both. To check on me, I mean. And you certainly are dedicated to your exercise program." This as another crack of thunder sounded outside.

Beatrice said, "Can we help you bring anything inside? Groceries? You're up with the chickens today, Eleanor."

A rush of color flamed across Eleanor's cheeks, which seemed like an odd response to Beatrice's offer of help. Eleanor mumbled, "Yes, I was out early. No, there's no need to help me carry anything. I was out for a coffee—that's all."

Her eyes once again didn't meet Meadow's or Beatrice's gaze. Meadow and Beatrice glanced at each other, and then Beatrice said briskly, "Let's head inside, then. If it's all right with you, Meadow and I want to wait for a few minutes. At least until the thunder has stopped."

Eleanor's face registered dismay until she quickly said, "Of course. You wouldn't want to leave with the thunder and lightning."

She walked past them into the house, and Beatrice muttered to Meadow, "Although walking in an epic flood was apparently all right with us."

Meadow gave her a reproachful look. "At least we're checking on her. That was the goal, right?"

Among other things. Like asking Eleanor to try to back off from Lyla before Lyla put a restraining order on her.

Eleanor seemed as if she were just going through the motions—almost as if she were in some sort of fog. She automatically found several glasses in a cabinet, poured some iced tea in them, and handed them out. Eleanor looked vaguely around her for a place for them all to sit, as the thunder and lightning kicked up a notch outside.

Eleanor said slowly, "The last time you were here, I

had a better idea where we should sit. But I've been moving things around . . ."

Meadow beamed at her. "We saw all the stacks you'd made. It looks like you're making great progress with your . . . clearing out."

Although Meadow had again tried to be careful with the words she used, Eleanor still winced at the *clearing out*. "I'm not sure I want to get rid of *all* of it," she said in a defensive manner, crossing her arms over her chest.

"Naturally," said Beatrice soothingly. "Of course you wouldn't. But it looks as if you're organizing your things in a very logical way—at least that's the way it seemed to me. A give-away, a keep, and a throwaway pile, right? That's the way I do it, too."

Eleanor's shoulders, which had been bunched up, seemed to relax at Beatrice's words. "Yes, that's right. Except sometimes I move things from the give-away and the throwaway piles to the keep pile," she admitted ruefully.

Meadow's eyes opened wide. Beatrice recognized the look. It was Meadow with a mission. And for once it wasn't directed toward Beatrice. Beatrice gave a relieved sigh.

"I know!" said Meadow excitedly. "It's so, so hard to go through things yourself. But this is the sort of project that I *love*. I would *love* to help you with this, Eleanor."

One of the cats came in and stared haughtily at Meadow. Eleanor reached down and distractedly stroked it. Then she brightened. "Meadow, that would be great. You can help me when I start second-guessing what I'm doing. Maybe you can help me keep focused, too."

"It's the kind of project that can't be tackled all in one day," said Meadow, waving a hand around expansively. "You'd get burned-out and frustrated. But if I came here every day for as long as it took . . . Say, nine o'clock each morning? Then I think it would go a lot faster."

Eleanor nodded, starting to get excited. "I've gotten to the point where I feel weighed down with all this *stuff*. I want to get my life back. I want to do more of what I really enjoy doing, which is working with flowers. I've always done really small-scale work as a florist because I don't think I had the confidence in myself to try to do more. But now . . . I want to really grow my business. And I want to move out eventually. I really don't want to be in this big house all by myself. Well, with the cats, too. Even then, I think I need to cut back, especially if I'm moving to a smaller place—it's just not fair to them. I've got three cats to care for and I love them, but I have a feeling that if I'm going to be realistic, I need only two."

Beatrice blinked at her. "You're actually looking to find a home for one of your cats?"

Meadow frowned at Beatrice. "Surely *you* don't want a cat, Beatrice. What would Noo-noo say?"

"Oh, Noo-noo would be totally appalled, the way she was when I took Smoke in before I gave him to Savannah. No, I'm thinking about Miss Sissy," said Beatrice.

Now both Eleanor and Meadow were staring at her as if she'd suddenly gone insane.

"Miss *Sissy*?" asked Eleanor. She made a face. "I'm not sure her house qualifies as a good home for one of my babies."

Beatrice said, "Let me explain that the cat would actually be shared between Posy at the Patchwork Cottage and Miss Sissy. I agree that Miss Sissy likely doesn't need complete responsibility for a cat right now. But Posy was saying that she'd like to share a cat with Miss Sissy and take some of that responsibility off her. The cat could be a shop cat some of the time, and some of the time could be at Miss Sissy's house. Miss Sissy has completely fallen head over feels for Savannah's cat, Smoke."

Meadow nodded with sudden comprehension. "I see. And, yes, that's true about Miss Sissy, Eleanor. Beatrice and I saw her out during our last walk, and she'd quilted a cat mat for Smoke. With tassels! But I think she's probably driving Savannah nutty, because Savannah wants to hog Smoke all for herself."

Eleanor said slowly, "Well, I certainly have a lot of respect for Posy. That's an arrangement that I'll seriously consider. Thanks for letting me know. I wanted to personally place a cat with a new owner—I'd never put one of my babies into a shelter." She glanced around them again. "Here, let's go into the living room. I think I've got a few good spots to sit down in there."

Sure enough, there was a stack that was the perfect size for Eleanor and one for Meadow, and Beatrice was even able to unearth an armchair with little trouble.

Eleanor looked pleased. "I'm making better progress in here than I'd thought. Now if I could only get my financial things in order as well as I'm getting my physical things in order."

Meadow grimaced. "I hate working on bills and things. Hate keeping up with it and tracking it and coming up with a budget. Bleh."

"Unfortunately, I do, too. And I've gotten to the point where I have to pay very close attention to it. I have a cousin who has been advising me on the phone—helping me to work through all the bills and organize them. It's been tough," said Eleanor, looking tired just thinking about it.

Beatrice asked delicately, "I thought you'd said that Trevor's insurance money was going to help you balance everything out."

Eleanor's face was pinched. "That's what I'd thought. But the truth is that it wasn't anywhere close to balancing out things. We were in a much deeper hole than I thought. That's what's behind my decision to sell the house. I've really *got* to sell the house before they start foreclosure proceedings at the bank. It would be helpful if, once I pay everyone, if I could have some income to start out fresh."

Meadow said, "Maybe when I'm helping you go through everything, we'll find some items that you can sell at the church yard sale. That could at least give you some pocket change, if nothing else. And a lot of your things appear to still be in their boxes."

Eleanor brightened. "I'd forgotten that the church had a yard sale. That would be a lot easier than me trying to attract people over to my house. A lot of people go through the church sale, don't they?"

"They certainly do," said Meadow emphatically. "Why, Ramsay and I made three hundred dollars there last year, and we didn't have nearly the items that you'll have."

Eleanor smiled at her. "It's wonderful to see things

starting to come together for me." Then a shadow crossed over her features, as if she'd been reminded of something unpleasant.

"It really is coming together, Eleanor," said Beatrice. She was trying to tread carefully into the topic of Lyla. "And you seem like you're doing really well. That's one reason Meadow and I are here, as I mentioned before—to check on you. You've had a really stressful time, and a scary one. I know stress affects all of us in really harsh ways."

Eleanor's eyes narrowed. "It seems as if you're tip-toeing around something, Beatrice. It's okay. You can get right to the point. What's this about?"

Meadow gave Beatrice an encouraging nod of her head.

"I bumped into Lyla Wales in the parking lot when I was leaving the Patchwork Cottage yesterday. I startled her, as a matter of fact. She seemed to think I might be you," said Beatrice.

Eleanor flushed. "I can't abide that woman. What did she say?"

"One reason I wanted to talk with you about Lyla is because she mentioned the possibility of a restraining order against you," said Beatrice. "And I thought, in a small town like Dappled Hills, that would make your life very difficult."

Eleanor's shoulders slumped. "Were you able to convince her not to?"

Meadow said, "Of course she was! Beatrice is a won-der when it comes to being persuasive."

"I asked her not to ask Ramsay about a restraining

order. And I told her that I'd come talk with you about your . . . following her around," said Beatrice, carefully avoiding the word *stalking*.

Eleanor nodded. "Thank you, Beatrice. I guess this is another part of my life that needs an overhaul—like my house and my finances. It's just really, really hard. I feel like Lyla is getting off scot-free and that she was the cause of everything."

"Everything?" asked Beatrice softly.

Eleanor shook her head. "No, you're right. I've made her into a scapegoat, but she has nothing to do with the way I accumulated all the stuff in my house and the way our finances got so messed up. But, you see, Lyla and I were friends. So I took this really personally. And then, of course, she *is* responsible for Trevor's death. I feel it in my bones. And someday she's going to pay for it."

Meadow said sternly, "Make sure that you're not the one who's making her pay, Eleanor, if that's even the case. Just to let you know, Lyla's equally convinced that *you're* the one responsible for Trevor's death. So, who knows? Maybe both of you are wrong and it's someone else. Because there are other people with motives."

Now Eleanor looked uncertain, but said in a strong voice, "I doubt that."

Beatrice hesitated and then said, "Eleanor, Lyla also said that you had a knife in your purse at the wedding. That you threatened her at the reception."

Eleanor's face flushed. "What? No, I . . . What's she talking about? The only thing in my purse that night was a couple of tissues and my car keys." But Beatrice noticed she wouldn't look them in the eye. "Besides, it's not as if Trevor were killed with a knife. Lyla is trying to divert attention away from herself. Because *she's* the one with the motive."

Meadow stood up and looked out the window. "Okay, it's finally looking better out there. In fact, it's not even raining." She glanced over at Beatrice. "We should probably head out before it starts pouring again. Eleanor, how about if I start helping you organize tomorrow morning?"

"Perfect," said Eleanor with a shy smile. "And I'll get in touch with Posy about the cat . . . after I've mulled it over today." She paused. "I've got a lot to think over today."

Beatrice and Meadow put on all their rain gear and grabbed their umbrellas from the front porch. They gave a wave to Eleanor from the end of her driveway, then saw her wave back and go inside her house.

Meadow said, "Well, what do you make of it all? Can we cross Eleanor off our list of suspects? She's so totally convinced that Lyla is the culprit that I don't think we can seriously consider her the killer, can we?"

Beatrice said thoughtfully, "I'm not so sure. What if Eleanor *did* murder Trevor, planning to assign the blame to Lyla? Wouldn't that make the ultimate revenge? She'd have gotten rid of both Trevor and Lyla."

"It's possible. At least maybe now she'll stop shadowing Lyla. Stalking Lyla like that is basically playing mind games with her. And if she'd play mind games like that, maybe setting someone up for a murder charge wouldn't be that much of a stretch," said Meadow. "Although I do really like Eleanor. I like that she's trying to fix all these different things in her life. She was pretty quick to realize that she needed to change her dealings with Lyla, too, when you brought it up."

"Only because I mentioned the fact that Lyla plans to put a restraining order against her. But I do think she's very motivated to take charge of her life now, which is wonderful. And Posy will be glad to hear about the cat," said Beatrice. She looked over at Meadow. "Did you think she was acting sort of oddly when she got out of her car, though, at the start of our visit?"

Meadow frowned. "Not really. I mean, we probably scared the life out of her, you know?"

"It seemed to me as if she wasn't simply startled to see us—she was really taken aback and didn't want to visit right then. Or that maybe she was hiding something," said Beatrice.

"You're just being fanciful. We scared her, and she didn't want company because it was early in the morning and her house is still a disaster area. You're over-thinking it, Beatrice."

But the more Beatrice thought about it, the more convinced she was that she wasn't overthinking it.

After lunch, Beatrice got a phone call.

It was Meadow, speaking in a highly excited voice. "Have you heard? No, I guess you haven't heard. Why would you, considering that I'm the one living with the police chief, after all?"

"What happened, Meadow?" asked Beatrice with as much patience as she could muster.

"It's Patrick Finley. He's . . . dead."

Chapter Eighteen

Beatrice took a deep breath. "Dead, as in, He's had a heart attack or died of some natural causes? Or dead as in . . ."

"*Dead* as in . . . we don't know. It's all very frustrating! Ramsay says they suspect foul play, but they don't know for sure," said Meadow. "He either jumped or was pushed off the greenway trail that he usually runs on. He plummeted off the cliff and fell to his death. They found a note tacked onto a tree. It was a suicide note with a confession of Trevor's murder."

Beatrice tried to take it all in. "So this happened at the greenway trail, but it could possibly have been murder? How would someone know where he was unless they followed him?"

"Ramsay spoke with Mrs. Finley, and apparently he had been walking three days a week in addition to the racquetball. He was pretty dedicated," said Meadow wistfully. She was no doubt thinking that her own exercise goal was difficult to maintain. "Anyway, he always took the same route, and he was always back at the same time each morning. So, she phoned Ramsay as soon as he deviated from that schedule and told Ramsay where to look for him."

Beatrice said, "If it *was* murder, it sounds like the killer knew his pattern and followed him out there. Did the police get any evidence at all? Physical evidence, I mean? Or do they know what time this happened, exactly?" asked Beatrice.

"Forensics was going over the area, but evidence will be tough to come by, considering that the trail is used by most of the town of Dappled Hills. And, yes, they're thinking it happened during the time of our walk," said Meadow meaningfully. "I mean, obviously *before* it really started pouring down rain and lightning."

"So, Eleanor could have done it," said Beatrice quietly. "If Patrick were murdered. Eleanor could have been returning back home when we saw her. It wouldn't have taken too much strength if she'd caught him off guard. Did you tell Ramsay?"

"I did. Although I reminded Ramsay, like I'll remind you: What reason would Eleanor Garber have to kill Patrick Finley? I can't figure out why she'd have done such a thing," said Meadow in a distraught voice. "I can't see it. And I volunteered to help her with her clutter from now until the end of time."

Beatrice said thoughtfully, "She might have done it out of revenge. If she thought that Patrick had been the one behind Trevor's murder. Or maybe *Patrick* knew that Eleanor was the one responsible for Trevor's murder, and he met her out there to try to blackmail her."

Meadow's voice was doubtful. "Hmmm . . . I don't think so. Not him. He seems financially solvent to me. I can't see him pulling a Trevor and trying to squeeze money out of people."

Beatrice said, "One other thing: If he was murdered and the killer made it look like suicide, then maybe the murderer's motive was to remove suspicion from himself and focus it on Patrick. Considering that a confession was found nearby. That could have been Eleanor or any of the suspects." She paused, thinking. "Did Ramsay say if the confession note was handwritten?"

"He said it was a typewritten note," said Meadow. "And, really, who types out a suicide note? I think that's one reason why the police think that it was murder. If you're feeling desperately guilty over having committed murder and you're considering suicide, do you really take the time to fire up your computer and type up and print out a note?"

"Good point," said Beatrice. "No, you'd probably grab whatever paper was nearby and scribble something out. Did Ramsay mention whether Patrick Finley's wife commented on his mental or emotional state? Had he seemed worried or upset or anything lately?"

Meadow said, "His wife was in total shock. She couldn't believe that he'd kill himself. Denise said he'd been worried weeks ago, but he'd been very upbeat and much happier since then."

"That could reflect a before-and-after attitude toward Trevor's death," said Beatrice. "He was worried and feeling desperate that Trevor was going to reveal that he'd botched that operation. Then, after Trevor's death, he felt a sense of relief that he wasn't going to be exposed. And

Denise is right: that doesn't really reflect the mind-set of someone who wants to kill himself." She hesitated. "I suppose Denise is a suspect? I know spouses are usually always suspects in these types of cases."

"She's not, no. There was an early-morning prayer breakfast at the church, and she was there during the entire time during which Patrick could have died. It was when she returned and saw that her husband hadn't come home yet that she called Ramsay." There was a pause. "There's something else." Meadow sounded a bit uncomfortable.

"What's that?"

"While Ramsay was calling in the state police, he was checking the area for a possible witness. You know, a lot of people exercise in the morning on that greenway before work. Daniel Kemp walked into the parking lot a few minutes after Ramsay arrived at the scene," said Meadow.

"Walked into the parking lot? He'd been exercising on the greenway?" Beatrice's heart sank.

"That's right. He told Ramsay he didn't see anything. But that was the second crime scene he was present at recently, so that wasn't very good." Meadow hesitated. "It's not like he really had a motive. He didn't even know Patrick Finley. He only knew what Trevor had told him about him."

"Yes, but remember: he could have made it look like suicide to deflect attention from himself as a suspect," said Beatrice slowly. "And that 'suicide' does seem pretty suspicious."

"Well, we don't know anything *yet*. The police are still investigating. But I'd like to get this cleared up. I don't enjoy being suspicious of my friends. Are you planning on asking another round of questions?"

Beatrice rubbed the side of her head, feeling a pounding headache coming on. "Yes, that will be my plan. And I'll try to do it in as unobtrusive a way as possible, considering that I've already gotten a warning one time." She thought for a moment. "I guess Lyla and Daniel will likely both be at the spring festival, so that might be a good time to talk with them. I wonder if Posy could get Eleanor to go there with her."

"I have a feeling that's going to be a no. After all, Lyla will be helping out in Posy's booth, right? For that 'petting zoo' for quilting that she's doing. Those two probably need to be kept apart, or Lyla really *will* put a restraining order on her. Besides, we already know that Eleanor was out at the time that Patrick Finley was killed. It's not as if she could deny it," said Meadow.

"Exactly. But I want to follow up with her, anyway, and see if I can get more information about why she was out. She acted as if she were hiding something. And it felt as if she really had something on her mind, too. Maybe I could get her to share it with me," said Beatrice.

Meadow said, "Or I can dig and see what I can find over our cleaning-up session later on. I'll let you know."

Beatrice hung up the phone and absently stared outside for a minute. Noo-noo looked up at her with worried eyes, and wagged the nubbin that was her tail. She reached out to pet the little dog. She felt as if she needed a bit of a break from the case. There had been so much to absorb the past few days—from the incident with the intruder to the odd visit with Eleanor and Patrick's death. She looked over at the clock. She could always check in with Posy. Maybe she could even give her a heads-up about Eleanor's cat, and to tell her not to be surprised if she got a call from her. And Posy's sweet manner always made Beatrice feel more relaxed.

Fifteen minutes later, Beatrice walked into the Patchwork Cottage. She glanced around apprehensively, expecting to see the throng of new customers in Posy's shop that she'd seen the past couple of times she'd been in there. But the shop seemed quiet. Beatrice felt guilty over her sense of relief.

"Hi, Beatrice!" said Posy cheerfully, as if she wanted nothing more in the world than to have Beatrice walk in through the door. "Want to have some fresh-squeezed lemonade with me? I feel like sitting down for a few minutes, and you have perfect timing."

"Yes! I'd love it," said Beatrice fervently. The feeling of normalcy that she got from walking in the door of the quilt shop was wonderful.

Posy and Beatrice sat together on the sofa in the center of the shop with tall glasses of lemonade in their hands. "How is everything going?" asked Posy with a warm smile. "I haven't seen you since our nice visit at supper the other night."

Beatrice's eyes opened wide at the thought that Meadow *hadn't* spread news of Beatrice's incident with the intruder all over Dappled Hills. But, then, Meadow had been very disturbed by the whole thing. Maybe she was trying to put it behind her. And she knew that Ramsay wouldn't talk about it, and that Piper had been very busy at school. So she took a deep breath and said, "Posy, if you don't mind keeping what I'm about to tell you under wraps. Tell Cork, by all means, but I didn't want folks worried about me. Because I'm fine."

Now Posy's bright blue eyes were alarmed. "Oh dear!"

Beatrice filled her in quickly, and Posy's eyes grew larger and larger. "But you see I'm just fine. I guess I've simply been asking a lot of questions around town and making someone worried. That's all. I'm going to keep going, but be more subtle. And a lot more aware of my surroundings."

Posy said, looking a bit confused, "More questions?"

"Unfortunately, Patrick Finley was found dead today. The police are treating it as a suspicious death, since they don't know for sure that it was murder," said Beatrice.

Posy frowned, thinking. "Patrick Finley. Do I know him?"

"You probably don't. I didn't at first. He does some volunteering at the church, but he works in Lenoir. He's a surgeon. So, now I do have more questions that I can ask. But I'll tread lightly, of course," said Beatrice. "I'm thinking I might be casually able to ask some questions while I'm at the festival. By the way, how are your preparations going for that?"

Posy beamed at her. "For the quilting booth? Very well, thanks. I'll have a sewing machine and some basic supplies, and hope to show everyone that quilting can be an easy craft to learn. I'm excited about it."

"That's wonderful, Posy." Beatrice snapped her fingers. "I remembered one of the things I'd wanted to tell you about. Eleanor Garber was talking about giving away one of her cats to a good home—she wants to downsize some. She said she'd probably be getting in contact with you soon about it."

"She already has," said Posy, eyes twinkling. "And thanks so much for the networking. Eleanor said that she had a mature cat who is a real sweetheart that she's thinking of for Miss Sissy and me."

"*Mature cat?*" asked Beatrice. "Is that code for *elderly*?"

"No, I think the cat is something like seven years old. But the best part is that she's supposed to adapt to change well—she doesn't mind if Eleanor changes out the cat food or the location of the litter box. Her name is Maisie, and she's supposed to be really laid-back." Posy took a sip of her lemonade.

"Have you told Miss Sissy about Maisie yet?" asked Beatrice.

"No, I was scared to, in case something happened and our arrangement fell through. Miss Sissy would be so crushed if that happened," said Posy.

Beatrice could easily imagine Miss Sissy kidnapping Maisie under cover of darkness. "That's probably a very good idea."

The bell on the door rang, and Posy looked up as a customer walked in. "I'd better run and help her," she said quickly.

"Of course," said Beatrice. "I should head home, anyway. Noo-noo will be ready to be fed."

The door rang again, and Harper came in. "Maybe I'll just say hi to Harper for a minute before I go," Beatrice said quickly.

Posy hurried off to help the customer, and Harper raised a hand and smiled when she saw Beatrice. She walked over to the sitting area and gave Beatrice a hug.

"It's good to see you," she said. "See, now that we know each other, we run into each other all the time." She sat down on the sofa next to Beatrice. "And I'm glad you're here, because I've been meaning to call you. I know I sort of dumped a whole bunch of emotions and . . . stuff on you the last time I saw you. But I felt so much better after we talked."

Beatrice nodded, and paused to pick exactly the right words. "Were you able to have a conversation with Daniel, then?"

Harper smiled at her and said, "Actually, it was Daniel who had a conversation with *me*. I understand that was your doing, and I'm very thankful."

"Oh, he would have spoken with you about it," said Beatrice quickly. "It was just a matter of when. I wanted to move things along a bit—that's all."

"I'm so glad you did," said Harper. She smoothed down an imaginary wrinkle in the crisply ironed black slacks she was wearing. Then she added in a thoughtful voice, "It explained a lot of things. Not everything, but a lot. Daniel is very protective of his mother in so many ways that it makes sense that he'd try to prevent something negative about her from getting out."

"I could see it, too," said Beatrice. But how far would he go to protect her?

"I only wish that he'd trusted me with the information. I told him that it couldn't matter less to me who his father was. After all, his father really is the man who raised him. Yes, it would have caused a scandal back in the day, and it's clearly something his mother wanted to keep hidden—probably to protect *Daniel*. But today, people likely wouldn't think twice about it. I know I didn't. And I wish that Daniel had entrusted that information to me." Harper looked wistfully at Beatrice.

Beatrice said, "Daniel didn't entrust it to me, either—not in that way. I knew what to ask, unfortunately, because of what I knew about Trevor and his habit of blackmail. You know, of course, that's why Daniel was so reluctant to share his secret with you: he shared it once with someone he trusted, and Trevor turned on him."

Harper nodded. "Daniel told me that Trevor had tried and failed to blackmail him over his parentage. But he should know that I'd never betray him like that." She hesitated. "And I know the fact that Trevor tried to blackmail him also makes him a fairly strong suspect in the case."

"I haven't talked to Ramsay about Daniel's parentage," said Beatrice. "Although I did encourage him to tell Ramsay about it himself. I thought it would be better coming from Daniel, instead of Ramsay or the state police finding it out themselves, the way that I did."

The fine lines on Harper's face looked deeper as she thought it through. "I'll see if there's anything I can do to encourage him. But it seems like he considers this such a deeply private matter that it almost physically hurts him to share it with others. And he'd know better than most that it would only add to his motive for murder. Right now, the police simply think that Daniel was angry at Trevor for his behavior. Adding blackmail to the mix?" She shook her head.

Beatrice added cautiously, "I understand that Daniel was at the scene this morning, too."

Harper stared at her, a frown creating a line between her eyebrows. "This morning? Daniel was off so quickly to his office. I mean, he went out to exercise on the greenway, as he usually does. Then he came home to take a shower and rush to the office. He did say that there'd been an accident there. Is that the accident you're talking about?"

"It wasn't an accident. The police aren't sure if it was a suicide or a murder," said Beatrice.

Harper drew in a deep breath, her eyes focused on Beatrice's. "Who was it, Beatrice? Who did they find out there?"

"It was Patrick Finley. The doctor I mentioned—the one I'd seen at the wedding reception and at the funeral," said Beatrice simply.

Harper put her fingers to her temple, massaging it as if trying to absorb the information Beatrice was giving her. "Why? What did the note say? Do you know?"

"Apparently, the note was a confession. But there's some question as to whether Patrick Finley wrote it. It was typewritten—a somewhat unusual choice for a suicide note. And his wife stated that he wasn't feeling depressed or anxious at all, that he'd been behaving normally for the past couple of weeks," said Beatrice.

"And Daniel was there," said Harper, her voice sharp. "He was at the greenway."

Beatrice said, "Harper, I know it doesn't look good. But you know Daniel. Does this really seem like the kind of thing he'd do? Kill someone to cover up a murder? Plant a fake confession near a body?"

Harper's voice was strong. "No. The Daniel that I know would never do something like this." She paused, and her voice was more uncertain. "But do I know the real Daniel?"

Chapter Nineteen

The next day was fairly quiet. Beatrice, trying to keep her promise to take her investigation slowly, stayed inside. Piper came by with spaghetti, garlic bread, and wine, and regaled Beatrice with particularly amusing stories from school, making sure to keep everything light and fun and stress-free. "We had a first-grade field trip to a farm in the middle of nowhere," said Piper. "The little girl who sat next to me on the bus told me knock-knock jokes the whole time. The situation got even more dire when the bus broke down and we had to wait for another bus from the school to take us to the farm."

Beatrice laughed. "What about Georgia? Was she on the bus, too?" Georgia also taught first grade at Piper's school.

"She was. But she apparently knew about Becca's knock-knock addiction, because she chose to sit many seats away. The forty-five-minute bus trip turned into a two-hour odyssey." Piper paused, eyes mischievous. "Knock, knock."

"Who's there?" asked Beatrice, a smile tugging at her lips.

"Broken pencil."

"Broken pencil, who?" asked Beatrice.

"That's what I'd like to know! Becca, as usual, couldn't remember the punch line."

There was a light rap at the door. "Must be Meadow," murmured Beatrice, standing up from the small wooden table. "She has an unerring ability of knowing when I'm finally starting to relax."

Piper laughed. "You know you love her. Even if she does drive you crazy sometimes."

Beatrice opened the door and broke into a smile. Ash Downey, with his handsomely dark features, rugged build, and crooked grin, stood there with his mother. He was casually dressed in dark track pants and a gray zippered sweatshirt. "What a nice surprise! I haven't seen you for a while, Ash." She stood back and let Ash and Meadow walk by her into the small dining area off her tiny living room.

Meadow caught her arm and gave it a squeeze. "I saw Piper's car in the driveway and couldn't resist dropping by! You don't mind, do you?" Without waiting for an answer, she said, "The children are just so darling together, and Ash was in Dappled Hills, helping me lug some furniture around at the house. Ramsay likes to pretend he won't pull something if he moves furniture, but he *will*, and men are so stubborn. Best to let the young move heavy things, right?"

Beatrice was only half listening as she watched Ash

and Piper give each other a tight hug and light kiss on the cheek. Piper's gray eyes lit up when Ash walked into the house, her whole being focused on him, as if everyone else in the world had disappeared. It was then that, more than from anything Piper had told her, Beatrice realized that these two were clearly destined to be together.

"Ash, how is the teaching going?" asked Beatrice. "Piper was just entertaining me with tales from her school. Of course, you're teaching on the opposite end of the spectrum."

Ash was an adjunct at Harrington College, about thirty minutes away. He was a marine biologist who'd lived and worked in California before moving back to North Carolina months before to be closer to Piper. At first, Piper had been surprised by his abrupt move, and worried that he'd sacrificed too much for a relationship that was still in the early stages. But now, as Beatrice watched Piper reach out for Ash's hand as he sat down at the table next to her, she saw that her daughter had overcome that emotional hurdle and was completely content and relaxed in Ash's company.

Ash's bright blue eyes twinkled at Beatrice. "Sometimes I think that college freshmen and first-graders *do* have a lot in common."

Piper said, "Except you don't have to hear knock-knock jokes on a broken-down bus, maybe."

Ash grinned. "I wouldn't put it past some of them."

"Have y'all eaten?" asked Beatrice.

Meadow said, "We have, although we both usually have room for more. Don't we, Ash?"

Piper stood up. "You know, when I was getting

some ice, I thought I spotted a large container of ice cream in Mama's freezer."

Beatrice arched her brows. "The remarkable thing about that is it's unopened! Usually, eating ice cream is my stress relief."

Meadow raised a hand in alarm. "Now, now, Beatrice! None of that! No talk of stress or of *the case* tonight. We're here to distract and amuse!"

And they did, until they were all startled to see that the time on the clock was nearly midnight.

The next morning, Beatrice decided to keep with the nonsleuthing schedule and plant some flowers in the backyard. Wyatt had called once while she was working out there with Noo-noo, making sure they were still on for the festival. Beatrice was glad that his voice sounded even and upbeat and that there was no sign of worry or stress—a sign to her that Harper hadn't shared with him her worries over Daniel. Wyatt, having been his minister, must have known about Patrick's death. But, apparently, he was unaware that his own brother-in-law had been spotted near the crime scene. Beatrice hated to bring it up, since the police weren't certain that it was actually murder.

The evening of the festival was clear and pleasant. There were people visiting from all around, since Beatrice had never seen many of the festivalgoers around Dappled Hills. The location of the sprawling fairgrounds was on the outskirts of Dappled Hills, and the surrounding mountains provided a beautiful view. There were striped canvas booths with Frisbee golf and fishing games for small kids. There were booths with arts and crafts for sale—glassworks, exquisite candles, quilts, children's clothing, and jewelry. And there was food galore, from the church bake-sale booth, which was decorated with a rolling pin on the outside of the tent, to cotton candy, hot dogs, and deep-fried candy bars.

Wyatt held Beatrice's hand as they walked by the booths, and a constant stream of church members greeted him with a smile and a wave as they went by. "I feel as if I'm part of a parade," said Beatrice dryly.

There was a main-stage area with local performers. Wyatt and Beatrice watched a group of cloggers, as Wyatt ate a steady progression of fair food. The women wore traditional clogging dresses with bright blue, tiered skirts over crinolines, and they whirled and snapped down their heels in time to the lively music. The male cloggers wore Western attire, with white fringe on their blue-checkered shirts and on the sides of their white pants. They spun their partners and then clogged next to each other in pairs.

"It's a good thing this festival is only once a year," he said, patting his stomach. "My arteries would really protest otherwise."

"I don't know how you stay so thin," said Beatrice, laughing.

"Well, if I ate enough chili cheese dogs, that wouldn't happen," said Wyatt.

"Or pies?" asked a voice behind them teasingly. They turned to see Georgia and Tony grinning at them. Beatrice noticed that Georgia's clothing style had become softer, more feminine, and more body-conscious since she started dating Tony. She was pretty in a coral-colored floral sundress. Tony had dressed up for the occasion and wore khakis and a golf shirt.

"Good to see y'all here!" said Wyatt. "But, no—no pie-eating contest for me. I wouldn't dream of competing against you, Tony. Especially not after eating a chili cheese dog, cotton candy, and a funnel cake."

"That's wise of you," said Georgia, beaming. "Especially considering that Tony hasn't eaten all day, in preparation for his big event."

"Well, I have to protect and preserve my championship, right?" asked Tony.

"But I'll be happy to play horseshoes with you, Tony," said Wyatt, pointing across the fairgrounds to where the horseshoe-pitching competition was taking place.

"Maybe later," said Tony. "I'd better focus on the pie eating first."

"But you'll likely be comatose on sugar after that," said Wyatt with a grin.

"That's so." Tony scratched his head as he remembered. "Last year I went straight home and took the longest nap you can imagine."

"How many pies do you usually eat?" asked Beatrice, feeling a bit bemused.

"Last year I managed to eat four pies in three minutes," said Tony proudly.

It made Beatrice's stomach hurt.

"And that's without using his hands, remember?" said Wyatt. "The contestants basically put their faces right into the pie and eat it."

Beatrice looked again at Tony's crisply ironed khakis and navy blue golf shirt. "So, you're going to be covered in pie, right?"

"Not *completely* covered. That would be like the twelve-and-under group. They end up with pie *everywhere*," said Tony.

Beatrice shook her head. "I think if I compete in anything, I'd have to choose the checkers competition. That's a lot more my speed."

"And not nearly as messy," added Wyatt.

Beatrice asked, "Have y'all seen Posy's quilting 'petting zoo' yet? There are so many booths here that I'm not sure where to even begin looking."

"We have, and she had all kinds of folks in there! It seemed like it was very popular. Even little kids." Georgia pointed out the general area of the booth. "Savannah's helping her out now, and Meadow pitched in some. Miss Sissy came with Posy and is sort of *not* helping."

"I can only imagine," said Beatrice.

Wyatt said, "We should walk Miss Sissy around the fairgrounds a while. We could get her a funnel cake. You know how she loves to eat. That might give Posy a bit of a break."

Beatrice could certainly tell he was a minster. Adding Miss Sissy to their evening hadn't exactly been in her original game plan. But she hid a grimace and nodded pleasantly.

"Actually, it won't only give Posy a break—it will give Savannah one, too. She's helping Posy out, but Miss Sissy is hounding her about Smoke and when she can come by for another visit," said Georgia. "So, you'd really have done your good deed for the day."

"Who else have you seen here so far?" asked Beatrice.

"Oh, we rode the Ferris wheel together, so we got a good overview of the whole place," said Tony, gesturing to the Ferris wheel looming over the fairgrounds. "In fact, the view up there of the valley is amazing, if you haven't seen it, Beatrice. Let's see. I've seen Ramsay, but it sort of looked like he was on duty. He was greeting everybody and being friendly, but I could tell he was here officially."

"So, Meadow is at loose ends," said Beatrice. Which could mean that this date with Wyatt could soon turn into a small group.

Georgia nodded. "Oh, and I saw Harper and Daniel here. I know y'all will want to catch up some with them. They were watching the cloggers dance."

Tony said, "Hate to cut this short, but I probably should head over to the pie-eating contest."

They hurried away, and Wyatt gave her hand a squeeze. "Where to now?"

"We should check in at Posy's 'petting zoo' for quilting," said Beatrice.

"Ah, that's right. To rescue Savannah and Posy from Miss Sissy," said Wyatt.

And, indeed, Miss Sissy did seem to be driving everyone around her crazy. Her hair was even more wildly unkempt than usual, and she'd spilled something on her long floral dress. "Don't touch that!" she snarled at a young woman who was examining the sewing machine.

"Now, Miss Sissy, remember what I was telling you. This is a *petting zoo*. So everyone is allowed and even encouraged to try out a sewing machine and give quilting a go," said Posy patiently. But she gave Beatrice a concerned look.

Savannah, who apparently was assigned to help visitors at one of the sewing machines, rolled her eyes at Beatrice.

"Might break it!" said Miss Sissy.

"I'm sure no one will break it," said Posy confidently. But the young woman was already thanking them and abruptly hurrying from the tent. Posy sighed.

"Might destroy the quilt!" said Miss Sissy, gesturing to the very basic quilt that was on the sewing machine.

"The point is that it's easy enough so that even someone brand-new can learn to do it," said Posy, smiling earnestly at Miss Sissy.

"Poppycock!" growled the old woman.

Wyatt quickly intervened. "Hi, Posy! And hi, Miss Sissy. Miss Sissy, I was wondering if you'd do Beatrice and me the great honor of enjoying the festival with us. We'd love for you to. And we thought you might enjoy a funnel cake or a deep-fried candy bar."

Miss Sissy's eyes lit up. Then they narrowed as she squinted at Beatrice with an assessing look. Beatrice gave her a weak smile that likely wasn't very convincing.

"And then we can talk more about your next visit with Smoke," offered Savannah as a desperate encouragement.

"Okay," said Miss Sissy. "Let's go eat." She sprang from the booth, and Wyatt and Beatrice leaped to follow her. Beatrice thought she heard a collective sigh of relief from the booth behind them.

Wyatt looked as though he might be experiencing a stomachache. "Actually, I've already eaten a ton of food. But we, uh, wanted to get your opinion on the festival food."

"Would have to eat a lot to have an opinion," said the old woman cannily.

"Of course you will," said Wyatt.

Beatrice was quite willing to chip in in case Wyatt ran out of cash. It would be worth it to keep Miss Sissy occupied.

It was a good thing that Beatrice did have cash on her. Miss Sissy not only ate a funnel cake, but she also ate a bacon-wrapped caramel apple, a corn dog, deep-fried butter on a stick, and a huge plate of onion rings.

"Miss Sissy, I do believe we should have entered you in the pie-eating contest," said Beatrice dryly.

"But then Tony would have lost," said Wyatt, "and he was so serious about defending his title."

Miss Sissy ignored them both. She appeared to be scanning the horizon for new foods to try.

A round-faced short woman with large eyes scurried across the path ahead of them.

"June Bug never slows down, does she?" asked Beatrice in amazement. "I'd have stopped her so we could talk, but I can tell she's bolting off to somewhere."

"Her cakes are in high demand tonight," said Wyatt, nodding. "And it's June Bug's rolling pin that we're using as decoration on the outside of the tent, so she's even pitched in with decorating, too. I don't think you'd have been able to stop her to talk. She asked me how many cakes she should supply for the sale, and I told her to bake only a couple. I didn't want her to wear herself out or spend too much money, since she'd be out of pocket, with the bake-sale proceeds going to a local charity. But she told me on the phone that she'd have more cakes in her car, just in case. I'm guessing she's off to get them because hers have sold out."

Miss Sissy said fiercely, "June Bug has good cakes."

"She certainly does," said Wyatt in a calming tone.

"Let's go to the bake-sale booth," suggested Miss Sissy in a wheedling tone.

Beatrice felt her head start to throb.

"We will, Miss Sissy. But we don't want to be carrying a cake around with us while we're walking around the festival, right? Why don't we go there later?" said Wyatt.

"They'll all be gone!"

"I think June Bug brought plenty of cakes. But if they somehow *are* all gone, I can still get one for you later. June Bug is at the church, cooking for us, all the time," said Wyatt.

"Maybe you could run and get her a snack," suggested Beatrice. She looked desperately around her. What hadn't Miss Sissy eaten yet?

"There!" said Miss Sissy, pointing an arthritic finger at the deep-fried candy bar truck.

"Okay," said Wyatt, looking relieved that there was no more talk of a cake. "Why don't y'all wait here, and I'll go get it? It looks as if there's quite a line."

Wyatt headed off to the food truck, and Beatrice was startled as Miss Sissy abruptly sat down on the ground. "Miss Sissy?" she asked uncertainly.

"Legs tired," she said with a sniff.

There weren't any benches nearby. But Beatrice didn't particularly feel like sitting on the ground in her nice outfit, so she stood next to her and bestowed reassuring smiles to passersby who gave the old woman concerned looks.

A moment later, she spotted Daniel. He was looking around him as if searching for someone, but then frowned as he saw Miss Sissy, and strode over. He was dressed, as usual, in suit pants and a button-down shirt with a tie. But at least he'd forgone the jacket. He peered at Miss Sissy solemnly through his black-framed eyeglasses.

"Is everything all right?" he asked, mostly to Beatrice. He didn't quite meet Beatrice's gaze, and Beatrice realized that he seemed to feel awkward around her—likely due to the fact that she knew the secret about his past.

"Oh, Miss Sissy decided to have a seat, that's all. There wasn't exactly a good spot for it, so she chose the ground," said Beatrice.

Now Daniel's gaze met hers. And it was amused. "Maybe we should put caution tape around her. I'm afraid people won't see her and will trip over her and go flying."

Miss Sissy was ignoring them completely.

"By the way," Daniel said, frowning now, "I heard a terrible story from Meadow about you. I was so sorry to hear about it. She said that someone had stuck a gun in your back when you were trying to get inside your house recently."

Beatrice froze. Because she certainly hadn't told Meadow about the gun; she'd known it would only make her more upset. And she'd expressly asked Ramsay not to say anything, and he'd been grimly convincing that he wouldn't. So how did Daniel know about it?

Her mouth suddenly dry, Beatrice swallowed hard and said, "I don't recall telling Meadow that there was a gun involved in the incident." It sounded like more of a question when she said it.

Daniel's eyebrows pulled together as his brow creased. "Didn't you? Oh, I must have confused her story with one of the ones I heard about in court the other day—I was at the courthouse all day long, and incidents start running together. At any rate, I'm so sorry to hear about it, Beatrice. Are you all right?"

Beatrice repressed a shiver. "Yes, I'm fine, thanks. It was very scary at the time, but no harm done in the end." Except now she was wondering if Wyatt's brother-in-law was her nighttime intruder.

"Harper told me about it all the next morning—I guess she must have talked with Wyatt on the phone. Terrifying. I suppose it was some druggie trying to force you inside to raid your medicine cabinet or something. That type of thing goes on, although I hadn't heard of anything like it in Dappled Hills. It could just as well have been me—I was out that evening, too. I'd been visiting Mother at Mountain Vistas, and then picked up some takeout so Harper wouldn't have to cook anything," said Daniel.

Beatrice was wishing that it didn't sound to her ears as if Daniel were changing the motive of the intruder's visit and offering an alibi for himself all at the same time. She nodded at Daniel in response.

"Well, glad to hear you're all right, but hope that nothing like that happens again, Beatrice. I'd better run and find Harper." He smiled at Beatrice, and then gave Miss Sissy a polite good-bye. Miss Sissy scowled at him.

Wyatt was quickly heading back their way with a deep-fried candy bar in his hand. Daniel spotted him and hastily left. Maybe he was feeling uncomfortable that Wyatt surely knew his secret?

Wyatt wore a bemused look as he watched Daniel hurry away. "Everything all right with Daniel?" he asked. He leaned down and handed Miss Sissy the deep-fried candy bar. Beatrice had to admit that the thing, no matter how disgusting she'd thought it sounded, did smell amazingly enticing.

Miss Sissy, who always paid a lot more attention than anyone gave her credit for, abruptly said, "Poppy-cock!"

Beatrice looked at the old woman sharply. Was she spouting off nonsense as usual, or was she mistrustful of the convenient alibi that Daniel had given for the night of Beatrice's intruder?

Wyatt was looking quizzically at them both, so Beatrice quickly said, "Daniel was on his way to find Harper—that's all. He's doing fine."

Wyatt stooped down and held out a hand to Miss Sissy, who was still camped out on the ground. "Did you have a good rest?" he asked.

Miss Sissy decided to circumvent the question. "Let's go to the bake-sale booth," she said. She wore a mulish expression on her face.

"But, remember: then we'll have to carry a cake around with us. And you've already got a deep-fried candy bar to eat, right?" said Wyatt in a reasonable tone. "We said we'd head to the bake-sale booth later."

"It's later," said Miss Sissy flatly, before taking a large bite of her candy bar.

"Oh, look. Horseshoes!" Beatrice said in an unconvincingly surprised voice. She was ready to start focusing on something other than food. She was also beginning to wonder if it would ever be possible for she and Wyatt to have a date together with no one else butting in. Lately, it had all seemed to be retirement-home visits, casserole creation, and festivals . . . with a crowd.

June Bug, carrying a cake and with a flushed face, ran across their field of vision again.

Miss Sissy clapped her hands. "Horseshoes."

Wyatt said with a warm smile, "Would you like to play horseshoes with me, Miss Sissy? Although I should warn you that I'm considered a pretty good horseshoe player."

Miss Sissy *did* want to, and practically skipped over to the horseshoes.

"I hope she's a good sport," muttered Beatrice to Wyatt. "I'm not sure I can deal with a cranky Miss Sissy for the rest of the evening."

"I think they give everyone prizes, no matter what. They have candy for consolation gifts for the kids," said Wyatt.

They gave the man running the game some tickets.

"You go first," said Miss Sissy to Wyatt, gesturing impatiently at the horseshoes.

"You're sure? All right, then." Wyatt stretched his arms to loosen up a bit. As he stretched, he said to the man taking tickets, "This is possibly the only sport I've ever been the slightest bit good at."

He picked up one horseshoe and carefully made some practice pitching motions, lining up his arm with the stake in the ground. Then, sticking out his tongue in concentration, he pitched a shoe. Although it was lined up well to the stake, it fell short by a few inches. Wyatt stared at the stake in surprise. "I'm rustier than I thought. I should have practiced at home."

"You've got another toss, right?" asked Beatrice, trying to sound peppy.

"That's right. Okay, let me try again." Wyatt frowned in concentration this time, swinging his arm back and forth in several practice motions before finally releasing it. This time the horseshoe was a ringer on the stake.

"Whew!" said Wyatt, laughing. "I was starting to worry that I'd lost my touch." He turned to Miss Sissy who'd gotten distracted by the sight of an ice-cream stand. "Miss Sissy? Are you ready to give it a whirl?"

Miss Sissy narrowed her gaze, studying the horseshoes. These appeared, to Beatrice's eyes, to be actual former footwear from actual horses. They were a variety of different sizes. Beatrice realized they might be in trouble when Miss Sissy reached down to try the various sizes.

Wyatt, however, was blissfully unaware. "Miss Sissy, the way you want to pitch the horseshoes is with a sort of swinging underhanded toss." He gestured helpfully.

Miss Sissy shot him a scornful look as she hefted a horseshoe, measured the distance carefully, drew back her hand, and then tossed a shoe at the stake. It was a ringer.

The old woman crowed and clapped her hands.

"Wow. That was really good, Miss Sissy." Wyatt looked concerned. "All right. So, now you. . . ."

But the old woman was already picking up another horseshoe and squinting at the stake. She tossed it in front of her, and it flipped in the air before clanking onto the stake as another ringer.

Beatrice and Wyatt stared at Miss Sissy. Miss Sissy danced around, eyes gleeful.

"I think you may have played this game before, Miss Sissy," said Wyatt, still with his cheerful voice.

The next fifteen minutes demonstrated that although Wyatt certainly had a talent for horseshoes, as he pitched ringers and near misses, it showed more strongly that either Miss Sissy had an innate gift for playing the game or she had spent many hours playing as a young woman. And Miss Sissy wasn't talking.

Wyatt looked relieved as the game finally drew to an end. The man in charge declared Miss Sissy the winner and asked her to pick out a prize. The prizes were assorted large stuffed animals. Miss Sissy weighed her options carefully. In fact, it took her longer to survey the prizes than it had for her to size up the stakes when she was pitching. Finally, she chose a tremendous lavender gorilla with a maniacal grin on its furry face.

Beatrice frowned. "Will you be able to carry that yourself, Miss Sissy?" She reached out to help her, and the old woman drew back, clutching the gorilla protectively. Beatrice shrugged, giving Wyatt a helpless look. "What now?"

"What now?" sang out a voice behind them. "What now is that y'all have fun, and I get to spend time with my favorite senior."

Meadow bounced up, giving them both hugs and a reassuring wink. Beatrice decided that she'd never been happier to see Meadow.

Chapter Twenty

Miss Sissy was staring suspiciously at Meadow and clutching the lavender gorilla closely.

"Miss Sissy," asked Meadow, beaming at her and speaking with her most sweetly persuasive voice, "would you come explore the festival with me?"

Miss Sissy thought about this for a moment, and then nodded and started walking back toward the food vendors.

"Hope you've brought plenty of cash," said Beatrice. "Miss Sissy has been very hungry."

"I'm loaded," said Meadow airily.

Wyatt said warmly, "Thanks *so* much, Meadow."

Meadow gave a dismissive wave, "Oh, it's my pleasure!" Then she bolted off to catch up with Miss Sissy, who was walking swiftly toward a cotton-candy vendor.

Wyatt gave a relieved sigh, and Beatrice reached out to resume holding his hand, giving it a squeeze.

"What should we do now?" asked Wyatt. "We've eaten and visited the Patchwork Cottage booth and played a game. What's left?"

"We sit down and enjoy some music," said Beatrice simply.

A bluegrass group took the stage, bowing low in acknowledgment of the audience before a bald man launched into an up-tempo harmonica solo. There was a stout man wearing a straw hat and a suit and enthusiastically picking on a banjo, alongside a solemn old man nimbly playing a fiddle. The group was rounded out by a man and a willowy woman, both strumming guitars. The spirited beat of the music had the audience stomping their feet.

Beatrice and Wyatt sipped tall lemonades and listened to bluegrass music under a tremendous tent, with no one to talk to but each other.

Wyatt said with a satisfied sigh, "I've always looked forward to this festival. It seems like it comes at the perfect time every year—right when I've been overwhelmed with work and ready for a break."

Beatrice was glad to hear that maybe Wyatt was considering taking things a little slower . . . or that at least he recognized that things at the church had been especially busy lately. "Has the festival been around for a while?"

Wyatt nodded. "One of my earliest memories is of sitting on the Ferris wheel with my father and seeing the whole festival laid out below me. All the dozens of people, all the other rides, all the booths, and the mountains rolling around us."

"You must have loved that as a small child," said

Beatrice. She took a sip from her lemonade, enjoying the refreshing coolness of the drink.

"I was terrified," admitted Wyatt with a laugh. "My father had to get them to stop the ride to let me off. But, in my defense, I was very small, after all. How about you? Any frightening festival or state-fair memories lurking deep in your subconscious?"

Beatrice considered the question thoughtfully. "No, I don't think so. I don't think my parents were probably festival-going people. My early memories involve going to the Georgia coast. I remember playing on the beach at Sea Island, making sand castles and drawing pictures in the sand with sticks. My father taking me out in the ocean and help me catch waves on a raft."

"But nothing that scared you silly? I'm going to regret sharing my timid nature," said Wyatt, eyes twinkling.

"The sand flies were scary," said Beatrice with a laugh. "I'd yelp when they'd sting me and jump half a mile. And the Georgia heat was pretty frightening, if there was no breeze from the water."

Wyatt looked at her thoughtfully. "I think you must have been a very brave and self-composed girl. And nothing has changed." He reached out and held her hand, and they watched a young singer walk on the stage. For the next little bit, they sat together in comfortable silence.

After nearly an hour, they were joined by Meadow, June Bug, and Posy. "It's time!" said Meadow excitedly. "The judges are going to announce the quilting winners."

Posy beamed at June Bug, who sat upright in her

seat, an alarmed expression on her face. "June Bug, your quilt was absolutely lovely. I have a good feeling about the results tonight."

Meadow gave June Bug a sideways glance. "Breathe, June Bug!"

June Bug, who did indeed seem to be turning blue, gave an obedient nod and a gasping breath while maintaining the look of alarm.

The quilting judge, a good-natured-looking middle-aged woman who was very stylishly dressed, walked onto the stage and tapped the microphone to get the audience's attention. "And now I have the results for the quilt show," she said.

The woman put on her reading glasses and peered at her notes. "First of all, let me say that it was both an honor and a very difficult task to judge such wonderful-quality quilts. I do a good deal of judging all over the Southeast, and I've not seen finer quilting anywhere than I've seen in this mountain community. So congratulations to all of you—on your skill and your creativity."

There was a round of applause, and Beatrice muttered, "Enough stalling. Get on with it!" Beatrice was worried that June Bug was going to start holding her breath again.

"Third place is Posy Beck, with her lovely hand-quilted *Spring Flowers*," said the judge.

Meadow squealed, and the quilters took turns giving Posy hugs. Posy's eyes shone as she rose to accept her ribbon from the judge.

When Posy returned to her seat, Beatrice said, "That's honestly one of my favorites of your quilts. I just love the bright, cheerful squares with the flowers, watering cans, and rubber boots. It's so whimsical and fun. It puts a smile on my face, just like you do."

Posy blew her an airy kiss.

"Breathe, June Bug," muttered Meadow again.

"Second place goes to . . ." The judge squinted at her notes. "Well, somehow I can't read the last name. Or maybe she doesn't have a last name. At any rate, the second place ribbon goes to . . . Miss Sissy for her riotous *Sun Spots*."

"*Riotous* is right," murmured Beatrice. She'd seen the quilt the old woman had submitted. It was certainly amazing, with spiraling ridges of yellow, orange, and red cloth over a chaotic blue, black, purple, and green background of tiny patches. It wasn't at all traditional and it shouldn't have worked, but it did . . . very well. Beatrice couldn't tell if it was a sign of genius or a sign of a diseased mind. "Where *is* Miss Sissy?"

"I palmed her off on Ramsay," said Meadow. "He's probably having to feed her again. We'll pick up her ribbon afterward."

"And finally, our best in show," said the judge with a smile for the audience. "What an amazing quilt it is, too, ladies and gentlemen. Tonight, our best in show goes to . . ." She paused, perhaps enjoying the audience's anticipation or perhaps enjoying its rapt attention.

"For heaven's sake," said Beatrice irritably.

"Air, June Bug. Remember? Breathe," said Meadow.

"To Annabelle Frost!" said the judge.

"Who?" said Meadow in astonishment. "Annabelle Frost?"

June Bug let out the jagged, pent-up breath. "Me! It's my real name." Her eyes were wide with shock.

Beatrice gave her a quick hug as the quilters cried out with excitement. "Well, go up there, June Bug! Claim your prize."

June Bug said, "Can you give me a push? My legs don't want to work."

Beatrice stood up and gently pulled her by the arm, propelling her toward the stage. The quilters gave June Bug a standing ovation as she shyly took the ribbon from the beaming judge.

As the festival started wrapping up and the band under the tent made its good-bye, Wyatt looked apologetically at Beatrice. "I'm afraid that's my signal to go help take down the bake sale. Do you mind? I'll call you tomorrow, and we'll set up a time to have lunch together."

"How about if I help out for a few minutes?" asked Beatrice. "With everyone leaving at once, it will be crazy trying to get out of the parking lot, anyway."

So they both headed over to the bake-sale tent, where the church members excitedly told Wyatt that they had raised five hundred dollars for the local children's charity. Beatrice helped remove the unsold cakes and load them back into the church van. She also put several folding chairs into the back of the van. She was looking around for more to do when Wyatt said, "Thanks so much, Beatrice, but I think we've got the rest. I really appreciate the help."

"All right. I'll listen for your call tomorrow, then," said Beatrice. It was now dark outside, and the parking lot was a fairly good walk. She set out on it.

She was close to the Patchwork Cottage booth when she saw June Bug zipping by again, carrying tote bags on both arms. This time, though, June Bug paused when she saw Beatrice and gave her a bright smile.

"June Bug, it sounds like your cakes were all a huge success. I heard that the church made five hundred dollars for the sale," said Beatrice. "And not only that, you got a best-in-show ribbon for one of your quilts. That's a really big night!"

June Bug beamed at Beatrice, lit-up round eyes in her round face. "I'm going to hang the ribbon in my house," she shyly confided to Beatrice.

June Bug shifted the weight of the tote bags, and Beatrice automatically reached for one to help her.

"You should hang your ribbon in a place of honor. And you deserved an award. Your quilts are amazing," said Beatrice. "I loved *Sunset over the Mountains*. The smoky blues and grays and the reds you chose were so vibrant. And piecing it together from so many tiny bits of fabric?" Beatrice shook her head. "It was truly magnificent. How do you create that type of look?"

June Bug tilted her head to one side, as if she'd never really thought about what went into it. Then she said, "I place the pieces where I want them. Sometimes they're a slightly layered on each other. Then I pin them until I can sew them together. Posy's shop has so many colors and so many fabrics! I love it there."

"Well, I can't wait to see what else you'll come up with. It's all very exciting," said Beatrice. June Bug was self-taught, which boggled Beatrice's mind. She'd run into artists like that in Atlanta when she curated folk art, but those types of artists were few and far between.

June Bug's eyes shone. "Lyla was one of the judges, you know. It was nice of her to choose me for a ribbon."

"Well, I don't think being nice had anything to do with it—the quilt was very deserving," said Beatrice.

"But Lyla *is* really nice, though," said June Bug. "I remember at the wedding reception, she helped me clean up even though she wasn't part of the catering team, like I was. And she's cleaning up now for Posy." June Bug gestured at the tent beside them that they were walking behind. "I was trying to clean up fast at the reception, and Lyla was going even faster than I was!"

Beatrice said slowly, "So Lyla was cleaning at the reception? I didn't even notice that. I'd noticed her coming and going, but didn't pay attention to what she was doing."

June Bug was happily prattling on while Beatrice nodded automatically but kept thinking about Lyla. Could Lyla have been clearing away evidence of some kind at the reception? Why else would she have been helping out the caterers?

June Bug abruptly stopped talking and squinted across the fairground. "Oh! There's Posy with my quilt from the show. Got to go." And she hurried off.

Beatrice was all the way to the now-deserted gravel parking lot when she realized that she still had June Bug's tote bag hanging on her arm. She sighed, peering inside. It held a cake tray and the rolling pin that Beatrice remembered hanging as decoration on the outside of the booth's tent.

Should she try to go ahead and get it back to her, or would it be all right to return it to her the next time she saw June Bug? Beatrice was rapidly feeling very tired from all the walking, despite the vigorous walks she'd endured recently with Boris and Meadow. It was tempting to just take the bag home with her. But then the thought of the little woman searching in confusion for the bag or needing the rolling pin for cakes the next day made her groan in acquiescence and turn around.

And as she turned, she spun right into Lyla Wales, who was standing very close behind her.

Beatrice gave a startled laugh. "Lyla, you and I have got to stop this habit of running into one another in parking lots. Let's have coffee sometime instead."

Lyla's red mouth bent in a smile, but her eyes were hard. "Yes, we'll have to do that sometime," she said rather unconvincingly.

Beatrice tried again to think of some form of conversation starter, because she wasn't sure what Lyla's intentions were, so she didn't want to accuse her of anything outright. And her car was certainly nearby . . . very close to Beatrice's, actually. She remembered Posy's tip about Lyla's secret weapon to keep her sewing machine's foot pedal from sliding away. Beatrice cleared her throat and said in a carefully neutral and casual tone, "By the way, I know your secret."

Lyla's eyes narrowed. "That's not exactly the smartest thing to admit, is it, Beatrice? And here I was, thinking how clever you were." She put her hand inside her loose-fitting jacket and pulled out a gun.

Beatrice's heart started beating in her chest so loudly that she was sure that Lyla could hear it. "As a matter of fact, Lyla, the secret I was referring to had to do with using a pot holder to keep your foot pedal still. But, clearly, you have other secrets that I don't know anything about."

Lyla's eyes flickered with annoyance. "Whatever. It was time for your nosiness to be over, anyway. I heard June Bug talking to you when I was clearing out the Patchwork Cottage booth. I knew you weren't going to be like June Bug and assume that I was cleaning up at the reception out of the goodness of my heart."

"No. You're right about that. That was the only way to get rid of evidence, wasn't it? You were being very helpful . . . too helpful. Nobody helps a professional caterer clean up. You'd finally had enough of Trevor Garber, hadn't you? He wouldn't leave you alone. He was following you to work and badgering you at home. You felt like it was only a matter of time before everyone in town was going to know. Maybe you'd get fired for having your personal life interfere with your business. Plus, you were desperate for your husband to stay in the dark, weren't you?" asked Beatrice, fighting to keep her voice steady.

"There was no reason for Julian to know," said Lyla expressionlessly. "Our relationship was going fine and suited me perfectly. Besides, I didn't want people all over Dappled Hills to start yapping about me and Trevor. And Trevor was starting to lose it."

"I was thinking that it must have been really tough to slip sleeping pills into his drink, but it probably wasn't, was it? After all, no one was on the lookout for anything but normal wedding behavior. You were in and out some to get food—a normal occurrence at a wedding—and you *had* to pass Trevor to get to the food," said Beatrice.

"It was completely necessary," said Lyla in that same brisk, unemotional tone. "Trevor was a loose cannon. It wasn't a horrible death in any way. He simply fell asleep and didn't wake up."

"It was a horrible death because it was unnatural and happened too soon," said Beatrice sternly. She'd temporarily forgotten about the gun in her indignation over Trevor's untimely death. "And a tragic one, because he was trying to turn his life around at the time."

Lyla snorted. She glanced around the dark parking lot as if suddenly realizing how exposed they were. She gestured to Beatrice's car with her pistol. "Get into your car, and no funny business, Beatrice. We only have Eleanor's word that Trevor wanted to change. How could I be expected to sit around and wait to see if he was going to suddenly stop stalking me at work and showing up at my house? Eleanor is about as nutty as a fruitcake, anyway. She stepped right into Trevor's shoes as soon as he was gone, following me to the office and showing up at my house."

Beatrice reluctantly unlocked her car and got into the front seat, automatically putting on her seat belt as Lyla trained a gun on her and climbed into Beatrice's passenger's seat. "But Eleanor's motives were different, weren't they? She was convinced that you were responsible for Trevor's death. And she was right."

"She was convinced that our *affair* was responsible for the whole mess," corrected Lyla. "And in that sense, Eleanor was right. I wish I'd never become involved with Trevor."

Beatrice took a deep breath. "You say that, but you obviously must have had feelings for him, too. I overheard you say that you wished you and Trevor had loved each other at the same time."

Lyla flushed. "That was actually the real tragedy. And the fact that Trevor was so unstable, which I'd had no idea about when we started seeing each other. I'd thought he was this upright, thoughtful anesthesiologist. That's what all appearances indicated. Who knew that he was going to go off the deep end like that?"

Beatrice was feeling desperate to gain more time. She wasn't sure where Lyla was planning on making her drive, but it couldn't have a good outcome. If she could only keep Lyla talking, maybe someone else would enter the parking lot. Unfortunately, the field the parking lot was in was huge, and the nearest car was Lyla's. It was also unlit by any type of streetlight. Still, anything had to be better than driving somewhere else.

Beatrice said, "So, after he'd ingested the drink, you walked back through the tent and made a point to help the caterers pick up discarded plates and glasses, including Trevor's. Although I'm not sure how you'd have picked up his glass without putting fingerprint evidence all over it."

Lyla shrugged. "It was a cool evening. I had a long scarf that I'd thrown on over my dress. I wiped down the glass after I'd taken it. That's all."

"A doctor that Trevor worked with was lurking in the background," said Beatrice thoughtfully. "I saw him looking in on the proceedings a couple of times. It seemed as though he was waiting for a chance to talk to Trevor alone. So he was focused on Trevor, clearly. He must have seen you coming over to the table and doctoring Trevor's drink."

Lyla shrugged. "Start the engine, Beatrice. We're going on a short drive. And, yes, he apparently either did see something or else he was able to fill in the blanks. Patrick Finley was a smart guy, but, then, doctors usually are."

Beatrice's gaze desperately flickered around the empty parking lot. No one was there. Slowly she put the keys in the ignition and turned. "But Patrick wasn't smart enough, was he? He clearly talked with you about what he'd seen. He basically signed his own death warrant then."

"That's a dramatic way of putting it," said Lyla with a dry laugh. "He did arrange to talk with me about it. I'd thought at the time that he knew more than he did. I guess he only saw something out of the corner of his eye, although he pretended that he knew everything."

"Was he trying to blackmail you with the information?" asked Beatrice with a frown. She really couldn't see it, although it had been such a focus in the murders, what with Trevor trying to get out of his financial trouble.

Lyla rolled her eyes. "Please. Not that guy. Whatever his vices are, I'm pretty sure that blackmailing people isn't one of them. No, he simply decided that he was tired of being a suspect in a murder investigation. He was giving me the opportunity to talk to the police before he did. He seemed to think that a confession would help the authorities go easier on me, or something."

"When did he tell you to turn yourself in?" asked Beatrice. "Was it at the greenway trail?"

"He'd called me from the hospital and told me to meet him before his usual walk the next morning. I had a pretty good idea what he wanted to talk with me about. I brought my gun along and printed out a handy-dandy suicide note to bring with me," said Lyla.

"So, he tried to convince you to turn yourself in, and then he set out on his walk," said Beatrice.

"That's right. And he was an unsuspecting lamb, I have to admit. He put his headphones on, turned on his music, and started walking. I walked right behind him, and he never knew I was there. I had my gun just in case something went wrong, but it was so much more convenient when Patrick paused to play a different song on his iPod—and I ran right at him and pushed him off the cliff." There was a hard note of satisfaction in Lyla's voice.

Beatrice reminded herself to take a deep breath. Now she knew exactly what she was dealing with. Lyla wouldn't think twice about getting rid of her. "You made sure he was dead and then posted the suicide note."

"Well, there was no 'making sure he was dead' about it—the guy tumbled off a cliff. He was a goner, all right. But, sure—I put the suicide note up with the confession. I figured I might as well take some of the heat off myself, after all." Lyla squinted to look into the distance. "Start driving, Beatrice. I don't want any sort of posse to come after you. Head out the gate and take a left."

Left was near nothing. Left led out to the middle of nowhere. Beatrice really didn't want to turn left. There was that gun to think of, though.

"This gun," said Beatrice. She cleared her throat as she slowly started driving toward the gate. "This must be the gun you were using the night you came up behind me when I was returning from dinner with Posy."

"It's a good way to motivate someone to do what I want," said Lyla dryly. "You were being far too nosy, Beatrice. It's really your downfall, if you think about it. You didn't have to get involved with all this. You didn't see anything at the reception. You didn't know what happened to Patrick Finley. You could have been free and clear. But you couldn't seem to stop yourself from digging."

"What were you planning on doing that night you showed up at my house?" asked Beatrice.

"Well, I certainly didn't want to shoot you outside. Considering your closest neighbor is the police chief, that might cause more interest than I wanted. But I did want to get rid of you. I could tell you were getting closer to finding out the truth, and you weren't leaving it alone. I was hoping to scare you off the case. It felt like you were trying to find proof that I'd killed Trevor," said Lyla. She thrust the gun a little closer to Beatrice. "Start driving."

Beatrice shook her head and eased her foot off the accelerator as much as possible as they drove over the gravel of the parking lot. "I wasn't. I was definitely trying to learn who was responsible for killing Trevor, but I had no preconceived idea who that might be."

"My mistake, then," said Lyla with a harsh laugh. "But now you know the truth, and I've got to get rid of you, anyway."

"The only reason I know that you killed Trevor and Patrick is because of what you're doing right now," said Beatrice as calmly as she could. "I hadn't connected the dots before this."

"Oh, I think you had, Beatrice. I heard you talking to

June Bug, remember? Whether you realized it or not, you'd connected the dots, all right. So, let's go."

Beatrice suddenly stopped the car, putting the brake on.

"What are you doing?" Lyla's voice was more like a snarl.

"I've changed my mind. If you want to kill me, you're going to kill me right here, Lyla. No second location. Go right ahead and shoot me here in the festival parking lot. I'm not going to be a party to my own murder." Beatrice glanced down at June Bug's bag. If she could just get her hands on that rolling pin.

But Lyla was paying too much attention. "Stop it right there, or I'm shooting you in that hand. I'm not going to say it again: start driving."

So Beatrice switched to plan B. She started driving—fast. Beatrice stomped her foot on the accelerator, flooring it in the nearly deserted parking lot. She twisted the wheel hard to the left and hit the brakes just as hard. Lyla slammed into dashboard and was knocked unconscious, slumping over in the passenger's seat.

Beatrice grabbed June Bug's rolling pin in case Lyla started stirring and threw Lyla's gun far away from the car. With shaking hands, she pulled out her cell phone.

Chapter Twenty-one

As luck would have it, Ramsay was still at the festival. When he got Beatrice's phone call, he came running to the parking lot, removed Lyla from the car, and put her in handcuffs in the backseat of his patrol car. Then he called the state police to report the arrest.

"What happened?" he asked grimly. Beatrice was sitting in the front seat of her car, feet on the ground, feeling a bit sick to her stomach. Ramsay was standing in front of her with his notebook and a grim expression on his face.

"Lyla came after me. She overheard me talking with June Bug about the fact that Lyla had helped the caterer clean up after the wedding. She decided to force me to drive out of here at gunpoint," said Beatrice. She was amazed how calm her voice sounded. At some point tonight, she was sure this was all going to really hit her hard.

"But she'd tried to come after you before, right?"

asked Ramsay. "She was the one who approached you with a gun the other night?"

"That's right. Apparently, she thought I was getting too close to figuring it all out. Maybe I was and didn't realize it. She wanted to get rid of Trevor because he wasn't leaving her alone and she was worried about losing her job and husband and reputation around town. Lyla put ground sleeping pills in Trevor's drink, expecting we'd all think he'd just had too much to drink. She cleared away his drink and some others before anyone discovered Trevor was dead instead of drunk," said Beatrice.

"And Patrick Finley?" asked Ramsay. "What did she tell you about that?"

"She said that he saw her at Trevor's table when he was lurking around at the wedding. He was tired of being a suspect and wanted Lyla to give herself up to the police. But Lyla had no intention of doing that. They met that morning at the greenway, right before his usual walk. He thought their conversation was over and started out on his walk, headphones in. But Lyla followed him. She'd planned to kill him all along, of course—she'd brought the printed-out confession letter with her."

Ramsay said, "It sounds like things were starting to unravel for her. So, Patrick knew what she'd done. And she suspected that *you* knew what she'd done. Was she going to end up killing half the town of Dappled Hills, then?"

"I don't know about half the town, but I suspect there was going to be at least one more victim: Eleanor Garber. I'd heard from Lyla that Eleanor was basically stalking her—following Lyla to work, following Lyla around town, trying to intimidate her," said Beatrice.

Ramsay shook his head. "I don't know why Lyla didn't come to me. I could have talked to Eleanor and asked her to drop it. She probably would have. If she hadn't, we could have signed a restraining order."

"I think Lyla was hoping it was going to go away. But what it meant was that Eleanor followed Lyla to the park that day that Patrick was killed," said Beatrice.

"But why didn't Lyla see that coming? Seems like she'd have known that there was going to be a witness," said Ramsay, eyebrows raised.

"I think either Lyla had become accustomed to it and was so focused on getting rid of Patrick Finley that she didn't even pay attention, or else it might be that Eleanor was being more surreptitious about following, since Lyla was getting more vocal about it. Either way, Eleanor put two and two together. But I think Eleanor was trying to figure out what to do with the information that she had. She was acting very strangely when Meadow and I arrived at her house the morning Patrick died. It seemed as though she had something on her mind. But by the time we left, it was almost as if she were trying to figure out a course of action. I don't know if she was going to turn Lyla in or if she was planning on picking up where Trevor left off with blackmailing."

"I'll send an officer over to check on Eleanor, just to make sure everything is all right over there," said Ramsay grimly. Then he squinted across the gravel parking lot. "What on earth?"

Beatrice looked in the direction he was staring in

and saw Meadow, mouth agape at the sight of Lyla in the back of the police cruiser, and Miss Sissy scowling at them and clutching the lavender gorilla that was nearly as big as she was.

The rest of the evening was a blur. Once Meadow had absorbed what was going on, she sprang into action. While Ramsay spoke to the state police, she assigned Posy the job of driving Miss Sissy and the gorilla home, connected June Bug with the tote bag of bakeware, and then sat protectively with Beatrice until Wyatt got there. "Trying to force you to drive to a remote location! Waving guns around! The very idea!" she kept bellowing, glaring at the police cruiser.

Then followed a longish period of time when Beatrice recounted much of what she'd already told Ramsay to the state police.

Finally, Lyla was driven away, and the state police finished questioning Beatrice. Meadow, still fuming, drove away. Wyatt said to Beatrice, "Why don't I drive you home? Are you feeling shaky?"

She smiled at him. "No. No, I'm all right now. Just suddenly very, very tired. I appreciate the offer, but I'm fine to drive myself home. Then I'm going to let Noonoo out and then head straight to bed."

Wyatt nodded. "I understand that, but I'm going to follow you back home and make sure you're safely tucked in for the night. And I'll plan on coming by tomorrow morning to check on you—not too early, though, I promise."

The amazing thing, thought Beatrice as she finally dropped sleepily into bed thirty minutes later, was that while Meadow's overprotectiveness irritated her, she found it oddly sweet in Wyatt.

Beatrice slept like a rock and was startled when she saw the clock read ten o'clock. Had Wyatt come by and she hadn't heard him? He should already be at the church by now.

She quickly got ready and ate a small bowl of cereal. The phone rang as she was washing out her bowl.

It was Eleanor Garber. "Beatrice!" she said. Her voice sounded as if she'd been crying. "Are you all right? Ramsay came by this morning to fill me in on the arrest and what happened last night. I feel so terrible."

Beatrice said gently, "Everything is fine, Eleanor. You were right about Lyla, after all—she *was* responsible for Trevor's death."

"And Patrick Finley's," said Eleanor's voice, still sounding teary. "And the intruder at your house— Ramsay told me about that. And then last night. Everything could have turned out so differently."

"But it didn't. I'm fine, and Lyla is behind bars. And everything can go back to normal," said Beatrice calmly.

Eleanor gave a harsh laugh. "Or, in my case, I can try to make everything normal. Beatrice, I have a confession to make. I was still following Lyla that day that she pushed Patrick off the mountain. I was more careful— that was all. I decided that I was done trying to upset her by having her see me. I wanted to get something I could use against her, since I was convinced she'd murdered Trevor. I thought that even if I caught her doing something *immoral*, like having an affair with another man, that I could hold it over her."

"When did you find out that it was more than something immoral?" asked Beatrice.

"Lyla was acting kind of strange. For one thing, she'd had this talk with Patrick Finley, and then she waited for him to walk away before she followed him onto the trail. The walk wasn't very long, which was odd. I knew it was about to rain, but it still seemed weird to me. Lyla wasn't dressed for exercising, either. She was dressed for work. It all seemed weird to me, so I hung out awhile," said Eleanor.

"What did you see?" asked Beatrice.

"I saw it start pouring down rain. And I didn't see Patrick come back out of the woods. I waited longer, thinking that maybe he had gotten pretty far away and it was just taking him a while to walk back. But he was such a big guy—kind of heavy, you know. I knew that he wouldn't have been able to get very far. I didn't *know* anything, though. Now, however, I feel like there was something I should have done. I should have gone out on the trail myself to see if he needed help." Eleanor choked up.

"You didn't know that anything had happened," said Beatrice. "Even if you'd gone out to make sure he was all right, there was nothing you could do to help him. And the storm had really kicked into high gear around that time, right?"

Eleanor's voice sounded relieved at Beatrice's reassurances. "Yes, it was pouring rain at the time. I wasn't sure what I was going to do—I kept thinking about it on the way home. I did feel pretty certain that foul play had happened and that I'd witnessed something important. But, to my shame, I decided to keep it to myself and not tell Ramsay about it until I'd decided what to do. After all, I'd *wanted* to catch Lyla doing something bad. Once I had, though, I wasn't sure if I wanted to send her anonymous notes about it or blackmail her about it or turn her over to the cops. What if you'd died last night because I hadn't reported what I'd seen?"

"Nothing happened," said Beatrice firmly. "And now it's time for you to move on."

Eleanor said, "You're absolutely right. Meadow is coming over in a few minutes to help me work through the clutter here. I've already found a small house across town that I'm going to rent. And I'm determined that this be a fresh start for me. Which reminds me of the other reason I called you: to ask if you could take Maisie over to Miss Sissy for me. Good-byes are tough for me, and I think it would be easier if I handed her over at home."

"I'd be delighted to. And, judging from what I've seen from Miss Sissy and Smoke, I think Maisie will be very happy with Miss Sissy. Actually, she'll likely be spoiled rotten," said Beatrice dryly.

"Good. Now if Miss Sissy doesn't really care for Maisie, let me know and I'll take her back in a heartbeat. I don't want to foist her on Miss Sissy."

"I will, but I don't think that's going to be a problem. I'll drop by your house later this morning, if that's okay," said Beatrice.

"Perfect."

Beatrice was letting Noo-noo back in and looking for her keys so that she could head to Eleanor's house when Wyatt pulled into the driveway, waving cheerily at her.

"You're in a great mood," she said, smiling at him as he strode down her front walk. She could wait a while before going over to Eleanor's house. They settled down in the living room on the sofa.

"That's because I'm finally taking a vacation," said Wyatt with a grin. "I haven't actually taken a break for years. We don't have any assistant ministers, as you know, but we have a whole layperson team. I made a couple of phone calls this morning, and they were so excited by the idea of being able to rotate giving sermons and ministering to the congregation for the next month. I'd somehow thought that it would be a big burden for them, and I'd tried to avoid it. But, apparently, they'd been really hoping for the opportunity to put their training to use. And happy, they said, that I was taking a break."

"Everyone needs a break," said Beatrice gently. "Even from a good job. It's so important to be able to relax." Then she laughed in surprise at herself. "Well, listen to me. Who knew that I'd ever be able to extol the virtues of relaxation? I think I realized last night how exhausted I was. So, what are you planning on doing during your sabbatical?"

Wyatt's eyes crinkled in a smile. "I was hoping that we could relax together. Not in an all-the-time-together way, just many more visits than we've been having. If that's all right with you."

Beatrice felt her heart give a leap. "That would be perfect."

"Maybe we could start today? I enjoyed the last picnic we had, although it's been so long ago now it's like a distant memory. I checked the forecast, and the weather is supposed to be beautiful. I thought I could pack us a lunch," said Wyatt.

"Oh, I can put some lunch together, too," said Beatrice quickly, before Wyatt gently shushed her.

"No, I want you to genuinely take it easy today. I was so worried about you last night. I felt this wave of both stress and relief, all at the same time, when I heard what had happened. It was your quick thinking that got you out of that situation." Wyatt's eyes were serious now. "It made me realize how valuable our time together was and how little we actually had. I decided to start making amends."

Beatrice reached over to squeeze Wyatt's hand, and they sat enjoying the quiet of the living room for a few moments.

She asked, "Do you know how Patrick Finley's wife is doing? I enjoyed meeting her that day when we were putting casseroles together."

Wyatt nodded. "Denise is doing about as well as can be expected, under the circumstances. I think the news that Ramsay has arrested the person responsible for Patrick's death will also help to give her some closure and put this all behind her."

"And Daniel and Harper?" asked Beatrice quietly. "I know there was quite a bit for them to work through."

"There sure was," said Wyatt with a sigh. "I was sorry that they had to start their married life with so many sudden issues. I visited them this morning, as a matter of fact, before I came over here. I wanted to let Harper and Daniel know that Ramsay had made an arrest in the murders. I thought . . . well, I thought it would help relieve their minds that Daniel was no longer under any sort of cloud of suspicion."

Beatrice felt a momentary twinge of guilt as she reflected that she'd rather strongly suspected Daniel, and not very long ago. But that was all part of working through the case. And Daniel didn't know how suspicious Beatrice had been of him—a good thing. "I'm sure they were glad to hear that it was all over."

"They were. Although they felt bad about Lyla. And, I think, surprised." Wyatt paused, leaning over to rub Noo-noo, who put her head against his leg. "Daniel told me, as well, that he'd had a long talk with his mother at Mountain Vistas yesterday morning. I was so glad he did. I suspected that the reason his mother had hidden the information on his parentage from him was because she was worried that he'd be hurt. And Daniel was worried that *she'd* be hurt. In the end, they talked everything through, cleared the air, and ended the visit with a hug. It couldn't have gone any better."

"I'm so glad to hear that," said Beatrice. She glanced at her watch and saw that it was getting close to noon.

"I'm sorry. Did you need to go somewhere?" asked Wyatt, quickly making to stand up.

"Oh, it's no big deal. Eleanor Garber asked if I could run by this morning and take her cat, Maisie, over to Miss Sissy. She and Meadow are clearing out the house so that Eleanor can move," said Beatrice. She saw Wyatt's eyebrows fly up and laughed. "Miss Sissy will be sharing the cat with Posy—never fear."

"Why don't we run that errand on the way to our picnic?" he asked. "Miss Sissy will be delighted, I'm sure. While I'm at it, I meant to ask if you'd be free to-morrow night for supper. I thought that maybe we could eat with Daniel and Harper." He stood up and fished his car keys out of his pocket.

"That would be great!" said Beatrice. She hesitated. "You know, Posy will probably be just as delighted as Miss Sissy to receive Maisie. She's bound to be pretty sad over Lyla's arrest—they were such good friends." She stood up and collected her pocketbook from a nearby table.

"Why don't we invite Cork and Posy, too?" suggested Wyatt, holding the back door open for Beatrice to walk out.

"Even better!" But then a thought occurred to Beatrice, and she frowned. "Except then Meadow will feel left out. And Meadow is *already* feeling left out because you and I are spending more time together."

Wyatt chuckled. "All right, so Meadow and Ramsay, too. The more, the merrier. In fact, let's make it a barbecue over at my house. It can be a celebration."

"A celebration?" asked Beatrice.

"Of friendships—old, new, and changing." And hand in hand, they walked to Wyatt's car.

Recipes

Harper's Wedding Day
Cucumber Spread

6 ounces whipped cream cheese
1 medium cucumber, seeded, grated, peeled, and drained on
   paper towels
1 tablespoon grated sweet onion
Toast points

Mix together the cream cheese, cucumber, and onion.
Allow to sit, covered, in the refrigerator for one day.
Serve chilled on toast points.

Warm Mushroom Spread

1 block low-fat cream cheese
1 small can of mushroom bits and pieces, drained
½ teaspoon grated sweet onion
1 tablespoon milk
Toast points

Preheat oven to 375 degrees F. Mix together the cream cheese, mushrooms, onion, and milk. Pour into a small casserole dish. Bake fifteen minutes or until bubbling. Serve warm with toast points.

Wyatt's Favorite Hot Dog Chili

1 pound ground beef
1 tablespoon olive oil
1 cup water
1 tablespoon chili powder
1 dash Worcestershire sauce
1 tablespoon dried chopped onion

Add one tablespoon oil to a skillet and brown the beef over medium heat; drain off excess fat. Add the water, chili powder, and Worcestershire sauce. Bring the ground-beef mixture to a boil. Add the onion, and reduce to a simmer. Cover the skillet and simmer for 25 minutes.

Asparagus Casserole

3 tablespoons butter
4 tablespoons flour
2 cups milk
⅔ cup grated sharp cheese
½ teaspoon salt
¼ teaspoon paprika
2 cans green asparagus, drained
2 hard-boiled eggs, sliced
Crushed buttery round crackers

Preheat the oven to 350 degrees F. Melt the butter in a saucepan over medium heat. Stir in the flour until smooth. Gradually add the milk, and stir over medium heat until thickened. Blend in the cheese, stirring until melted. Season with the salt and paprika. Layer the cheese sauce, asparagus, egg slices, and more sauce in a 2-quart casserole dish. Top with the crushed crackers. Cover with foil and bake for one hour.

Quilting Tips

Rubber shelf liners under a sewing machine will help keep the machine from moving while you're working.

CD holders make handy holders for fat quarters.

Instead of dampening thread to thread a needle, dampen the eye of the needle instead.

Use scrap pieces of batting to easily pick up loose threads from your floor.

When traveling, instead of taking shears on the plane with you (which are likely to not be allowed), bring along a container of dental floss, and use the floss container to cut your thread.

Empty over-the-counter medicine bottles make a handy and safe repository for used sewing needles.